SEEKING SIRIUS

SciFi Suspense with a Metaphysics Kick

Crystal Ceres Time Travel Books #1

DogStar Press

Seeking Sirius

August 2014

Published by DogStar Press
P.O. Box 1793, Fairfield, IA 52556
www.DogStar-Press.com

For my husband, Allen

Profound thanks to Coyle Schwab
Master Cessna 195 Pilot

And to my father, Gene Edwards, from whom
I have my love of reading

Prologue

Cold from the hard cement seeped up through her trousers. "Hello?"

The word 'disoriented' barely described her state of mind. Worse, she felt bone deep that she should be remembering something...but just couldn't.

On the other hand, the incredible feeling of happiness—even relief—flooding through her was very nice. *Why am I so relieved?*

As she rolled her head and uncrossed one leg to stretch out a cramp, an acrid odor penetrated the haze. "Huh, motor oil." With that, she studied the space more closely. "Oh, this is the hangar."

I should go. She'd just got her hands on the ground to leverage up when a small aircraft passed by the open door, filling the air with its rumble-roar. The sound was unmistakable. Adrenaline prickling, on instinct she grabbed the white plastic bag beside her and sprinted, barely avoiding a wooden crate before pushing out into the sun.

At that very moment the silver and red airplane lifted off the runway. She chased after the craft a short way, crying out "No!" But it was obviously too late. As the plane banked toward the ocean she moaned, "Why did Alexa leave?"

A dread welled up. Could Mac have told? *No way.* Baffled, she stared at the plane droning in the distance.

Scorching blacktop brought her back, and Rachel yelped, "Where are my boots?" While jumping from foot to foot, her gaze rose from her painted toenails to the faded cargo pants she wore. And somebody else's yellow T-shirt—with a smiley face? *Not my clothes.*

The plastic bag in her hand contained a newspaper so she dropped it to the ground. With tender feet no longer being sizzled, she could study the environment. This was the small airport she'd known since childhood. The air shimmered in heat, puffball clouds sailed by in the sky, cicadas shrilled their magical music. Everything was as it should be. Yet it felt as if the whole world had changed.

A man had ambled over from the terminal, his old Jedi Master pullover stained with engine oil. He grumbled at her, "Rachel, what are you doing here? I thought you were flying with Alexa."

"Hey, Morty." Turning to him, she threw out her arms, and said, "I don't know." A memory of laughter with Alexa brought it all back. "Oh yeah. I went to the hangar to get the newspaper you sold me." She turned to watch the plane disappear into the clouds. "And well, it looks like Alexa left without me."

Morty shook his head. "Why did you want that old thing anyway? You already know what happened."

"It's so weird," she said, rubbing her face. "I can remember being with Alexa in the plane." Rachel almost fell off the bag when a gust of wind kicked up. "But maybe the memory is from when I flew with her before."

Morty waved at her, muttering something about people being nuts, and turned to leave. She picked up the bag to follow and unfolded the thick bundle to peek at the newspaper. "Hey, you sold me a paper with writing on it." In disbelief, he grimaced and reached over to take it. At that moment, though, Rachel recognized the scribbles as her own. Hard to miss the all-cap style she cultured while dating an engineer.

Bright purple ink screamed at the top:

ONLY FOR THE EYES OF MAC OR RACHEL
RACHEL, IMMEDIATELY CONTACT MAC

She pulled the newspaper to her chest. "Never mind," she said in a small voice. "It's fine."

As Morty headed back to the office, Rachel shifted from heel to heel, rereading the note. Even a third and fourth pass made no sense. More odd, her writing also flowed around the margins, mentioning places and people she'd never heard of.

She tiptoed to the nearest shade at the hangar before stopping to locate her mobile phone in a pocket. The autodial went through to the right number, but instead of Alexa it was their friend Becky who answered. "Rachel? You calling about Alexa's phone? She left it here..."

"I need to find Mac."

Chapter 1

At the far end of the tiny airport, Alexa Jane Alden radioed the tower and announced, "This is November5337Victor, departing on runway Bravo-2." Seconds later, the Cessna 195 reached takeoff speed and Alexa pulled back on the yoke, grinning as the plane lifted into the sky. That almost human leap always gave her a rush. It was one of the experiences that kept her flying.

Still, this particular takeoff had gone kind of strange. She could no longer ignore the odd twisty sense that began while the plane had been taxiing. In fact, the feeling had grown to a conviction inside her that something just turned very wrong.

Alexa glanced around the cockpit: The motor sounded normal, and no smell of burning engine oil or anything else could be detected. Vibrations were minimal. It shouldn't be those old pre-flight jitters, because they always disappeared by this time. Alexa frowned and wrangled her hair back into a barrette. The emotion was astonishing. Almost despair. She hadn't felt something that strong in years.

Maybe she should have listened to her instinct fifteen minutes earlier, a clear intuition to leave Donny Dixon behind. He had arrived more than twenty minutes late and then delayed them another ten minutes to go to the airport office. *And I woke up before dawn to get in my meditation so we could leave early.*

At that moment, Donny sat in the backseat of the plane, crinkling paper and tossing things from his duffel bag. He gave a grunt of satisfaction before sticking a faded Cubs baseball hat over dishwater hair, and topped that with the communications headset.

By the time her plane approached cruising altitude, the sadness plaguing her had begun to disappear. Still, she felt it might be a good idea to scan the airport. Tucking a curl behind her ear, Alexa twisted to peer out the window. Two figures, barely discernible, stood on the airport's empty tarmac.

Her friend, Rachel Mulligan, also turned back around from looking at the field. Settling back in the seat, she even appeared to shiver a bit.

"Wonder who's down there," Alexa said into the headset. "Think there's a problem?"

While rubbing her face, Rachel said, "I don't know." Then she checked her mobile phone and considered for a moment. "Nah. They'd call, or radio you if anything was wrong."

Alexa opted to review her standard to-do list: *Handled that detail. That's done. Okay. Yes. Oh, oops.* She picked up her backpack from the floor between the front seats and felt around inside. Then she investigated each pocket on her cargo pants. "You know what, I forgot my cell phone."

Rachel flipped her hand, and said, "They know my number." After that, Rachel took up her puzzle book and filled in another blank. The purple ink from that funny pen could about blind a person.

The plane began pitching, to the point that even Alexa's pack bounced around on the floor. After some time working to keep wings level, Alexa realized the strange sensation was almost gone. Brushing a red-gold wisp from her face, she glanced at Rachel, whose outfit practically glowed neon. "I see that you're wearing your man-killer uniform."

"That cute gallery owner in Nassau mentioned he likes kids," replied Rachel, while ducking her head. "I want him to really notice me this time."

Her friend had been refining the look since high school. That exact pink shirt with a deep V-neck, supercharged by a push-up bra, had once attracted the attention of every guy in a bar. Alexa smiled, remembering how the men had almost fallen over each other.

Personally, she never felt the need for such efforts. Attracting male attention had never been a problem, though she wouldn't mind being a bit less petite.

Rachel paused from biting a cuticle. "I thought Mac was supposed to fly you to the Bahamas."

"Called away on business, as usual," said Alexa, without taking her eyes off the plane instruments.

"Do you really think he'll take time off to go with you to the Himalayas?"

With a resigned nod, Alexa acknowledged it would be a stretch for Mac. Her parents had trekked in that region before they were married and she wanted to replicate their route. Her mother's stories about esoteric destinations had tugged at her since she was a little girl. After a honeymoon there, with her parents honored, perhaps she could settle into her own life. "I hope so." After a shrug, she said, "There's still a lot to do. Thank goodness, we still have almost a week before the wedding."

Armstrong MacPhearson, her lovable workaholic fiancé, had called two days ago about a quick flight to close a business deal, explaining, "I know, I'm supposed to come get you. I received a message from Brahmaji. Still, my new investor suggested this deal. And for Fahlsteder to fund the new lab, I must bring back a signed contract. I told you that investors need a lot of strokes. I'll be back to help with the wedding details as soon as I can, I promise."

Alexa didn't bother to protest, since airport sounds were obvious in the background.

However, if Mac thought a signed contract would clinch the deal with his investor, what a shock when last night Sterling Fahlsteder telephoned Alexa directly; a surprise since she'd barely met the man.

Fahlsteder announced to her an intention to leave the Bahamas, perhaps forever. Her heart clinched; Mac had been so excited about his interest.

Before the man hung up, he asked, "Do you still intend to sell your airplane?" When she said yes, he seemed to relent a bit. "If you get it here tomorrow, I may decide to stick around." His tone implied that, otherwise, he'd leave. When she didn't quickly agree, he offered encouragement with, "I could make it worth your while."

She'd tried to contact Mac, but her messages on his cell phone refused to produce a response. Ultimately, the thought of losing an opportunity to sell the aircraft helped her over any reluctance about piloting.

In the plane, Alexa verified their bearings. They were on course to Nassau.

Rachel said, "I'm amazed you were willing to do the flying this trip."

"Everyone at Becky's house last night had an opinion," said Alexa, and grimaced. "Someone would say, 'you can do it.' Then they'd all go quiet. It was obvious they were thinking about my grandfather's death." Then she confessed, "To tell you the truth, it came down to selling the plane. If this man buys it, we'll have the down payment for the cottage I told you about."

"As nice as your family home up north?"

"Nice enough," said Alexa, waggling her hand. Again, she silently reviewed her decision. *Flying to Nassau makes sense. Let it go.*

She jerked to the present when the aircraft leaped to the right by maybe a football field, lost altitude like a rock, and drifted to back on course, leaving her insides somewhere behind. "What is this?" she muttered. "The weather forecast was perfect earlier." Alexa looked over at Rachel. "You're unfazed by this turbulence, aren't you?"

Her friend threw out her hands, as if to say "sorry."

Funny how different they were. Through the years they might bicker or rant at each other, and once disastrously competed for a guy. Yet that didn't matter between them.

Maybe to distract her, Rachel began effusing about the contents of the white plastic bag on her lap. "I am so glad I went to the hangar for this. See, I scored a Sunday *Times*!" She hefted the newspaper up and down. "The paper was in a corner of the airport store and it's a week old. But that's okay. I loved reading it in New York." On the front page she pointed out a photo of her favorite Yankee, and slid the paper back into its bag.

Donny stuck his head forward between them. "You gals want some coffee? It's the best the airport can offer." Evidently, he'd decided to offer an apology of sorts.

When the plane's nose dipped and lurched, he steadied a paper cup with steam coming through the hole in the plastic top, before handing it over to Rachel. Alexa declined. "I have tea in a thermos."

Donny said, "Also have some bagels and cream cheese," and Rachel stretched her hand to receive a bagel encased in cellophane. At the sight of a hunk of cream cheese smashed into the wrapping, Alexa wrinkled her nose. Donny shrugged.

At least he'd brought food. He'd been mooching off her friend Becky for days, even considering nobody in town had ever laid eyes on the guy before he showed up for the first time about a week ago. Alexa included him today only because of a request from Becky— who always was a sucker for a cute dimple.

After a sip, Donny leaned forward again. "My grandmother has raved about the Bahamas ever since she visited there five years ago on a cruise." As the plane bounded twice, he held onto the back of Alexa's seat. "I also found this map with the latitudes and longitudes of old shipwrecks."

"You hunt pirate treasure?" joked Alexa.

Donny looked away out the window. "I guess."

At the same time, Rachel said, "Yeah?" as she twisted to take the map. She unfolded the paper, then turned it around a couple of times, almost hitting Alexa in the eye. At last, she lined it up with the horizon and pointed at a dot on the map with her pen. "This is Bimini."

The pen had to be from her eight-year-old son, Sammy. He was crazy about a space man from a recent movie, and that cartoon character bobbled around on a spring on top of the white plastic. Using it, Rachel then pointed toward a smudge on the water, to the right of them. "And there is Bimini on the ocean. I've heard of several wrecks near there."

"Cool," said Donny. "Besides Atlantis ruins around here, they're also supposed to be on the Yucatan and maybe some near Portugal. I heard that storms uncover new stuff all the time." He lowered his voice into the scary register. "And there were a couple of good ones here recently." Rachel chuckled.

The whole Atlantis thing made Alexa cringe. She said, "If you believe in that, and the fairies, I have a parcel of land for you with only a few alligators." Donny sat back and got quiet.

At last, the plane stopped bounding through the skies and Alexa began to relax.

"Dolphin pod below." Donny had the excited tone of anyone from the middle of the country. He'd mentioned his hometown was in Nebraska.

A few moments later, Alexa was happy to announce, "All right, I think we found an altitude with smoother air currents."

With the plane in good order, she reached to reposition her backpack. She also took time to verify the wrapping around the "very important package" given to her last week by Brahmaji, her family's meditation teacher. She had put it in the wall safe at the house of another of her high school buddies when she arrived ten days ago, and picked it up this morning. It would be a relief when she could deliver the package to Mac, per Brahmaji's instructions.

With that thought, Brahmaji's words when he gave it to her appeared in her mind. "Please hand this to Mac when he comes to you." *Huh. Didn't exactly wait for Mac to come to me.* An old twinge of concern pricked inside her. But then her intellect kicked in. Shouldn't be a problem.

Everything was quiet for few minutes, giving Alexa the opportunity to realize her nose tickled. She scrunched it around, trying to get rid of the itch, but that didn't work.

About the time she noticed the smell of ozone, a flare of light nearby about blinded her. But the plane's instruments showed normal. "What was that? It didn't come from inside."

An odd luminosity began coursing around them. In her peripheral vision, she noticed Rachel craning to see around outside the plane.

Then mountain-size clouds began manifesting in front of them. Some parts were dazzling white, others scary dark. Pretty, when viewed from the ground. *But up here, they make me nervous.* Alexa scanned the horizon for the best way around the thunderheads.

A glimpse of the ocean below showed waves churning at crazy angles, producing huge whitecaps. Soon after, the plane began to jerk like on the end of a cat toy. Alexa glanced at Rachel, whose face reflected her own shock.

Suddenly, a fiery column shot up in front of the plane, scintillating. Donny pushed between them and called out, "Oooooh, ET." Blinding brilliance began at the water and zapped up straight out of sight.

On top of everything, a downdraft caught the plane. Alexa cried out, "Jeez, strong!" But she almost felt grateful for something to focus on. Another downdraft, and the nose dropped further. No way to avoid that light column. "Too close. Going through!"

From one moment to another, brightness enveloped them, outside and in.

Energy pulsed, tingling.

Effulgence stretched, redder and redder to darkness.

Alexa felt a swirling, whirling, toward a single point.

Just as she realized that the plane was really flying forward, not spiraling in a dangerous dive, the tumult inside her began to circle down, quieter and quieter away.

Last sound she heard was a whispered "oy" from Rachel.

Then utter silence. No sensation. No smell. Five seconds passed, ten seconds, fifteen, twenty, infinite seconds.

Chapter 2

From stillness, a rumble barreled through Alexa's chest. From darkness, blue light burst, hurting her eyes. Something lamented in higher and higher registers. Then all resolved to sky, drenched with driving rain.

Which almost obscured the view of ground rushing up at them.

The airspeed was approaching the red line.

"Pull up! Pull up! Pull UP!" howled Donny.

Alexa had already begun wrestling the nose off its collision course. She popped out the throttle knob and with both hands drew back on the yoke. The plane groaned. She continued coaxing it to resist the relentless pull toward trees, beach and ocean. Still they hurtled downward. Her heart raced, practically reaching out in front of the plane.

Through the front window, she could almost pick out the foam on ocean waves.

A heart-stopping moment later, G-forces doubled her weight, like she might drop to the ocean depths. *Finally!*

Wings wobbled, protesting stress; but the plane had changed course. Alexa's ears popped as the craft climbed away from that threatening watery grave. Clouds streaked by the windows.

After a bit, the wind's screech retreated to its normal rush, broken only by the splats of raindrops. Alexa eased the throttle in and granted power to the engine, feeding its roar. She reached out her senses. The plane felt okay.

At last, with the craft stabilized at a safe altitude, the pulsing in her ears slowly retreated, the pounding in her chest gradually eased. Flying low under the clouds, Alexa let out her breath and heard the others do the same. As long as the storm didn't force another emergency, they were safe. Bless her grandfather, insisting those many times that she practice pulling out of a steep dive.

It was Donny who noticed the landmass close by. "That's no

island. How did we get back to Florida so quickly?"

At last able to focus on something outside the plane, Alexa identified palm trees on the beach below. She glanced to the west past Rachel, where flat open land lead to the sun, which shone through a sliver of sky. Rachel and Donny followed her gaze, and began announcing more details.

"No buildings," said Rachel. "Anywhere."

"Dolphins below," shouted Donny. "Lots of them."

"Are they following us?"

"Over there to the right, there's a bay," said Donny.

"And a building," said Rachel. "Have you ever seen anything so pretty?"

Reluctant to turn her attention away from the plane, Alexa demanded, "What are you two yelling about?" At Rachel's touch, Alexa followed her line of sight out the window. "Whoa!" She banked the plane. "What's something like that doing here?"

Football field-size and two or three stories tall, the white structure glimmered in the low light. Columns along the front were topped with zigzags in blues and greens. A dome on the roof spanned almost the middle third of the structure. Smaller buildings nearby showed through greenery, and it all totaled the area of a small town.

Donny poked his head in between them. "The temple, the darkness, the light. I think it's safe to say, this is not Kansas."

Alexa sniffed. "Understatement of the year." She gestured around them. "How did we get to Florida? We were past Bimini."

"Maybe we're over the Everglades?" suggested Rachel.

"Guess so. Where else could be this empty?"

Ocean on one side. On the other side stretched an expanse of low trees punctuated by sharp grass-covered hillocks, unbroken by human structures. If roads were anywhere, Alexa couldn't see them. Mountains rose, far to the right. *Mountains? In Florida? Must be huge clouds.* Rain drizzled in a soft patter.

"It's getting dark," said Alexa, "although I can't understand how that can be possible." She shook her head. "It should be mid-morning." As they flew by the town again, she fretted. "We do not have unlimited fuel. What say we put down, there on that lawn area in front of—whatever it is." People began running out of the building. "Make sure your seat belts are tight."

The makeshift runway lay parallel to the water, from where a stiff breeze blew. She'd had plenty of practice with the prevailing wind at her town further north in Florida. To slip into the landing, Alexa maintained the plane's nose slightly toward the sea while also banking to increase drag. At thirty feet above ground, a strong wind shear forced the craft's nose up at the wrong time. But Alexa brought it back into position, right before touchdown.

A series of deep ruts made it feel as though they were a basketball being wildly dribbled. She pressed hard on both brakes, fighting for control. No way she could halt before the plane would run over a sharp boulder, though, so she steered hard left. Same time, a gust caught the wing. *Will we flip?* Alexa momentarily released the brakes and turned the nose back into the wind. The craft remained upright. They were almost stopped.

Then a ravine, hidden by tall grass, appeared directly in front. Before she could react, they plunged. Four feet. To an abrupt stop.

Alexa bungeed into and off the steering column. Same moment, a distinct thwack came from the direction of the propeller. The engine stopped dead. Her grandfather had assured her that the Cessna was designed, in the 1940s and '50s, to land on almost any kind of surface. Evidently not into a small canyon.

Except for her nose thrumming from that connection with the yoke, she was okay. Engine and electrical circuits switched off, Alexa asked, her voice a croak, "Everybody all right?"

A drama-laden whimper from Rachel was actually a good sign.

"Man," murmured Donny. "Yeah. Okay."

Rain chittered on the aluminum wings and the windshield. While Alexa verified the plane's status, Rachel and Donny started shouting about something. It was obvious they were upset, but that didn't prepare her for the sight when she looked up. Around the plane, yards away, was a wall of people. Mostly men, a few in toga-type garb and others in short or long gowns. Everyone in white.

Inside the plane, Rachel murmured, "They look like enchanted ghosts."

One man, taller than the others, came to the front of the line on Alexa's side and cupped his hands before yelling, "Do you speak English?"

The sun had set, and Alexa wasn't sure if he could see them inside the plane. Nevertheless, when she nodded yes, he continued. "Are you hurt?"

Alexa glanced at Rachel and Donny, then shook her head at the man.

"Please remain in the plane until we can transfer you to a safe room. You may be deathly infectious for us, and we for you. Please stay where you are."

Infectious?

The man gestured for everyone to step back. It appeared they were making two lines with a wide space between, leading from the plane toward the huge building.

"What is this place that contagion would be a problem?" She'd never heard of a hospital for humans in the Everglades.

"Hey," said Donny, "a short dude is pushing against our door."

Rachel dropped her phone on her lap, complaining, "There's no signal, at all! How can I contact my son?"

It took perhaps twenty minutes before they received permission to exit the plane and bring everything with them. Despite the lush smells beckoning, Alexa kept her attention on luggage. A few minutes later they huddled under the wing. She looked around for which direction they should take.

Donny picked up from the ground three lengths of white material, evidently left by the little man. "What're these for? They won't keep us dry."

Alexa cupped her hands and called out, "Where are we? Can we go to Miami or somewhere? If you would call a taxi or something, we can leave and not be a threat to your group." The guy opened his mouth to respond, closed it and shook his head. She said, "The plane's propeller is broken. I need to contact someone for a part."

"Sorry, not possible," he replied. "If you would cooperate at this time, my father will explain it all later."

Every person in that wall had a cover over nose and mouth.

"Do we have a choice? Where are we? Who are you?"

The guy looked pained. "You are in no danger, except for the potential for infection."

"Is this a hospital? What's so contagious?"

He scratched his head.

Alexa commented low to Rachel, "What I'd really like to do is contact the police."

The guy said, "We will not hurt you. You can leave later. Nevertheless, we must take precautions." After a moment, he added, "Please."

Alexa blew out her breath and said to Rachel, "Okay. Looks as if they're serious about this." She began tying a scarf around her nose and mouth. The other two made eye contact before copying her.

On the path to a small building less than a hundred feet away, through the drizzle and a silent human gauntlet, Alexa stopped to reposition her bags. Because she was essentially moving to Nassau on this trip, she had more stuff with her than usual. And there was no pavement around. When Donny took the larger suitcase she whispered, "Thanks."

The single room in the stone building was sparsely furnished: one table and a tall metal box standing beside it. They were alone. "No feminine touch here," commented Rachel. On the table was a pile of linen sheets, which they used to dry off.

About the time they finished, a man coughed for their attention. It took a bit, but Alexa located a small spherical speaker up high in a corner. He asked, "What are your names?"

Alexa flicked her eyes to Rachel and Donny, who shrugged. She asked back, "Why do you need to know? Where are we? And who are you?"

Thereupon, the guy from outside came on. Alexa recognized his voice. "Never mind, not necessary. What is necessary is for each of you to take a turn in the test unit." Involuntarily, all three looked at the tall box beside the table.

"No way am I going to do anything until I call my son," declared Rachel.

No response.

The three of them eyed each other and glanced around. *I could wind Rachel up into a scene, and they'd have to come in to deflect maximum destruction.* However, no doubt she'd be the one to bring Rachel down. Since neither of the other two moved, after a heavy sigh Alexa volunteered to go first.

She opened the door on the box and stepped inside, fighting panic as she closed it behind her. But as soon as the lock clicked a light came on. After a slight hum, there was warmth, then intense cold, and then an undeniable prick on the index finger she'd dutifully inserted into a receptacle, per instructions through an intercom above her head. A woman asked her to breathe deeply. After that, the request was for her to please disrobe entirely.

Alexa said, "You have to be kidding."

"Your clothes may harbor germs and viruses."

Alexa debated. "For whom. What is the health emergency? We haven't been anywhere with an outbreak or anything."

"From your belongings, we can verify there isn't one hopefully," came the guy's voice.

This was getting out of hand. "Is this some kind of joke?" No answer. *Just want the whole thing to be over.* "Well, you'd better not watch."

A powerful blue light and a moment of heat seemed to flash-fry her skin. Afterwards, the woman said, "At your feet are robes. Please put one on. We will test and sterilize your clothes and belongings."

When Alexa exited dressed in white, Rachel's eyes widened. Knowing the drama Rachel was capable of, Alexa thought it best to not mention all the details beforehand. "These folks must be sensitive to everything," she said. "I think it's okay though."

Rachel came out last. "Spooky," she whispered, while covering her mouth and nose.

Alexa asked, "Are you all right?"

Rachel nodded and impatiently shooed her at the door. "Let's go anywhere other than this freaky building."

Following instructions, out they trudged into the mist and through the dark to a nearby house, Donny in front of her and Rachel behind. The long robe Alexa wore slapped her legs with every step. Despite those brave words back there, without the distraction of her luggage, all the people standing in line about fifty feet away were unnerving.

Eventually they passed under a lighted arch into another small stone building. When the front door slammed shut behind them, all three jumped. Rachel muttered, "What next?"

The bright central space of the house included the entryway where they stood. Three open doorways showed on each side. Enough illumination spilled into them to identify beds in the three rooms on the right. Windows must be open because the same smells of wet greenery as outside wafted through the hallway. At first, everyone huddled near the door.

When nothing more happened, they began to investigate their surroundings.

As Rachel returned from the middle room after testing the bed, she moaned, "I can't just stay here. I need to call my son." She strode over to the front door, but it was locked from the outside. "What are we? Prisoners?"

From the back room came a low *zzzpft*, and Donny yelped, "Yow!" He trotted out, warning, "Don't try to climb out the window. I got zapped by some Klingon force field."

"You're joking," said Alexa, already on her way to examine the front bedroom.

In the dark, a bed and a table were discernible. At the window she tried blowing. Nothing happened. Next she tried brushing the hem of her sleeve. *Zzzpft.* Sparks all but flew. "Where did this technology come from?" Perhaps this was some secret military place. Alexa noticed someone out front, about twenty feet away, and whispered, "Yeah, guard us."

Back in the central area Rachel was pacing. She groaned theatrically. "A.J., where are we? What do we do?"

It'd been a long time since Rachel had used just her initials.

"Donny," said Alexa, "did you try your mobile before we left everything with them?"

He looked up. "Yep. Negatory on the signal."

Rachel stopped cold and pronounced, "Oh m'god, they took our passports."

Alexa gave Rachel the same look she always did when her friend began her drama routine. She had precious little extra energy to deal with all that, considering she was fighting her own anxiety. "They have our passports, yes, with everything else. They didn't specifically take them." She put her arm around Rachel. "It is all strange. However, this doesn't seem to be a jail."

Judging by the wild look, Rachel's imagination was going into overdrive. Alexa braced herself, knowing how far her friend could go on a tangent.

"What if we're caught on some island out of time, or something," said Rachel, almost hyperventilating, "and we can never go back, and they're all really ghosts out there, who can't get out of a time loop."

Alexa clamped her lips closed, managing to not smile, and tightened her hug around Rachel. "I bet we don't have all the information yet. There has to be a logical explanation for this."

Huffing, Rachel broke from Alexa's embrace. "I have to think as a parent."

"Which you did. You told me you arranged for Sammy to spend the night with his best bud, in case you stayed over in Nassau. Right?"

Rachel appeared unconvinced.

"Probably tomorrow it'll all become clear. And I'll be able to send a message to Mac, at least. And you to Sammy."

"Please," snorted Rachel. "Keep the optimism to yourself."

At that moment, Donny came out of the middle room on the other side of the building. "Coconuts in here." He pointed to the front. "That room is a kitchen." Moments later, he raised his voice from the back. "And this is a living room." He ambled over to Rachel, who remained near the front door. "All the conveniences of home, if you happen to be on a coconut diet."

Alexa called out from the kitchen. "Anybody like oatmeal? Besides pots and pans, that's it in here."

Rachel said, "I'm exhausted. Shouldn't it be late morning?" It appeared she was about to cry.

Donny, ever the optimist, said, "Maybe they gave us a sleeping drug. Tell you what, we can all cuddle up together and I'll keep you safe."

Alexa couldn't think of a comment to blast Donny appropriately without taking him down to cinders. Rachel locked eyes with her and they both shook their heads in disbelief while silently turning to go to their own beds. As Alexa closed her door, the lock clicked on Rachel's.

Alexa also felt exceedingly fatigued. Perhaps it was the darkness. Not able to locate a light switch, she had to grope around the bathroom. The toilet included a tank at head height with a dangling chain to let the water slosh. Perhaps they'd landed on some British protectorate island.

Eventually, she climbed onto the single bed and sat. Tired, and wound tight. The entire morning scrolled through her mind, scene by scene. What about the propeller? What was the name of the company for Cessna replacement parts?

It was all incredibly strange.

Except for that moment in the plane right before everything disappeared. She had to admit that despite all the odd things leading up to it, that feeling had been familiar, in a good way. Similar to some lovely experiences while meditating when she was young. *An experience of Beyond.*

Alexa adjusted the blanket over her legs. With her right hand she fingered her engagement ring, the one that upon sight both she and Mac recognized as perfect.

Did all this happen because I didn't stay put and wait for Mac? It was almost too big to take in. "Mac. Can you feel me? I'm here, wherever here is."

Chapter 3

Hunger awakened Alexa.

The sun had to be high in the sky, judging by the shadows. Ocean sounds made their way past billowing white curtains and the small room's lemon-colored walls glowed behind simple wood furnishings. Lovely.

Even so, she recognized nothing.

A mental image of Mac flashed in her mind; his long legs crossed at the ankles and feet on the edge of his messy desk. She smiled amidst the tug of sleep and stretched. Her muscles were a little sore.

Then the previous night's events burst into her mind and her instinct shrieked, *go to the plane!* Of course, reality also dawned. "Okay, got to locate a propeller and find someone to install it. Unless these folks insist on quarantine for a hunk of metal, too."

Belatedly it occurred to her. "They probably have a land line somewhere." With nothing else to do Alexa lay for a moment, hoping for inspiration. "Basics first. I'm starving."

In the kitchen, she began poking around the cabinets of rustic wood. She swept her hand across stone counters, and nervously eyed the high-tech stove.

As she filled a pot with water, Donny pushed open the kitchen door. "I heard Rachel moan. Loud." Stepping from side to side, he said, "Through the wall. She didn't respond when I knocked. And the door is locked."

When Alexa reached Rachel's door, heavy groans could be heard from the other side.

Donny brushed his hands on his trousers. "I feel kind of strange. Funny stomach, achy muscles. Do you think she does, too?"

Alexa knocked on the door. No sound inside. She pounded on it. Nothing.

She was about to yell for Rachel's attention when the front door banged open. People in shiny Hazmat suits rushed through and headed straight for Rachel's door, where Alexa and Donny allowed themselves to be jostled aside.

One of the people held a little metal cylinder to the door, after which it opened, allowing that crowd to rush into the room. They conversed quietly in a language Alexa couldn't identify. After a bit they barreled out, guiding a stretcher with Rachel on it. Sweat plastered her hair and she tossed her head side to side, to the point the oxygen mask barely stayed on.

As they guided Rachel's cot out the front door, a man said, in a heavy accent, "We will return tonight. Stay out of that room." He jerked his head at the closed door.

Gone. The hallway dropped into a well of silence.

Alexa tried to recall more precisely what she'd seen. *There were no wheels on the stretcher, nothing under it.*

On the temple steps Iain Newcastle smoothed errant wrinkles from his linen suit. The aircraft stood at parade rest on the lawn below; present and accounted for, exactly as the family legend predicted. He'd doubted the whole thing all along. *Until now.*

Walking toward him was his sister, her blonde hair the perfect setting for a flower the hue of her coral silk outfit. "Is that it?" She peered more closely. "Ah, guarded." She studied it for a moment. "I thought it had trouble landing last night."

Newcastle nodded. "Something is missing on the front. They must have towed it to this position." They gazed at the silver and red myth, bright under the sun. "Haven't seen any of the people."

"I may have," replied Penelope. "They took a stretcher with someone on it from that guesthouse," she pointed at a building, "to a side door of the temple. Woman, I think," she said. "Dark hair, not red."

Newcastle brushed back his own fine blond hair. He couldn't understand why he would feel relieved with the last bit of information. If truth were told, it would be hard to know if this turn of events helped or hindered his assignment.

Chapter 4

In the guesthouse central hallway, Alexa and Donny stared at the front door after it closed.

Donny broke the quiet. "Do you think Rachel will be okay?"

In shock from how bad Rachel looked, Alexa replied, "I hope so." Since she'd seen her friend in much worse situations, however, she added, "Rachel usually bounces right back." Alexa searched Donny's face. "You said you feel bad, too."

Donny tried the front door. It remained locked from the outside. "Not enough to call those suits in here again," Stretching his shoulders, he said, "But I'm going back to bed. Call me if something happens."

After he closed his door, Alexa picked at her white robe. "I need to clean up."

Her bathroom resembled the inside of a geode, with every item crafted from stone. A basin of rose perched on a white marble ledge. The rose stone tub rested on a honey-colored stone floor. While she was soaking, a sunbeam slanted in and lit up the rose color around her. "Beautiful," she murmured. "Must have cost a fortune to ship this stuff." She used white linen sheets to dry off. Afterward she nibbled on coconut.

She must have dozed through the afternoon because at almost dark she awoke again, feeling ravenous. Delicious smells were detectable, seeping into her room from within the house.

In the kitchen, she found a tall, thin man with a shock of white hair and bushy eyebrows. He obviously was the one banging pans and lids. The man wore a threadbare uniform that could have been in a World War II movie. *Wonder if he's involved in those battle reenactments.*

"Hello, sir," Alexa said. The spices were rich and savory. "This smells terrific. Can I help?"

He glanced up and a smile spread big. "Eh, lass, aye. Would you mind moving those plates a wee bit closer to me here?"

As Alexa complied, she asked, "How is Rachel? When they took her away, she looked pretty sick."

"Rachel, aye." He stopped, his face taking on a serious mien. Alexa's heart skipped a beat. "She is all right," he said. "Stable. But we will have to coddle her for a bit."

Almost weak with relief, Alexa asked, "What's wrong with her? Nobody said anything, other than we could all be mutually contagious."

"Rachel has a virus," said the man. "One that can be nasty, if the person doesn't receive the correct attention right away. Therefore, we were on the lookout for it and caught it in time. And since the two of you have not come down with the symptoms, it seems you won't suffer from it."

"Both of us felt achy."

"That is all right," he replied. "It's your immune system fighting it off."

Alexa arranged and rearranged small items on the counter. "Are you the father of the young man? He said you would tell us what's going on. Since the cell phones don't work here, is a land line available anywhere?"

He smiled at her. "I am Murdoch Callaghan. You may consider me your host."

"Where are we? The Everglades?"

"You are on Adalans, at the healing temple. Not Florida." He turned toward the door. "Are you hungry?"

Her stomach growled. "Yes!" *Not Florida?*

"Good, let's call your friend and take our plates to the dining room."

On their way to Donny's room, Alexa asked, "Adalans? Is this some kind of military installation, on Cuba or something?"

Callaghan rapped twice on the door and said, "Mister Donald, come to supper." Next, he stepped across to the middle room between the kitchen and living room. He reached in, moved his arm a bit, and the space lit up.

As he left, Alexa stuck her head in. The table and chairs were the same golden wood as in her bedroom. She scanned for a fixture, since she'd not yet figured out how to turn on a light in her room. No specific point, simply the walls seeming to glow. "That's fascinating."

Callaghan had headed to the kitchen. She caught up with him. "So, what kind of place is this?" Her tone was becoming more insistent. Donny came up behind her, as she demanded, "Where are we?"

Callaghan stopped and turned, his eyes switching from Alexa to Donny and back. He glanced at the window, which by that time showed nothing but blackness, and nodded as if answering his own question. "Are either of you familiar with the star constellations?"

"For navigating at night I learned the stars fairly well," said Alexa.

Callaghan must have made a decision because he headed for the front door. "All right, it's dark. Let's look at the sky."

When the two stepped out the door, in concert the response was, "Wow." Several huge circles of gaseous light, each with a twinkling star in the middle, filled much of the sky. A few other stars appeared four or five times bigger than usual. The illumination was as if from a full moon, though no such orb showed its face.

"Are we at a high elevation?" asked Donny. "No that would be difficult, with the ocean nearby."

Alexa scanned the sky. "I can't see any of the constellations that should be there." *Were we somehow transported to South America?* "I'm not as familiar with the stars in the southern hemisphere."

Callaghan shook his head, and said, "It is." He stopped, and pursed his lips. After a moment, he said, "This is all because." But he interrupted the flow again.

Alexa stifled a scream.

"It is because we are looking at the stars from a different point of view." After rushing out with that statement, the man drew in a deep breath, threw his head back and studied the sky. "The stars are this bright because we are standing on a planet in a solar system close to the Orion Nebulae." He pulled his gaze to them and said slowly, "In other words, we are far, far away from Earth."

Alexa heard his words. They made no sense.

Donny's Adams apple moved as he swallowed hard and blinked twice slowly.

She looked up into the night. *All I want is a quiet life in a little house with Mac.* "Really, truly, this is not the time for a joke."

Callaghan watched them intently. "I spent a long time wishing it was a joke, a dream."

Alexa shook her head, and worked to keep from screaming at the man. *Some people will go to incredible lengths for…for…whatever.*

"Where are you from?" asked Donny. He didn't seem to notice Alexa's glare for granting any logic to the conversation

"Scotland. I had been in the Bahamas for a year."

Alexa broke in. "That's so quaint: 'in the Bahamas for a year.' I have to say, you have all the right words," she spat. "But everything you're saying is impossible. So please, just give us the truth."

Callaghan's eyes telegraphed pain. "I am sorry. This is the truth."

Alexa tried again. "All right, *sir*. I'll play along. Tell me, then, just how much will you demand for us to get home. I warn you, though, nobody is rich here, so I question your game. But just spell it out, so we can get home."

Callaghan ducked his head. "I am sorry, lass. But as far as I can tell, there is no method for returning."

"Unacceptable," she decreed.

Donny interrupted. "Okay, let's just say what you're telling us is true. Then, the question is: how did you get here?"

"In much the same manner as you, I believe," said Callaghan, giving a shaky almost-laugh. "However, I could not find a place to land my plane. So, I crashed in the ocean the smoothest I was able and swam to shore. Later, in case others came through in an aircraft, I arranged for the lawn to be cleared." He looked

Alexa in the eye. "My apologies that it became a wee rough in the meantime. Its repair began today. Your plane is safe."

Alexa stared at him. She recognized that the man was trying to help her feel better. His statements, however, were impossible.

"Exactly when did you arrive?" asked Donny.

"The Japanese had recently bombed Pearl Harbor. I was in the Bahamas, collecting intelligence for Great Britain."

"That's around seventy years ago," said Donny. "Were you two years old?"

"Nay, I had been in the Royal Air Force for some time." Callaghan then looked up at the sky.

Since he didn't seem to be relenting from his outrageous story, Alexa followed his gaze to the sky, which admittedly was very *not* what it should look like. *None of this is really happening.*

An answer popped into her head. She turned to Callaghan. "Let's just say you're telling the truth, and we are actually on a different planet." She closed her eyes, marveling at how ridiculous that last statement sounded. "The right question, therefore, is: How often does this transport happen? And how do we make it happen again?" *Mac. Must get to Mac.* "I need to go back."

Callaghan pursed his lips. While opening the door to the house, he said, "I am sorry, Alexa, but is not common. And even if it was, your plan would not work like you think. Come inside and I'll explain more."

As she turned, Alexa noticed people strolling along the path in front of the house. And did not care.

Inside at the table they tried Callaghan's food: a golden mashed potato-type concoction with spicy vegetables and sparks of mango. After two bites to take off the hunger edge, Alexa asked, "Why can't we make the strange light happen and fly into it?" In her mind, she began figuring out how to make a strong enough wooden propeller. The food felt like a rock in her gut.

"Or, how far are we from Earth?" put in Donny.

Considering the way he kept asking questions, like visiting a new country, Alexa couldn't figure out if he was upset—or just stupid.

Callaghan's expression became speculative. "Adalans is about nine hundred and fifty light years from Earth. If you were to look from Earth in the direction of the Dog Star, or Sirius, we are beyond that."

Donny perked up. "Cool! In researching Atlantis, I remember that Sirius is considered to be the Dog Star in many cultures. The Egyptians noticed it appeared right before the Nile did its flooding thing each year. It also was connected to Shiva, as a companion. And both the Cherokee and Pawnee American Indian tribes? They regarded it as an end point for, like, a path for souls or something." He stopped when he noticed the look Alexa was giving him.

Stupid. Donny must be stupid. "I don't suppose you could remember something actually useful," she commented, in a tone that could blister paint.

Donny mumbled something like, "actually, this is a God-send."

"Are you kidding me?" demanded Alexa, leaning at Donny.

Callaghan jumped in. "In fact there is a path, in a manner of speaking."

Alexa felt her face screw up. The man must be pulling their chains, all around. "Okay, this sick joke is ending. Right now. I really need to let my fiancé know I'm okay, and Rachel really needs to contact her son."

"I wish it was a misguided jest," replied Callaghan, keeping his calm. "Nevertheless, you are very far from Earth. And since you traveled about nine hundred and fifty light years—"

"In seconds?" interrupted Alexa, incredulous.

"Aye. It also seemed no time when I made the trip." Callaghan took a deep breath and rushed on. "Lass, somehow against all known laws of physics for us, you are also about nine hundred and fifty years into your future. This is the year 2962, in standard Earth time."

Newcastle and Penelope strolled, out for an evening's stroll. He aimed this way and that, all the while keeping his younger sister engaged with gossip about family and friends of family.

Gradually, slowly, he brought them down the path from the temple, to walk past a certain guesthouse. His pulse pounded. The gravel crunched under his shoes and the breeze boded well. He asked Penny, "Why did you leave school early?" He had to distract her, because she would not be able to keep her emotions off the point of this visit.

"That again." She took the bait. "I thought you would be the last to pester me about leaving school." Penelope's brilliance in math and science also made her quick to become bored with the institutions their family insisted she attend. "I know perfectly well how to dress and dance. And I can converse in four languages. I do not understand why I must attend stupid schools that cater to mindless children."

"When you're home," said Newcastle, "you are almost always at the stables, exercising the horses."

"I have found being out of sight is helpful in sidestepping the idiot boys our dear bossy brother always tries to foist on me." Penelope tossed her head. "I plan to marry Captain Pearson, and that is that."

There. Newcastle almost crowed. They were past the guesthouse without Penny noticing. And with her obsessing about the captain, he could probably turn them around to make another pass.

He doubted Pearson was aware of his imminent fate. But thank the stars, the situation would not be his problem.

Newcastle surreptitiously studied Callaghan and the woman on the building's portico. He bet old Callaghan was breaking the news. It certainly sounded like it.

The man with them was probably the one to contact. Perhaps this whole expedition might all turn out all right.

Nevertheless, that idiot Corky also strolled nearby. Iain never could understand how Corky had made it from class-clown to the prime minister's assistant. What was he doing on a walk, at this moment, near this house?

Chapter 5

Early the next morning, Callaghan strolled into the guesthouse after a quick knock. "Good morning to you both," he boomed. "Good news, you are cleared to move about."

Alexa strode out of her room. She'd been barely civil as the gentleman left the previous evening, and had hardly slept, wracking her brain to figure out a solution. "I need to make certain. Is there any method, any possible way at all that we can get back to Earth?"

A kindly look came into Callaghan's eyes as he turned to her. "You can go to Earth, aye. But it will be Earth in the year 2962, or whenever you arrive."

"Hold on," said Donny. "It's possible to get to Earth? There's interstellar travel?"

Callaghan nodded. "Aye." He held up one hand while fishing in his pocket with the other. "Here, the doctors asked me to ask the two of you to take these." He reached and placed in their hands three pills each. "They will help protect you from all the beasties around today."

Alexa leaned forward and accepted the pills. "Can we communicate to our time?"

Callaghan's gaze was sympathetic. "Not that I know of."

She wouldn't simply lie down and go passive. "Surely the light thing is good for something. Does it go both directions?"

"I understand that wherever you go through it, it is always forward in years, which would not help. It's not the same as wormholes used for travel. Wormhole. Strange name, eh?"

A couple of knocks at the open door showed two small men. After Callaghan gestured for them to enter, they placed Alexa's luggage, Rachel's backpack and Donny's duffel in the central hallway.

"Here are your belongings," said Callaghan. While Alexa righted her larger roll-on, then the smaller one, and placed her backpack on the big one, Callaghan said, "May I suggest a tour of the Temple?"

As Donny returned from dropping his bag in his room, Alexa asked, "Can we see Rachel?"

"Aye you can, through glass. She is still feeling punky, though I think a brief visit is safe."

All her ideas kept coming up against a brick wall. Alexa blew out her breath. "Just a sec, please." She extracted her computer from the pouch on the front of the small roll-on, opened it and switched it on. "Want to see if my computer works." *Photos of Mac and me, please be there.* The screen lit up. Her photos were safe. "There's no such thing as an Internet? It's not picking up any kind of signal."

"If you mean cyberspace, yes, there is."

"Ah. Documents in the cloud will be safe. Right." Alexa closed the computer and returned it into the pouch. Then she reached into her backpack for lip gloss, where she found it in the appropriate place.

But the package, the one in gold cloth entrusted to her by Brahmaji, was absent.

In a split second, all those old, and not so old, self-doubts hit. Not only had she screwed up somehow and not done enough to keep everything, everyone safe, now the item she'd promised to deliver was gone. Alexa frantically emptied her pack. "Something is missing." When Callaghan didn't appear surprised, she pressed, "Do your people steal?"

"Nay, lass, they do not. Not one of my people would take anything of yours."

Did it fall out? The landing was rough. "I need to swing by the plane. It's imperative I locate this item."

Callaghan turned to Donny. "Donald, do you know about an item belonging to Alexa?"

Donny moved his eyes from one to the other. "Uh, I don't think so."

Callaghan lifted his eyebrows slightly. "All right," he said, while opening the door, "let's walk to the Temple for the grand tour. Regarding the aircraft, perhaps we might go by there afterward? People are nearby, watching over it."

Alexa felt like stomping her foot and insisting they do what she wanted, right that moment. But good sense—from somewhere— kept her from throwing a fit. "I suppose so, if you're certain no one will disturb the plane. Speaking of the plane, the propeller is damaged. Is there technology around here to make a really strong wooden one?"

"I noticed the propeller," said Callaghan. "And I already have my team printing one."

It took a few beats for Alexa to understand what he meant. "Oh, you mean 3-D printing. That's really new. Well, new, at home. My home." She halted at the threshold. "But I don't think a plastic propeller would work on the Cessna."

Callaghan smiled. "You are correct. It would not. There are also metal printers."

"Hmmm." Alexa reluctantly followed him off the porch.

It was difficult to not be distracted by the beautiful morning. Basking in sunlight for the first time in eons, it seemed, she stretched. Flowers of all colors and sizes bloomed large, filling the air with rose and gardenia scents. Morning sun glinted on the ocean. People strolled across the green lawn in front of the temple, between the guesthouses and among a group of more official-looking buildings across the way. Most of the people, every one dressed in either a white toga or a simple white shift, were carrying items as if on errands.

A breeze rustled the leaves and played with Alexa's hair. A fear began tugging at her. "I just want to make sure, this place isn't— Purgatory or Heaven. We didn't die, did we?"

Callaghan laughed, deep and hearty. "Aye, I also wondered that for a bit. But you can be certain, we are all very much alive."

A few baskets about twice the size of those under hot air balloons, carrying as many as six people, glided toward the big building. She asked, "Are those things hovering on their own?"

"They are powered by crystals," said Callaghan. He stopped to look back and forth along the gravel path. "Which is the reason no one uses wheels around here, though I tried to introduce them at first." He glanced out over the ocean. "I'm happy to say everyone enjoys sailing."

Alexa coughed politely. "Considering when you left you are probably not aware that at times, crystals have been all the rage. A family near me filled several rooms with them. I can't say I ever noticed anything special."

Callaghan shook his head. "Let me explain about this place." He stopped and gestured to the large structure on a low hill. "This first part of the Temple is where the healers work and where Rachel is." He moved his hand toward the far side. "On down is an area for people wanting," he searched for words, "to refine awareness and sensitivity. As in, sensitivity to feelings and thoughts."

Alexa felt she had a handle on all that. However, Callaghan seemed to be talking about something else. She narrowed her eyes, prompting more explanation.

Callaghan leaned his head to the side. "People here spend a good deal of time with the crystals. Almost everything on this planet works because of crystals. The difference to Earth, is the big one here that boosts all the others."

"How big?" she asked.

He looked up at the temple. "See the dome? About that size."

Donny whistled. Alexa clarified, "One huge crystal, or a bunch?"

"The one I'm referring to is a single crystal, amazing clarity. There are other smaller ones, both similar and different. Each has a use." He glanced up and began climbing the steps. "Here we are. Let's enter."

The structure was of white granite. Steps spanned the front and at the top was a row of columns, all capped by designs in green, brown and blue that looked to be inlaid stone. Inside, the walls were decorated with a series of stone mosaics, each twice an adult's height and about twenty feet long. Callaghan gestured toward them and said, "Those portray major historical events."

Mac loves the mosaics in Turkey. Alexa's heart plummeted. *Mac.* She stared forward.

A circular opening to the sky in the middle of the dome over a central cavernous space allowed sunlight to pool on the floor. People milled in and around stalls full of produce and flowers. Many stopped, watching the three of them. All chatter ceased. "Everyone heard about your arrival," whispered Callaghan.

A tiny man sitting in the sunbeam in the middle of the hall glared at them, clambered up, pointed and began speaking loudly. Perhaps it was the language Alexa heard yesterday when the Hazmat suits came for Rachel. The man had a bony head and wore only a loincloth. He began pacing toward them, swinging a stout stick as long as he was tall.

"It's the little guy who came up to the plane," said Donny.

The two looked for guidance to Callaghan, who put up both hands to slow the process. The man continued advancing. He stopped at about fifteen feet and shouted, glaring at Donny, gesturing first to him then to the outside. He took further steps toward Donny, who began backing up while Callaghan watched carefully, and did not interfere. When Donny at last stood on the temple steps, the man stopped, turned around and quietly walked to his spot to sit.

Callaghan motioned for Alexa to follow him. Outside, Donny appeared outraged. "What was that all about?"

Callaghan folded his arms. "Remember I said the crystal increases sensitivity to everything? That means people are aware of the thoughts, intentions and recent activities of others. Including someone in another building, as in a guesthouse." He waited a moment. "Is there anything you might want to say to Alexa?"

Donny stopped pacing and spun to face him. "What do you mean, intentions and recent activity?"

"I'm speaking of an activity that would be considered harmful

43

to someone else."

Donny replied in a haughty tone, "Nothing to do with me."

Confused, Alexa turned back and forth between the two men.

"All right then, since you won't fess up, I will spell it out," said Callaghan. "You took something that belongs to Alexa. You were thinking about it quite clearly yesterday." Donny appeared dumbstruck, and he did not deny. Alexa studied him more closely. "In your favor," said Callaghan, "you seemed to be wondering if you could return it to her. Nevertheless you did, in fact, steal it."

Blood began pounding in Alexa's head. "A package wrapped in gold cloth is missing from my backpack. Come to think of it, this whole last week the contents of my luggage at Becky's house seemed rearranged." She stepped up to right in front of Donny. "You were searching my stuff!" Her lack of height didn't matter at the moment, since he appeared to feel she towered eight feet tall. "I need the package. Right now."

Donny glanced at the ground, then peeped up to the temple, switched to gazing off across the ocean, and finally looked at her. He groaned, said, "It's only a crystal," and raised his hands in confusion. "I can't understand why he wanted me to take it!"

She bore her eyes into his. "He?"

"The man wouldn't say his name," said Donny. He jutted out his chin. "I easily traced him though. John Lloyd."

Alexa nearly fell over. The same man who sat in the room with Brahmaji when she received the package? The man with whom she made an effort to carry on a friendly chat, because he seemed so alone? He had never really made much of an effort to connect with people at the school.

"He offered me much more than normal for this type of job."

"You do this all the time?" Alexa shook her head in wonder. "You're a professional thief!"

"Not professional. At least I don't consider myself that way," protested Donny. "When I realized it's a crystal, for god's sake, I wondered what all the fuss was about."

"Where is it?" barked Alexa. "What did you do with it?"

"I tried to leave it outside my window."

"No!"

Donny held up his hands as if to ward her off. "It's in the kitchen."

She had to stifle an impulse to shake the guy. She turned to Callaghan. "How long does the light column last, generally?"

Callaghan considered his response. "Somewhere between five and eight minutes."

Alexa nodded. "I thought so." She turned to Donny. "And what were you doing, to delay us the extra ten minutes at the airport?"

Donny groused a bit, then whined, "I was calling in to report that I'd be traveling with you." His words got quieter, to hardly audible by the end, "which was part of the agreement."

Alexa closed her eyes.

"If it helps, he wanted me to avoid hurting you."

Ice practically formed off her breath. "So. Avoid hurting me. But no problem with delaying us enough to get us sucked into the light column." Donny hung his head. "Because of that telephone call, Rachel's eight-year-old son is wondering where is his mother and my fiancé has no idea whether I am even alive. And we are theoretically stuck here forever." Her tone went acid. "Brilliant."

As Alexa turned toward the house, Callaghan touched her arm. "Lass, I found it in the kitchen last night and moved it to underneath the third drawer from the window."

Donny said, "I'm really sorry. I didn't mean to make all this happen."

Alexa shook her head, unwilling to give him a break.

Before she stomped away, she heard Callaghan say to Donny, "I checked the video and know you had the sense to expose it to sterilization on the first night you arrived. If you had not done so and thus put my people at risk, Donald, you would be getting used to the prison cell that would be your home for the rest of your life. See if you can demonstrate some good sense from now on."

Chapter 6

From behind a market booth with singing birds, Newcastle watched the interaction on the temple steps. Alexa, that should be her name, did not look happy when she stormed away. He wondered if his contact had botched the job. The man appeared absolutely bollixed.

Calculating that the guy would be well-primed for domination, he quietly approached the man from behind. "You are Donny, correct?"

"Yeah, what's it to you?"

A little upset, are we? "Actually it is of great import to me," replied Newcastle, stroking the bridge of his nose with his forefinger. "And I believe our interaction will be rather significant for you, since I am to complete a handsome payment for a job well done."

The Donny person looked at him warily. "What kind of job?"

Newcastle opted to match wary with cagey. "Our family lost a certain item. Some time ago, you agreed to obtain it for us."

Donny grunted and glanced at the guesthouse. "No idea what you're talking about."

Newcastle experienced a momentary impulse to take the guy by his low-class shirt and shake him, which would attract far too much attention, alas. To modulate his emotions, Newcastle conjured thoughts of a particularly lovely lady on TohuMu.

Perhaps a little reminder would assist his memory. "It is fortuitous you made it away, since the police were about to locate you." That focused the man's attention.

"Tell me something I don't already know." Donny glanced at his watch, and said, "Well look at that, how time flies."

Watching Donny's retreat, Newcastle smoothed his hand over the back of his head.

If only he had listened last year to his instinct about the engine design—the engine that failed *after* a full production run. If he'd done the right thing then, despite all the time spent on the design, his brother wouldn't now have the leverage to make such dire threats.

A quarter of an hour later Alexa sat on her bed, music player in hand and ear buds in place. A shadow momentarily blocked the sun in front of her. When she opened her eyes, Callaghan stood there with a concerned look on his face. She took out the earphones. "I'm listening to a chant. One that always calms me down." She bit her lip. "And I probably need some calming."

Callaghan shrugged. "A friend's betrayal is never pleasant."

Alexa shook her head. "I wouldn't count Donny as a friend. I don't know him well." She placed the player on the bed. "The question is, why would someone hire him to steal it? I mean, he's right. It is a crystal. The same as a really beautiful and much bigger one I saw before this trip. But it's not solid gold."

"The place you saw the big one, is that where you received this one?"

"Yes, at the school of my family's meditation teacher." Alexa leaned back against the headboard. "In fact, last week a friend told me something about it." The story had been garbled. She tried to order the details in her head. "After I left, a man who introduced himself as the boss of John Lloyd showed up at the school. And maybe he threatened some people, because Brahmaji sent everyone away that same night."

"You know this John Lloyd?"

"Kind of," said Alexa. "We spoke a couple of times. He seemed nice, if a bit stiff." Out the window, a tiny yellow bird jumped from twig to twig. "The big crystal disappeared from the school at the same time. Probably Brahmaji took it with him."

She gazed at the crystal in her hands: shorter than a pencil and scarcely thicker. Smooth and cool. Sun glinted off a metallic sheen on the outside, while inside light refracted into rainbows, like a transparent opal.

She stroked the sides. *Brahmaji, bring me home. Hah. As if.*

"Funny how I mocked the crystals here, and lo and behold, Donny managed to turn my life upside down because of one." She studied it. "I have no idea what to do with this thing, other than perhaps wear it on a necklace."

"Considering someone went to the trouble of hiring a thief, maybe—"

Alexa completed his thought by saying, "I should keep it under wraps." Nodding, she placed it into a pocket on her cargo pants and closed the clasp. "Um, this is crystal." She then gestured toward the Temple. "Everything around us here is crystal. Do you recognize this type?"

"Not completely" he said. "I have seen one here that is somewhat similar, but without the sheen on the outside. I'd say yours is from somewhere else."

"I guess I'll figure out what to do with it later."

Callaghan changed the subject. "Would you be interested in visiting Rachel?"

On the path to the temple they met the young man who had asked her and her friends to wait in the plane. In the daylight, he was obviously Callaghan's son. His name was Jesek, and he didn't seem to hold a grudge about her reaction that night. Before she and Callaghan entered a side entrance to the temple, the young man mentioned something about overseeing a project and departed.

"He looks barely twenty," commented Alexa, "hardly old enough to be a manager."

Callaghan watched his son turn the corner. "The crystals keep everyone younger looking than is common for us, and healthier. Which is the reason I am still around." He opened the door for Alexa. "Besides having completed pilot training, Jesek is also an artist, and is teaching people to use the printing press I built for him."

In the hospital area, Alexa stood at the glass window with a view into the room where Rachel lay, fast asleep. *I've never seen her look so bad.*

After they knocked softly, Rachel wakened and managed a weak smile. "A.J., you're okay." She drew a ragged breath, during which time she closed her eyes. "I was worried."

Alexa and Callaghan stood in an empty corridor that could be in any hospital at home. The few white-coated men and women busy in nearby rooms echoed the norm a thousand years ago. "I'm fine," said Alexa. "I understand you will be, too."

Rachel nodded slightly. "Have you been able to call anyone?"

Her friend had no idea of their whereabouts, or whenabouts. Springing that kind of shock on her at that moment would be cruel. The thought of Rachel not ever seeing her son again made Alexa feel sick. "It's tougher than I thought. I'm still trying."

Chapter 7

As Callaghan closed the door to the hospital wing, he invited Alexa on a walk. "The park near your guesthouse is in full bloom." *Perhaps I can pick up some useful information.* "Yes, please."

The park included trees and plants similar to those at home on the East Coast, including dogwood, fig, live oaks, a pine grove in the distance and even a stately magnolia. Low gray shrubs mounded here and there. Birds flitted among branches and on the ground, and small animals were probably around, judging by the scurrying sounds.

After a few yards, Callaghan asked, "Are you aware people from almost every settled planet will be arriving soon, for a grand conference at the Temple?"

Alexa almost stumbled. "There are many settled planets?" She couldn't wrap her head around the concept, despite all the science fiction she'd read.

Callaghan chuckled. "Aye. Officially, five more. Though I've heard of others. It's been going on for hundreds of years. None are as crowded as Earth."

"When did humans come to Adalans?"

"That happened thousands of years ago, through the same light that brought you and me, evidently." Callaghan snagged something from a bush. "Do you like figs?" When Alexa nodded, he handed it to her and snipped another. "Perhaps all those legends about Atlantis breaking up were true. The story is that due to an emergency, people came here, using the light beam created by the crystals that connect Earth and Adalans. Soon after those people arrived here, the light stopped." He cut the air with his hand. "Perhaps because the crystals on Earth became covered by water and sand."

Callaghan tossed the fig stem into the brush. "A few years before I showed up, the light began to happen again. Sporadically.

Maybe the crystals on Earth are closer to the surface? However it happens, the light generally delivers to Adalans fish, or dolphins, or sea birds. Or coconuts." He stopped walking. "The reason I asked them to give you coconuts and oatmeal, which I import from Earth, was because those foods were the ones I could be fairly certain you all could handle."

Alexa said, "We wondered about that."

"Aye. However, food variety will increase with our visitors arriving."

After a couple of steps Alexa asked, "Why are these people coming here?"

"It seems there has been a change lately, in how easily everyone interacts. The hundreds of years since the twentieth century were quite different from our time. Which is good, considering what was happening when I left." He fell silent for a few yards. "In these centuries, people and cultures were generally not torn apart. And still aren't." Callaghan slumped. "Though new, troubling incidents are becoming more and more common. Even some piracy."

Alexa tilted her head to the side. "So, governments are coming together here to make new laws?"

"Nay," said Callaghan. "It's the spiritual leaders who want to convene. Most every religion is sending a representative, to identify a way to stop the change in trend."

Alexa tried to think of a similar reaction from her own time, and couldn't. Religious leaders foregoing their own interests and cooperating for a greater good—things *must* have changed.

Callaghan asked, "Do you want everyone to know from whence you come?"

Her gut reaction was a strong, "No. Please."

"We should move the airplane, at the least." He gestured to the temple and all around them. "Adalans is known to be unusual. But the plane is too much to explain away."

"Unusual?"

He searched for an explanation. "When the wormhole leading

here was first discovered about thirty years ago, explorers for the League of Planets expected the system to be uninhabited. Humans already being here was a big surprise."

Alexa asked, "Is it possible to put the plane in a shed or something?" When Callaghan said yes, she felt a little relief.

They were quiet for a few yards, during which she watched her feet as she walked, an activity that usually put her in a zone. Soon though, the loss of Mac and her life crashed in on her. Almost as bad as when her father died, when it seemed the last source of goodness was snatched away.

A bad time. Not a place to revisit. Her mind veered off.

Change of subject. Alexa angled her head to the side. "I asked you if this is a military installation and you said no. Is Adalans centrally located, or neutral or something? Why here?"

Callaghan smiled, granting her the point of logic. "Good question. Would you mind if I ask a few first?"

His request sounded suspicious. On the other hand, it might distract her thoughts. "Okay."

"Mac is your fiancé, yes?" She nodded, and Callaghan continued. "Do you have any family, other than Mac?"

Alexa massaged her neck. "Not really, because I don't count a second-cousin who stole my family home, in essence. I recently worked for that woman till I walked out after receiving notice about the house. Otherwise, my mother passed away when I was a child and my grandfather," her voice caught, "died five months ago. My one and only aunt, my mother's sister, she died two years ago. And my father," she sighed, "disappeared in a boating accident in the Caribbean when I was a teenager."

After a puff of breath, Alexa said. "You'd think I would have the good sense to not go near the Caribbean, considering my father disappeared there—and all the strange things that happen in that area. Are you certain that all those planes and big ships that have disappeared over time never showed up here?" As he nodded, she said, "It's just so bizarre. I guess they're at the bottom of the ocean."

She raised her hands in surrender. Memories seeped under the locked door. "Right before my father left, I accused him of always putting his pet theories about Atlantis before me. And look where I end up." A scene surfaced in her mind, with her wailing at her father, accusing him of not loving her. Her father had looked both pained and sympathetic. Before more of that old ache barreled through, she mentally slammed the door on it.

Callaghan was looking at her kindly, unaware of her selfishness then. "Do you look much similar to your parents?"

"I supposedly look like my mother. I have my father's eyes and hair. He was tall."

Callaghan persisted. "What were their names?"

Alexa turned to gaze at him quizzically. "Mary and John. Alden."

"And how many years ago did your father disappear?"

Where this is going? "Almost twelve years, I guess."

Callaghan switched his attention to out over the ocean, probably watching the three sailboats. Some kind of bird song twittered from a group of trees, and a small animal snuffled in the bushes.

Alexa tried changing the subject again. "How is it the bushes and trees and all the animals I've seen are like the ones on Earth?"

Callaghan turned around, scanning the forest. "The people who came here many years ago brought their crops and animals with them. The birds and dogs and cats are much as the ones you and I knew at home."

"My family always had cats when I was growing up," she said. "I like dogs."

"We even have some animals up there," he pointed to the mountains, "that may be extinct on Earth. We have sent some breeding pairs to Earth, when governments ask for them." He nodded across the ocean. "The plants native to Adalans are more gray and the local animals are small, no bigger than a dog." Then he pointed up to the sky. "The nearest planet in this system is almost entirely crystal. You cannot live there without protection.

Though since the galactics showed up, people do work there to mine the crystals."

"Galactics," repeated Alexa. "People from other planets?"

Callaghan nodded.

A hush fell between them. Perhaps he was watching how the ocean changed colors as clouds raced above.

Callaghan drew a deep breath. "Did you ever receive word about your father's disappearance?"

"Not really." *Wish he would let go of that ancient subject.* "His motorboat showed up in pieces, but not the small boat towed behind it. And his body never washed ashore." After a moment, Alexa continued. "I tried to convince Dad the night before to ask my grandfather about borrowing the plane to go to the Bahamas. But Dad didn't want my grandfather to know about the trip."

Callaghan turned to her. "Alexa, I am sorry. I don't know how to break this to you more gently." He touched her arm. "I know of one other person who was transported here, and I believe he was your father."

A bird screed up in the sky, maybe an eagle, and some critters were tussling down the trail. She stared at the man.

Her father. *Here?*

Alexa turned to Callaghan. "Why would you say that?" She searched around, half expecting her dad to step out from behind a tree. "Is he alive? Is he here?"

"Aye, alive!" said Callaghan. "At least, he was alive the last time we heard from him. But nay, not here." Callaghan's tone turned placating. "About ten of our years ago, a tall man appeared, in a rubber dingy on the inlet here. He said his name was John. His eyes were the most amazing aquamarine color, close to yours. He had red hair, though not as bright as yours."

"My God," she breathed. "Where is he?"

"When he arrived he was very concerned about his daughter. In fact, he left about a month later, intent on finding some method to go back to you."

Alexa lowered her head in disbelief. "Did he know about the time difference, about being in the future?"

"Aye," said Callaghan. "He said it should not matter, if he found the right person to help him. He was convinced a master, as he called it, would transport him back to you. And he went to find someone for that."

Looking up to the sky, Alexa said, "Dad always was a believer in metaphysical saints and cosmic masters. Do you know where he is?"

"Nay, I am sorry."

"When was the last time you heard from him?"

Callaghan spread his hands. "It has been years. He stayed in touch at first. When we didn't hear from him, I contacted the last place we knew he visited. They did not know where he went. However," said Callaghan, "your father's meetings on the different planets had an effect. Because of them, Adalans was chosen to host this conference. Some of those wise men your father spoke with will probably attend."

Alexa did not hear much of what Callaghan said about the assembly. Her mind whirled in a storm of frustration and confusion. She turned and strode along the path. Callaghan followed.

She stopped and spun to face him. "What is the likelihood of this happening to two people from the same family? How can I know you are telling the truth? About any of this?"

"Regarding our time and place, you can verify with any one of the people beginning to arrive tomorrow. Regarding your father and you," he moved his head from side to side. "I think it may have something to do with your crystal."

"You refer, I assume," said Alexa, "to the one I promised to keep safe until I handed it to Mac and which I have no idea about what to do with now?"

Callaghan cocked his head. "Yes. Is there any connection between it and your father?"

"Kind of. Dad also meditated. He learned when he married my mother because she was into it. Later, he took me to learn. The person who taught us, he is the one who gave me the crystal."

Callaghan nodded, studying a nearby shrub. "Although it isn't the same as crystals we have here, I did notice last night that it resembles one in a legend from my childhood in Scotland." He searched around and gestured to a nearby bench. "Did your father ever tell you the name 'Alden' is Scots?"

"I'm vaguely aware of that. My father had a book with ancestors and he would let me look at it when I was a little girl."

Callaghan said, "I enjoyed your father's company when he arrived, after these many years without my kind." He stopped, and crossed his arms before beginning again. "I mean, I am happy here. I have a marvelous wife and many wonderful children. Nevertheless, it was good catching up a bit about my own time."

Alexa couldn't help but feel his sadness. "Did you leave family behind in the 1940s?"

Callaghan nodded briefly. "Aye, my wife and infant son. I never had the heart to search through history to find out what happened to them. She was beautiful and kind. I hope she remarried."

It struck Alexa that she could begin to think of Mac in the far past tense. As in, he *was* handsome and witty and lovable and loving, but no longer, because he di…. No, she wouldn't even think the term. Internally, she fell to her knees, *no, no, no, no,* beating with her heart.

Callaghan did not seem to notice. "After a bit, your father and I compared our Scottish roots, and realized we both have a family story about the Ceres Crystal and its companion, the Key Crystal." The man looked at her. "Is something wrong, Alexa?"

Numb to the core, she shook her head.

"All right. This began long, long ago, when an enlightened sage arrived in Scotland from the west. He brought with him extraordinary crystals with which he wrought healing for the folk and awakened wisdom for their leaders. Stories of ceremonies and wondrous events were handed down. Some said great magic was done, miracles accomplished. Eventually, a golden age developed in Scotland under the rules of Alexander the Second and his son, Alexander the Third, including peace with England.

"Before the sage died, he trained a select few in safeguarding the crystals, an honor because simply caring for either of them bestowed good luck. As well, the man warned that, together, the crystals would be too strong for most people. Only one person in any generation in the world would be capable of evoking the crystals while also preserving them. Actual misuse could result in their destruction, including great loss of life.

"By the first part of the 1700s, a small number of Scots families in the north continued protecting Ceres and the wee crystal, the Key. Perchance the core of this group was in the east of Scotland, considering a town's name in that region. The families switched them around to share the benefit, always keeping the two separate while being careful to maintain secrecy.

"However, perhaps the legend was true about the Key always finding a way to reconnect with Ceres. Or maybe it was human nature." Callaghan laughed, not happily. "You see, one family decided it should hold both crystals."

He threw up one hand. "Their intentions may have been good. They were in the thick of efforts to assist the bonnie Prince Charlie, and conceivably they thought that with both in their possession the greatest power would benefit him. Nevertheless, within a few years of tricking the other families and bringing the two together, both crystals were stolen—by enemies from the nearest city in England. Shortly after, the Scots' cause was ground to dust at Culloden. That family lost its land, holdings and all its men folk, save one infant lad."

Alexa couldn't shake the impression that Callaghan felt personally responsible. It occurred there might be a connection. She asked, "What was the family's name?"

"Callaghan."

"Ah," she whispered. "And the Aldens?"

"They were the last family to hold but one of the crystals."

Chapter 8

After parting from Callaghan, Alexa met with Jesek to move the plane to a shed. It was a good thing they had already pulled it out of the ravine, considering that several floating baskets were necessary to even get it moving from its parked position in front of the temple.

Finally, with the plane secured in the building and the huge door locked, she waved to Jesek and headed to the forest where she'd walked with Callaghan. Some alone time and an opportunity for a little perspective on everything had become an urgent matter.

As Alexa turned the corner to locate a shortcut, she ran into a tall guy. *Hmmm. Make that a handsome tall guy.*

"Miss, I deeply apologize. Please excuse me." He spoke with an English accent, and held her arms longer than necessary, looking earnestly into her eyes. His touch, warm and dry, lingered.

"Thank you." Alexa raised an eyebrow. "You can let me go."

He released her with an apologetic smile and peered around, hunting for something. "Did you notice how some baskets towed the most amazing antique this direction? If I'm not mistaken, it was a Cessna 195."

Alexa cringed. Too much, evidently, to hope her plane would not be spotted by a galactic. The man in front of her was definitely not a local. Too tall, too blond, not wearing enough white. "It's a…" Alexa yelled at her brain to come up with something, "an example. Yes. It's a mockup of those ancient crafts. Built from a kit. Mostly balsa wood."

"Balsa? Wood?"

Alexa bit her lip. "And plastic."

"Ah." With no hint of sarcasm, he asked, "Did you build it?"

She shuffled back. "My grandfather. It was his. Now it's mine."

"I wonder if those kits are available anywhere. Sounds right up my alley."

"I don't think so." She swallowed. "I bet not."

The man gave her a sidelong glance and bent to whisper. "If you ever fire it up, may I be around? I love engines. I design engines."

Oh no. "I don't start it much. Fuel is costly."

"I'd wager so. In fact it's difficult to find that kind of fuel on Earth. Much less, this far from Earth."

"Yes," replied Alexa, in a tone to end the conversation. "Well. I was about to go this way. It's been--"

"What a coincidence," the man said. "I am headed in the same direction. May I join you?"

Why is it so difficult to resist someone with an English accent? "For a bit, I guess. Although," she broke off, and said in a little voice, "I was looking forward to some time alone."

⌒∗

Watching Alexa struggle, Newcastle felt a twinge of guilt. If he had gone through that ordeal he'd be fleeing to the stars. But he really must obtain her cooperation, and the most obvious method would be romance. "How about if we both take the little hill. It looks fun." He started out and was relieved when she didn't simply take off in the opposite direction.

As the gentleman his family raised him to be, he allowed Alexa to move ahead up the incline. Then when the dirt went steep for a moment, he got lucky. She slipped. And he made sure she slid directly into his arms.

Beautiful eyes. Which he had an excellent view of because he landed against a tree, with her face near his. Also her mouth. Her lips, tantalizing.

She pulled away and said, "Excuse me."

If he weren't careful she might catch him staring. "Not at all. My family insists its sons verify safety first." When she turned, he noticed an enormous diamond on her left hand. Romancing her might be a challenge, if she still felt connected to that man.

At the top, the woman took a stance squarely in the middle of the path, leaving no room for accompaniment.

Come up with something! Don't let her go. Desperate, he said, "I am here on business and if fuel for your balsa and plastic plane would be useful, I could arrange it."

"You have that kind of fuel, this far from Earth?"

Mockery, or amazement? Newcastle couldn't tell and became more intrigued.

She said, "I'm sure, though, I wouldn't be able to afford it."

Of course! She's probably in need of funds. He said, "In fact, I came to Adalans to purchase crystals. For our ships and production facilities. I have an ample budget, and we search for new types of crystals all the time."

The woman's face became withdrawn. *Wrong thing to say.* He blurted, "Do you know you have the most amazing aquamarine eyes?" He bent toward her for a better look.

She leaned away, appearing both bemused and flattered. "Thank you. My father's eyes were—are—the same color." After a polite smile she said, "I'll be going along now. A pleasure meeting you."

When she offered her hand to shake goodbye, to Newcastle's own amazement he brought it up and kissed her fingers. No more than a soft brushing of his lips. Something he'd not done since those historical dancing lessons as a teenager. Still, he certainly didn't experience a jolt similar to *that* during those lessons.

Judging by her widening eyes, she experienced it too and even checked him out more completely. But then she insisted on leaving him behind. "I'll just go along this way."

Newcastle couldn't manage a good response; past the probable foolish look on his face. Before she turned at a corner, the woman turned and waved. Since he still stood on the path, he waved back.

Chapter 9

An hour later Alexa arrived back at the guesthouse, without any significant improvement. Everything that morning seemed custom-designed to scramble her emotions. Her father popped into her heart. *Dad!* The issue was too charged though. She said a prayer for his safety and resolutely sealed it all away until later. Much later, depending on how likely it was that she could ever locate him.

Her thoughts also spun with extra torque because of her reaction to that man. Was it the norm in this age for a man to kiss a woman's hand? If so and it was that strong every time, she was in trouble.

On the guesthouse door hung a note with an invitation for a trip up to the space station with Callaghan's daughter, the galactic ambassador for Adalans. To join the group, she'd have to rush. The thought of an afternoon jaunt up to a space station made her mind reel, while another part of her skipped like a little girl.

Bridgeth Callaghan's appearance was as most people on Adalans, similar to American Indians. She appeared to be in her late thirties, though Callaghan implied her age would be in the fifties. Only her height, approaching six feet, proved Callaghan to be her father. Instead of wearing white, her green brocade robe over tailored pants of a deeper green seemed to be expensive pajamas.

Alexa found skimming the treetops in the basket to be like a hot air balloon ride she once took. This was not aimless drifting, however. Undeterred by a side wind ruffling their clothes, the basket made steady progress. And no engine sound, except a tiny whine only a person with exceptional hearing might perceive. They sailed about thirty feet above ground. The lift above trees happened more smoothly than most altitude gains in her plane.

An awning on top protected from too much sun, while rolls

of material on the sides under the awning might be flaps. The basket—woven of both grass and a stronger stalk—smelled like an import store. A thin board comprised the floor and planks on each side provided seating.

It seemed the basket knew exactly where it was going. Alexa asked, "Where is the port?"

"A bit beyond the first range of mountains. It will take about fifteen more minutes." Bridgeth turned to her and inquired kindly, "How are you handling this? It must be wrenching."

"Only when I momentarily accept the idea." Alexa turned to gaze across the ocean. "I'm supposed to be married. In less than a week."

Bridgeth brought her hand to her heart. "I am sorry. That is a profound loss." After a few moments, she continued. "I wish we had the time to allow you a more gentle process. However, with these delegates showing up, we had to choose between integration and keeping you in your house. Father recommended we give you a taste and let you decide."

"Can you give me an idea of what to expect? I've never been in space."

"Most everything off the planet will be brand new, I suppose," said the woman. "I wonder if the people will be different."

"Are you like the people I will meet?"

Bridgeth considered and nodded.

"Then humanity has not changed much. Bring on the technology. Maybe it will help distract me."

When they arrived at the spaceport, a shuttle was swooping straight down from high up in the sky. The craft appeared a bigger, sleeker version of those belonging to NASA, aerodynamics being aerodynamics, even hundreds of years later.

After they climbed a steep set of wooden stairs to board, Bridgeth turned to the crew and said, "Thank you, you can close the door."

"Hello!" hailed a man from outside. His basket skipped a couple of times as it landed and he held on to the sides to keep from being thrown out. "Please wait for me!"

"Corky," called out Bridgeth. "If you wanted to come, why didn't you speak up earlier?"

The man smoothed his expensive pajama set and longish brown curls as he rushed up the steps. "The request for me to come up side was late. Thank you so much for waiting." He headed directly to Alexa, smiling as he sat next to her. He began buckling the several seat belts and said, "I don't believe we've met. I am Lord Corcoran Esteban DeSoto FitzDermot Espinoza. So very wonderful to make your acquaintance."

No one spoke as the shuttle lifted off, almost straight up and without a huge rocket. Gravity tried to keep them on Adalans, momentarily tripling and almost quadrupling Alexa's weight. In minutes though, they were past the planet's atmosphere where freefall took over, hence the multiple seating restraints.

Alexa's hair floated out around her head. She smiled when the little gold heart on a silver chain that Mac gave her for her last birthday tickled her ear. She gathered in her locks and resolved no giggling. People nearby hopefully didn't know the facts of when she came from and she wanted to keep it that way.

At long last, Corky drifted away. Continuous chatter about the planet Varga and its wonders had been informative, yet wearing. After he departed, Bridgeth approached Alexa. "He is an example of the type you will meet."

Alexa asked, "How long to the station?"

"A few hours."

"Perfect. By chance, is there a place I might meditate?"

"Certainly," said Bridgeth. "Follow me."

Alexa glided behind Bridgeth, pulling or pushing herself along. They stopped at a bank of three horizontal sleeping alcoves. In each, there was room enough to sit up, though Alexa realized pretty quickly that in freefall "up" is debatable. She asked her hostess, "If I doze, will someone wake me in time to see the station from outside?"

"We always announce over the intercom thirty minutes before," said Bridgeth, "so relax."

Despite her intention, the ship's background noises soon lulled her asleep. She was in the middle of an intricate dream about Mac when the arrival announcement woke her. She hung there for a bit, gradually orienting herself. *I could almost cry.*

There was plenty of time to make her way to the viewing window, so Alexa pushed off in the direction of the head. Afterwards, unfortunately Corky seemed to be waiting for her.

"Miss Alden," he cooed, "so wonderful to have a little private time."

"Hello Mr. Espinoza. Or Lord Corcoran Esteban DeSoto FitzDermot Espinoza?"

"Oh, yes," he replied and briefly raised his hands. "My extravagant name. Everyone calls me Corky. Please, you also." After Alexa politely bobbed her head, he began to effuse. "Yes, I can see you are a lady of great refinement. In fact, it amazes me you are here on Adalans." When Alexa scrunched her eyebrows in confusion, he said, "The sweet Adalans is lovely and quaint, yes? But also, dare I say, a tiny bit backward? So much physical labor, since they disallow our robots."

Alexa's attention sharpened. *Robots? You have robots?*

Oblivious, Corky said, "You, however, are undoubtedly of a discerning character. I wonder if I may ever tempt you with a trip to my exquisite planet. And all its romantic and visionary and fabulous benefits."

Because the two of them were in close quarters and he effectively blocked her exit, Alexa opted to play it safe. "That sounds lovely."

He said, "In fact," with such gusto that he projected his body back against the wall. When he bounced toward her, his hand shot beside her head to rebound off that wall. "Excuse, please." He smiled. "Many of those benefits are available even on this station. Though I would so adore to show you my beloved Varga, is it not perfect that you need not wait to enjoy?"

Alexa smiled with her mouth and wondered where were all the people. "Well. Corky. It sounds wonderful. And I always enjoy perceiving beautiful things. Sometimes though, it is not possible for me to personally partake of every item I see."

"Not possible?" he replied with an innocent look on his face. "I wonder. Could it be that I may assist you in enjoying anything you might desire?"

Alexa blinked. He seemed a master of obscure statements. She'd worked to not say anything. Still, he exceeded all her efforts.

He continued. "Please know, if the block is due to a temporary small lack in finances," Corky nodded happily, "I am in the very fortunate position of being able to assist you."

Confusion remained triumphant in Alexa's brain.

"You see, people often are unaware an item they hold, which is of hardly any value to them, might actually be highly precious to another."

Alexa's bewilderment began to clear. To anchor herself, she backed up and grabbed onto a light switch behind her.

Corky wheedled, "Do you think, milady, you might possess a bauble? A trifle? A sparkle that, although pretty, might actually be rather useless to you?"

Comprehension crystalized in Alexa's brain and she did her utmost to maintain a blank look. All she knew was that this man asking about her crystal, out of the middle of nowhere, was far too strange for her tastes and not to be trusted. "Thank you, Corky, for your concern," she simpered. "If I can ever begin to identify anything in my life fitting your description, please believe I will endeavor to locate you." Eyes open fatuously, she prayed someone, anyone, would arrive in the corridor.

"Alexa? Are you here?" Bridgeth called out from around the corner. "If you want to see the station, you should come."

For a moment, the look on his face turned dark and mean, eyes burning as the crust on hot lava. Then the smiling Corky bobbed there, between her and freedom. "Of course. I understand," he said, and reached into a pocket. Alexa held her breath. He brought out a card. "Here is my name and contact information. Please believe I am at your service, at any moment."

Alexa slipped by Corky to follow Bridgeth, and mentioned nothing about the interchange, even while the passengers floated through a tube and exited the craft into a huge open space on the station. Everyone now walked on the deck. A scientist in the hundreds of years must have figured out artificial gravity.

When the others moved ahead, Alexa felt no one else might hear. "This Corky person," she whispered to Bridgeth. "Is he known for a short temper, as well as being pushy?"

The ambassador thought a moment. "Exuberant, yes. Even brash, when he is acting on behalf of his boss, the Prime Minister of Brasileria on Varga. But I've never known him to show anything other than pleasantness, even to the point of being obsequious." The woman glanced at the shuttle. "When I called you to view the station, I noticed your discomfort. We from Adalans are used to being aware of the feelings of others. But I detected only a short burst of anxiety from him after I said your name."

"He seemed to want to buy the item Donny stole from me," said Alexa. "I assume you know about all that?"

"Yes, father told me. I understand most everyone picked up on Donny's thoughts, considering how loudly he broadcasted. Perhaps it was mentioned to Corky?"

Alexa considered. "Perhaps. Or maybe I imagined it all."

Bridgeth nodded briskly and turned to follow the group.

Trundling toward them was a cart with a man on the back. He sported lime green paint on his face and arms. As he passed, Alexa stared hard when she realized the man was not riding. In fact the conveyance encased his bottom half, or his top half sprouted up out of it. She caught Bridgeth's arm. "Robots. Corky mentioned Adalans not allowing robots. Is that," she gestured her head to the retreating cart, "an example?"

Bridgeth glanced, said "Ah," and grinned. "Yes. You have now been exposed to a major technology difference to your time. If I remember correctly, bots had not yet become common."

"Robots, or 'bots,' had hardly been anything more than an extension of a machine, a method for building cars. Though my fiancé was working in that area." With this, again the question of past tense singed Alexa's heart. *No, Mac is working. Time is a river. He is still working.* She picked up where she'd started. "Mac is working on remotely controlled robots in the ocean." After Bridgeth nodded, Alexa asked, "Why the lime green?"

"When they have a human form, they come in many colors." Bridgeth turned toward the double doors. "At one point, it was the fashion to make the bots appear human. But problems arose, and these days that is outlawed on almost every planet except for Earth."

"And robots are outlawed on Adalans, in general?"

"Because they emit no emotions," said Bridgeth. "Being aware of emotions is our basis for security. All the delegates know ahead of time they will not be able to bring their bots with them downside." She stopped at the doors. "Are you ready for the whole show?"

Chapter 10

Surprisingly, Alexa found the space station more familiar than the planet Adalans. Stores and offices, and probably homey apartments, lined the hallways in all directions. It felt like a shopping mall. Entire walls broadcast news and advertisements, in full-human size. And there must be a food court nearby, including Chinese and Italian cuisine judging by the aromas. More important, she noticed a sale sign in front of a clothing store.

Bridgeth saw it too. "I have some time before my first meeting. Why don't we look for clothes other than the white tunics of Adalans for you and your friends?"

Alexa might have ordered outfits printed for her. Instead, she located a few ready-made sets for herself and some she thought Rachel would be willing to wear. Even a couple that a guy like Donny might find tolerable, though she hadn't really planned on getting any for him. When it came time to interact with the humanoid checkout bot—a peach-colored female form embedded in the desk—Alexa stopped. *Duh!* She turned to Bridgeth. "I have no way to pay since I'm certain my money will be useless here."

"I realized the situation, which is why I remained. Please allow Adalans to take care of this for you." Bridgeth paid and asked for the package to be sent to the shuttle. As they left the store, Alexa's stomach growled. Bridgeth laughed. "You weren't around when we had a snack on board. Please take this chit and let me know how the food is here. I must go to my meeting. Shall we rendezvous at the shuttle in about an hour?"

As Alexa searched for the best direction to locate the source of delectable smells, she noticed Jesek in the distance across a large common area. Beside him stood a tall man with shoulder-length straight brown hair.

A young woman walked up at that moment and gazed adoringly at the tall man. Jesek waved and Alexa gestured back. When the man followed Jesek's line of view, the grin that spread on his face was striking, to the point that when the intricately coifed blonde woman saw it, she frowned.

Being hungry, Alexa ignored an impulse to go visit with Jesek and, instead, allowed her nose to guide her to the food. Plates were clinking, somewhere. Her mouth watered, because of the spices. Still she ended up at the entrance to a dead end, the kitchen nowhere in sight.

One bot was nearby. No humans. *Okay, new experience, talking to a robot.* "Hello," she said. "Can you tell me how to locate the food court? I think one is nearby."

The bot rolled toward her. It was an upright metallic model with a stylized face, a type she'd seen a few times since leaving the shuttle. This one did not respond to her question. Instead, it kept advancing. When Alexa stepped aside to give passage, it sidled and moved as if to guide her further into the cul-de-sac.

"I'm sorry. Perhaps I should find someone else to help me."

At first the robot did not respond. When she made to walk around it, the bot took her by the arms and pushed her further and further into the deserted area.

"What are you doing?"

Its response was to stop. Then one hand took her in a grip she couldn't free herself from and the other began frisking her.

"Stop that!"

Without warning, the robot released her. Alexa glimpsed a tall man with long hair standing behind the bot. He wrenched up and ultimately dangled the bot by its arm. "Are you hurt?" the man asked.

As Alexa shook her head, his American accent registered somewhere in her awareness. All the while, the swinging robot ran its wheels, trying for traction. The man turned and carried the bot to a corner. Its wheels continued spinning and it still made no sound. He dropped the robot, then reached low on the base and must have triggered an on/off button because it abruptly powered down.

The blonde rushed around the corner. "You left!" she said to the tall man. "And didn't hear how well I mastered the old code." When she noticed Alexa, she demanded, "Who is this?"

Jesek arrived, glancing back and forth between Alexa and the bot in the corner.

Alexa said to him, "That robot attacked me."

"Impossible," the woman interrupted, in the imperious tone Brits are capable of. "Their programming absolutely prohibits that sort of thing."

"It certainly felt like an attack."

"Why would it attack you?" She seemed to doubt anyone or anything would consider Alexa as valuable.

Stung, Alexa retorted, "I don't know, maybe it also wants what I have."

After a start of surprise, the young woman took the time to study Alexa. In fact, her gaze became positively speculative. "I tell you what," she said in an almost sweet tone, "why don't you hand me the item. Thus, you won't be bothered."

The tall man spoke up. "Lady Penelope, I believe we have a dinner reservation." He took her arm and began walking away.

Lady Penelope appeared to want to remain. "But Pearson. This is important for us. I mean, for her. It's important."

The tall man smiled kindly. "Yes. However, you always prefer to be punctual. We are to meet the Consul and his wife, remember?" As he led the young woman away Pearson glanced back and made eye contact with Jesek, then cut his gaze to Alexa.

Jesek asked her, "May I show you around the station?"

He did his best to smooth the situation, but the encounter with the robot had shaken Alexa. After a quick bite at the elusive food court—fairly decent Chinese—she asked to go to the shuttle to wait for Bridgeth.

"That may be a good idea," he said. "It will be crowded, with the delegates arriving. We should make certain you have a comfortable seat."

At the double doors to the docking area, Alexa turned to him. "Are you coming down to the planet, too?" When he shook his head, she said, "Thank you for your help, just now and this morning, but I can take it from here. Also, please pass along my appreciation to Pearson and Lady Penelope." Jesek laughed and agreed to deliver the message.

Alexa turned toward the shuttle's portal. About halfway across the dock, a guy trotted up and began walking beside her. "Hello," he said in a cheerful, friendly manner. "I'm Zaire Chevalier. How are you?" He was cute, with medium dark skin, smiling brown eyes, and dreadlocks neatly pulled back with a yellow band.

"Fine, thank you," replied Alexa, and kept walking. She preferred to not engage in a conversation right then. Whether intended or not, Penelope's comments had resulted in some internal debate for her.

At about thirty feet from the shuttle, Zaire asked, "Might you be the beautiful woman who flew the remarkable aircraft over the temple on Adalans?"

The question caught her so off guard Alexa came to a complete standstill. "Excuse me?"

"An ancient aircraft flew in the skies over the temple and landed a couple of nights ago." He smiled engagingly. "You fit the description of the pilot."

She took off toward the shuttle. He might follow her to a chair, but not into the ladies room.

He kept up and peppered her with questions. "How is it, flying that aircraft? Is it different from piloting a shuttle? Its engine was noisy. Is it really powered by gasoline, instead of crystals? Where do you find fuel for it? How is it that such a craft is on Adalans? Why do you know how to fly such an ancient craft?"

At about this point he brought out a three-inch shiny ball, threw it up in the air and the ball began circling her. His questions came fast and hard. "Where is the plane from? Where are you from?" The ball seemed to be taking photos. "When are you from?"

He stopped about five feet from the shuttle. "Work with me on an exclusive." She raced through the door. "I'll shield you from all the others," he yelled, as she left him behind the corner.

Alexa did not stop until she located the sleeping alcove she had used earlier, leveraged her body in, and locked the door.

Chapter 11

After arriving on terra firma that night, the basket ride to the temple site through a quiet and gentle breeze almost put Alexa to sleep. *Downright civilized.* It certainly helped her feel better after the attacks on the space station by robot and reporter.

Along the way, Alexa got one question answered. As the several people in her basket quietly conversed, she wondered aloud about no one piloting. Someone replied, "Crystals onboard are attracted to other crystals at each destination."

She had to admit that Corky had a point. The presence of robots might always feel weird, but Adalans was a strange combination of basic and sophisticated. Woven grass being the only barrier between her and a thirty-foot drop to the ground didn't jive with glowing walls and hovering conveyances.

Exhausted and numb, she climbed into bed well after midnight.

To her dismay, in the morning with the room flooded with sunlight, it was clear that her luggage had been searched. She'd not touched anything last night, opting to simply lay her clothes on the table and sleep in the white gown from the first night.

Nothing was glaringly wrong. However, her tiny stuffed animals were moved and other belongings shifted around in the suitcases. *Donny has gone too far.* She yanked open her door.

He must have come out of the kitchen behind her as she headed to his room, because she didn't hear him until he spoke. "You got home late last night." He fell back a step when she whirled at him. "Whoa! What happened?"

"Someone searched my bags." Alexa pushed her face up at him. "Do you never give up?"

"It wasn't me! I swear!" Donny glanced at his own room. "In fact, now you mention it, I think the gear in my duffle bag was also messed with." He threw out his hands. "We were both gone yesterday afternoon."

Alexa began to pace. "I wonder if that Corky person paid someone to search while we were on our way to the space station."

"You went to the space station? How cool." Donny jammed his hands into his jeans pockets and scuffed the toe of one high-top sneaker. "How was it?"

Alexa wanted to resist this little interchange, having no desire for friendliness with Donny. Still, she didn't have the heart to deny his interest. "The flight up was," she nodded to herself, "incredible." She smiled. "Weightlessness."

"No," he said, drawing it out. "Too cool for words."

"The station is a big metal disk with windows every once in awhile. Inside," she considered and gave a little laugh, "was pretty similar to a shopping mall. Including the stale air."

Donny cackled. "Makes sense. I hope I can see it sometime." He turned toward the kitchen and then stopped. "Hold on, did you mention someone on the trip up?"

"Yeah," said Alexa. "It's pretty clear this man wants the… package." She couldn't explain why her intuition told her to keep its identity secret. "He tried his best to talk around the issue. But he wants it, I think."

"So you know," said Donny. "That's a relief."

"Know what?"

"The people who hired me? Back home? They still want your… package."

"Why do you say that?"

"This guy came up to me in front of the temple and asked if I obtained 'the item' for his family." Donny crooked his fingers a couple of times to bracket that word.

"What did you say to him?" *In other words, do I have to worry about you trying to steal it again?*

Donny appeared contrite. "That I didn't know what he was talking about."

Alexa tried to remember Corky's words. "The man in the shuttle didn't mention a family." She raised her hand to Corky's height.

"He's only a bit taller than me, with dark curly hair. And speaks with a Spanish, or maybe Portuguese, accent."

"No. Different dude," said Donny. "The man was tall, blond, British accent."

Newcastle lounged on a sunny terrace overlooking the front of the temple. People rushed everywhere, in frantic preparations for the arriving dignitaries.

He hoped they succeeded in changing the trends of time. His own family had lost a ship and everyone on it to the pirates.

For himself, however, he wished he were more secure on how he'd done with the Alexa woman. He'd become used to an immediate response in his interactions with the fairer sex, who reacted if not to his own experienced charm then certainly to the allure of his family. It was never even necessary to introduce himself to anyone.

She did seem to experience a similar shock to his impulsive kiss of her fingers. He must remember that little gesture, especially if it generally produced such an effect.

Nevertheless, Alexa abandoned him on the path and he'd not seen her since. He took advantage of her absence yesterday to try to locate the crystal. To avoid detection, he had concentrated on happy childhood memories. Nevertheless, he did not find the crystal.

His oldest brother had been exceedingly clear: Bring home the crystal, or be the first kicked off the payroll.

Now what.

Alexa came into view, walking across the open space. No mistaking her. It was too far to verify eye color, but the red curls pegged her. Newcastle paid his bill and strolled along a specific tangent.

Chapter 12

On her way to check in with Rachel, Alexa hoped no bad news about her friend meant good news. *Something going good, that would be a relief.* Particularly, considering how people—and a robot!—attacked her over and over again yesterday. Could the robot have been after the crystal? Why would a robot want a crystal? Lady Penelope seemed certain the machines would never take such actions.

Donny stole it from her. Corky did his best to buy it from her. And Penelope proposed to take something from her. Even that British man at the shack for the plane mentioned crystals and offered her money. Probably he was the one who approached Donny. Could Penelope and that man be related?

That British man. Exactly the type of guy who always gets what he wants.

She did need money. It had been downright embarrassing to depend on Bridgeth for clothes and food. What was she to do? *Oh, Mac. We had it all so well planned.* Watching her feet as she walked up the steps, Alexa failed to notice the person in front of her until at the top. It was that man. She strode by, keeping her eyes forward.

"Hello," he said, appearing beside her. "Nice to see you again."

Same as the reporter on the space station. She sped up.

"Going somewhere special?" he asked, his long legs having no trouble keeping up with her.

She halted, and he continued on a couple of steps before he stopped and turned. She demanded, "Who are you?" He looked stunned. He should be, her tone was not friendly. "Why do you want my crystal?"

Alexa had intended to appear fierce. But she couldn't concentrate on putting him in his place, because almost every head in the Great Hall swiveled toward her. She hadn't shouted. In fact she'd taken care to keep her voice close to a whisper. Still, everyone nearby was staring. Then it dawned, she'd yelled loud and clear with her emotions.

That man also realized the reactions around them and said in an irritatingly calm tone, "I am Iain Newcastle, and please believe me that I am not threatening you. However, you might want to tone down your emotions."

"I can see the situation," she snapped. "I want some answers, or you have not ever witnessed the emotions I will bring down upon you."

"Possibly. Nevertheless you don't know my sister. I assure you, try as you might it would be a challenge to surpass her abilities."

Alexa didn't resist when he began leading them out of the temple. She said, "Actually I met your sister, I believe. A certain Lady Penelope." It appeared he was unaware of their interaction. "My question for you is, how did you search our guesthouse without being noticed?"

He stepped back. "Why do you assume I was there?"

"Because I am not blind. I know when my belongings have been messed with. Also because Corky pestered me on the trip to the space station, and your sister was in the station to keep me busy."

"You know Corky?"

"Well, yes," she explained with exaggerated patience. "He tried his best to buy my crystal for you." She crossed her arms. "I'm not budging."

"He wanted the crystal?"

"Hah!" she said. "You admit you know about it."

"Wait, this is important. Corky, of the absurdly long name, tried to purchase the crystal from you?"

"Yes," said Alexa. She plopped her hands onto her hips. "What is it with you people? It's almost a thousand years. Can't you let go?"

⤚✕

Newcastle searched through his memory of the family legend. There was something about another party. A rather nasty character, if he remembered correctly. Possibly Corky? The witless twit overnight Wonder Boy? His mental efforts trying to place Corky in this little drama were interrupted by Miss Alexa.

"Well, Sir Charming? Any response?"

"As a matter of fact, my brothers received all the knighthoods. Listen, you may be in a bit of danger." He lightly touched her shoulder. "Let me buy it from you. My family can protect it. Besides, it was ours before you took it."

At last, he had her full attention. She stared at him, and asked, "Your last name is Newcastle?" When he nodded, she said, "As in the city in northern England, near Scotland?"

He felt his eyebrows shoot up. "Yes. My family's name was something else then. When we left for Varga, we took the name of our home city on Earth." He continued in his smoothest style. "Since that was hundreds of years ago, I assume it is all right to mention the reason for changing our name. It may have had something to do with a slight disagreement with certain parties, who made their antipathy rather plain."

She nodded. "I'll bet. Since it would make sense if your family stole the crystal from my group of families in Scotland! By the way, I recommend not trumpeting to Callaghan that little detail about your home city."

Newcastle rubbed his face. "Let me help you. Sell me the crystal. I'll pay handsomely."

She didn't even seem to consider his offer. "Did you just happen to be on Adalans and notice me as a person who might have something you want?"

He glanced into the temple. "The family legend predicted you would show up here, around this time."

"Legend. You're saying there was enough information to create a legend. One lasting nine hundred and fifty years."

"So, you're that old?" He regretted his words the moment they shot out of his mouth. When she turned to leave, he caught her arm. "I apologize. Overly glib on my part." She narrowed those beautiful eyes, requiring an explanation.

With a shrug, he gazed out over the ocean. "Unfortunately, the story became a little garbled over time. But here it is: More than a thousand years ago our family searched for two crystals taken from us. It took some time before we located them. John Lloyd, he did the searching."

Alexa put in, "Lloyd stipulated that I shouldn't be hurt."

"You knew Lloyd?"

"Yes."

"What was your impression of him?"

She looked off into the middle distance. "British accent. His hair was dark. He was short and kind of pudgy. Didn't talk much. Seemed somewhat lonely."

"Every once in awhile, you say things proving it all truly did happen."

"Oh. It happened. A couple of days ago for me. What's the rest of the legend?"

"The crystals disappeared again. Eventually, a young woman took one away and some old man evidently hid the other. Lloyd tracked the woman," he gestured to Alexa, "however, she escaped," he gestured to all of Adalans around them. "In some manner, not sure how, Lloyd got the idea that she, as in you, should show up here, about this time."

She asked, "How did you keep track of this? It's almost a thousand years!"

Newcastle shrugged a little, before saying, "The story and instructions were stored via various methods. They were meant to appear about every fifty years, to remind my family to perpetuate the information with the newest technology. From what I can tell, identifying a member of the family was challenging a few times. Luckily, a few essential elements seemed to have made it through." He gestured to Alexa with his head. "You are here and you have a crystal."

Alexa appeared skeptical. "Besides being informed you should steal, did the messages give you a reason? For stealing?"

He brought his hand to his chest. "We prefer to think of it more as reclaiming."

"I'll bet." Alexa stood there, waiting.

"This next part becomes a bit vague." He leaned against a column. "When we possessed the two crystals, everything was golden, we couldn't lose. We dominated the shipping industry. We controlled all the banks. Then the two disappeared. And it all fell apart."

"Yet during all this time, you stayed a family with a memory."

A new thought occurred to him. "I wonder if those reminders helped keep us focused? Sometimes, the surviving member was female."

Alexa rolled her eyes. "How good of your family to recognize a female."

"Her husband would change his name."

"It's been a really long time. Why remain fixated on something so small. It's not powerful, at least I haven't noticed anything like that. Except for attracting all this attention. And if it was, you'd think it should have at least kept me from being hijacked away from home!"

Newcastle said, "Supposedly having the two at the same time is worth it. Lloyd certainly believed so, and emphasized that it's important to obtain this one first. Let me buy it from you. One part of the legend mentions someone truly heinous. I don't want to think of you in danger."

Uneasiness passed over her face. "Am I in danger with you?" She lifted her chin. "What if I don't agree to sell it to you?"

Before he thought it through he replied, "You are in no danger from me." As he said the words Newcastle knew he spoke truth, despite any threat to his own wellbeing from his brother.

She stroked her forehead. Taking it all in? Perhaps he could convince her.

"I'll think about it," she said.

Chapter 13

As Alexa trekked through the corridors to Rachel's hospital room, her mind gnawed on her few facts. Stranded. No money. Depending on strangers. Consistently attacked and accosted, for a little piece of hard glass that as far as she knew could not be delivered to Mac as requested. And she couldn't fathom why it would be useful for anything other than some fairy tale. *Selling the thing might make sense.*

She hesitated outside Rachel's door. Crystal drama aside, no amount of money would help in what she must do now, inform her friend there would be no contacting her son.

In the room, Donny sat beside Rachel's hospital bed. Both of them bent over what appeared to be a game of tic-tac-toe, using Rachel's space-dude pen and the palm leaves used locally as a kind a paper. Rachel, who wasn't exactly doubled over in hilarity but had regained a healthier color, looked over when the door closed. "A.J., you're here. I've been worried they locked you up."

Alexa glanced at Donny, and wondered why he remained so intent on such a simple game. She said, "Nah, just running around. Wow, you look great."

"They say I can move into a room near other people soon." Despite the upbeat words, Rachel kept picking at the sheet. She peeked over at Donny, then said, "So, how is it going in your search for a way to get us back in time?"

All of a sudden, oxygen was absent from Alexa's lungs. "Search?" Donny cut his eyes to the door. *Hold on, buddy. You're not getting out of this.*

"Yeah," said Rachel. "Donny told me you were searching for ideas about time travel and ways to use them."

Alexa cleared her throat, found a smile, and opened her mouth, not totally sure what would come out. "I am. Clarifying. The feasible. And the impossible."

"Oh God, thank you, A.J." Rachel grabbed Alexa's hand. "I couldn't face life without some hope of seeing my son again."

Alexa swallowed hard. "I'm doing my best, my absolute best."

"If anyone can do it, it's you," replied Rachel, with more certainty than Alexa would ever feel. In the ensuing silence and still holding Alexa's hand, Rachel looked first at Donny then Alexa, almost a child anticipating the next miracle.

Not quite knowing how to deal with it all, Alexa gave a quick smile and escaped from the bedside. It wasn't hard to come up with an excuse to leave. Already heading for the door, she said, "I haven't eaten breakfast. See you this afternoon?"

If she hung out nearby the room, she could collar Donny. Or, come to think of it, she could put it off, since they weren't going anywhere. But Donny surprised her when only a few minutes later he walked up to her on the temple steps and stood to receive her wrath.

Not even trying to contain her emotions, Alexa barked, "Are you out of your mind?" Hands on hips, she demanded, "What was Rachel talking about? How did she get an idea like that?" When he just stared at the ground, she raised her hands and searched the sky for some kind of divine intervention. "You heard Callaghan. There is no way back to our time."

Donny peeked up from under his lowered head. "I visited Rachel yesterday. And pretty quickly realized she had no idea of where we are. But I couldn't dodge her questions." He smoothed his hand over one of the columns, appearing to be fascinated with the grain of the stone. "When I told her about us being in the future, she went berserk." He stopped caressing the column. "They nearly had to peel her off the ceiling. And the only thing that kept her from doing something *really wrong* was letting her think you were trying to fix it." He hung his head even lower. "Maybe I am out of my mind, but I couldn't bear to see her so upset."

"And why exactly were you there? She doesn't have what you stole, or anything worth stealing."

That sure hit home, considering Donny placed his arms across his stomach. Shaking, he said, "All my fault."

At least he realized it. Alexa sighed and turned toward the ocean, hoping for answers. She allowed herself one snort, and then declared, "I'll start at the library. But you can guess what I'll find."

Hours of fruitless searching later, Alexa realized she needed lunch. She'd completely forgotten about the breakfast that had been only halfway an excuse to flee from Rachel's room. Lucky for her, the kitchens were still serving.

Feeling much better afterward, she was happy to come across Murdoch Callaghan, studying a palm leaf in his hand. People rushed to and fro, all over the place. She asked, "How are preparations for the conference?" It dawned on her how she and her friends were likely monopolizing space destined to house delegates. And none of her hosts even hinted at their intrusion. "Can I help?"

"Aye, Lass, assistance would be gladly accepted," said Callaghan. "Bridgeth knows what needs to be done." He peered at her and asked solicitously, "How are you doing?" His tone was the same as when he told her about her father.

"Okay, considering everything," she said. With no clue about an impossible task, one may be excused for checking everywhere. "I have a question for you, though. Do you remember anything at all from my father about identifying a method to go back in time? Even nonstarters?" Which would simplify her investigation.

He tipped his head to the side. "He met with a number of the religious leaders arriving."

"So, logically, no one coming here showed him how to travel through time."

"Not necessarily," said Callaghan. "He may not have spoken with every group."

"Could we identify which ones he didn't consult?"

Callaghan considered for a moment, and said, "Are you thinking to pick up your father's quest?" A woman across the hall called out to him. He acknowledged her in the local language, after which the woman switched her attention back to the palm leaf in hand.

Alexa shrugged. "Sir, even if I think it's highly unlikely, I have to at least try. For Rachel's son, Sammy."

Chapter 14

By late the next morning, as faces and names blurred into a continuous stream, Alexa felt she'd acquired a passing handle on the conference attendees. Callaghan had asked her to assist in greeting new arrivals, pointing out she'd have opportunities to meet the right people.

In a way, it was comforting that even a thousand years later, people remained so totally human. One gentleman, dressed in robes that would embarrass a peacock, groused about a lack of conveyances. He represented a religion that had developed on Varga a hundred years earlier. On the other hand, the leader from a city named IbnArabi waited patiently with wives and children, while tents were erected to accommodate the tribe.

As the group headed away, children skipping beside mothers, Alexa took a moment to peek at the list Callaghan's secretary had slipped into her hand earlier. It cross-referenced the arriving groups with the ones who might have been questioned by her father. Her dad certainly visited the group from Qumran City. An elderly gentleman wearing a black fedora and long ringlets at the sides of his face had remarked that she looked similar to John Alden. "He and I met eight or nine years ago," he said. "John was such an earnest man, and on such an outrageous quest." He smiled kindly at her. "He so missed his daughter. Tell him hello for me." Alexa managed to not moan out loud.

It appeared from the list in her hand that her father did not meet with any Buddhists. Therefore in the process of helping the group from SriSriLanka, Alexa asked if it might be possible to talk with their leader. After checking back and forth with Bhikkhu Dharmapala's secretary, who wore a length of orange cloth wrapped around him and leather sandals, they finally agreed a time for that afternoon.

During the negotiations Jesek had been waiting for her, grinning.

As she walked away with the young man he spoke low. "I have some good news for you, I think."

Relieved to be off duty for a moment, Alexa searched for a corner they could get away to. But someone called for her help, again. Jesek laughed out loud at the face she made, and offered to find her later.

She mouthed, "thank you," before dashing away toward the group.

During lunch, Alexa allowed herself a tiny spark of excitement about the scheduled meetings: two groups that afternoon, a third in the evening and another the next day. *Maybe a way home.*

The first meeting that afternoon ended up taking place in the tenuous privacy of a noisy crowd, which limited how much she felt comfortable sharing. The stares directed her way were not actually unkind, more utterly confused, and she managed to walk away with some dignity, though no answers. The second meeting was at the Sufi's guesthouse and at first appeared promising because the group included a scientist. Alas, it turned out the woman distrusted much of quantum physics and wouldn't even consider the possibility of time travel.

Between appointments, Alexa alternately searched for and evaded people.

Corky dominated the avoid list. When he had arrived with the Varga contingent, he'd tried his best to arrange for her to show him to his quarters. She escaped only because Bridgeth intervened by assigning her a task.

In the afternoon, however, Corky managed to discover where she sat and settled in next to her during a meeting. "Hello, my beautiful one," he wooed.

A visceral repulsion nearly catapulted Alexa from her seat.

Oblivious, Corky again launched on the wonders of Varga, adding that they might leave on his lovely cruiser if she desired. Pretty quickly, he circled around to the subject of, "paying her enough to make her heart swoon for any funny little crystalline trifle she didn't need." She pointed to the speaker, implying the need for silence. When he finally departed—required by the Varga group for something official—Alexa dropped her head back on the seat in relief.

At the top of the want-to-see list was Jesek, but the fates refused to cooperate. Alexa caught sight of him once in the distance and when she waved to catch his attention he began wading through the throng in her direction. However, his father next to him must have asked a favor because Jesek suddenly turned and sprinted away toward the floating baskets.

Newcastle: also someone to avoid. Or so she thought. What to do with the fact that she unconsciously switched into flirtation mode when he showed up beside her in the dinner line? A little embarrassing the way she tossed her hair and made googly eyes at him.

He asked, "What do you think of our spiritual leaders? Any differences?"

"I've never been around this many religions at one time," she said. "People have been gracious and polite, despite a few tempers this morning." She raised her shoulders a tiny bit and dropped them. "I can't say I'm any better."

He laughed. "I can. I know many of these fine exponents. For example," he turned his gaze to a lady primly picking at her food, "you would never guess she has six previous husbands, each richer than the one before. A few of them left her a widow, though everyone of them lost most of their fortune to her." Next he moved his attention to a large man with a huge mustache. Newcastle momentarily mimicked the cleric's imperious demeanor so spot on that Alexa couldn't repress a giggle.

She didn't realize she'd tipped her tray until Newcastle took it from her hands. He ended up on the receiving end of hot soup down one leg.

As she moaned, "I'm sorry," he simply set down the tray and cleaned off the soup, betraying no anger or irritation in his quiet words of assurance.

Before they parted, the thought surfaced in her mind to agree to sell the crystal to him. At least Corky would be put off permanently. "Yes," she said.

People flowed around them, rushing to tables or leaving the area. Newcastle seemed unsure of her intent, as he repeated, "Yes?"

She clarified, "The crystal." *That smile of his is a keeper.*

"I want to clarify." He bent to hear her amidst the noise, and asked, "You will allow me to deflect from you the villain of legend, by selling me the crystal?"

Alexa's mind went blank. As people began surging past them to return to the conference, she and Newcastle received more than one look silently requesting them to please move. They shifted to the side.

She had begun the process and now felt compelled to carry through. Still, the actual word "yes" wouldn't come. She nodded mutely.

Newcastle tapped on his legs, and then reached for his pocket. "We can arrange everything this moment."

"Alexa," came her name above the crowd. When she searched, Callaghan was gesturing for her to come his way. He repeated, "Alexa, I have someone for you to meet." She waved to indicate she'd be there directly.

Glancing at Newcastle, she knew her agitation showed. He took pity on her, and said, "I will find you after the meeting."

A moment later, while smiling at the man Callaghan had introduced her to, Alexa tried to ignore a doubt welling up. *It'll all be okay. Probably.*

In fact, when Corky accosted her again amidst everyone flocking back to the meeting hall, it was easy to decide that offloading the thing would be a really good idea. Corky took hold of her arm and began guiding her away. "I understand you have a tiny crystal that's quite useless to you," he said. "I am certain you will be happy with what I can offer."

She pulled to a stop, staying near the crowd. "Oh, were you referring to that?" In her most innocent tone, she said, "I couldn't begin to imagine I had anything useful to you. But I am sorry, the item is promised." After adding, "to someone who inquired before you," she flashed a smile.

For an instant, the same meanness as on the shuttle burst from Corky. Almost a physical punch. He even raised his hand. Before he could follow through, however, she murmured, "Sorry," and rushed into the middle of a group passing by. She didn't glance back at him.

Though it was very, very good to hand over that headache to Newcastle, she had to admit to some nervousness about the transaction. According to Callaghan, her crystal had been important in the legend from Scotland.

But one, it was just a story; and two, what use could the little one be without the big crystal? Settling into her seat in the midst of as many people as she could locate, Alexa allowed herself a moment of relief. Besides, with the crystal question settled, there was more time and energy available to accomplish the impossible.

She sat there during the speeches, considering the next two possibilities for identifying a way to travel through time. "I might as well be looking up some magical incantations." Admittedly, the group scheduled for the next day was doubtful. She'd pursued it mostly to assure herself that all potential paths had been covered.

Whether the third and final meeting of the current day produced anything would become clear, eventually. At least, even if nothing developed, this group would be familiar.

At dusk she strolled to the group's guesthouse close to the ocean. A middle-aged man answered the door and then guided Alexa to the back left room. In there was Swami Ramakrisna, who appeared to be one of the most elderly of all the delegates visiting Adalans. He sat on a deerskin placed over a saffron couch, with a canopy of red silk above it. A brazier a few feet in front of him burned low, to ward off a slight evening chill. Without speaking, Ramakrisna gestured for her to sit on cushions near him. The assistant withdrew to outside the door.

Upon a nod from the gentleman, Alexa launched on her explanation. Ramakrisna listened intently. Sometimes he gestured with his head that he understood, particularly about Rachel wanting to return to her son and Alexa to her fiancé. After some time, she relaxed. *He believes me.*

When she mentioned also needing to deliver an item that her meditation teacher entrusted to her, Ramakrisna asked to hear more about it. Realizing some feelings of trust had developed, she brought out the crystal. In her hands, it was so cool and smooth. As she explained the entire story, he took it all in, not challenging anything as outrageous.

At the end of the story, he asked to hold the crystal—in such a respectful manner that it felt completely safe to hand it to him.

He cradled it for about a minute, before speaking. "In our lives, laws of nature are set, dependable, no matter where. It can happen, however, if deep silence is dominant that even gravity may be transcended. Some saints have floated. In all religions, holy men and women have discovered something beyond." His eyes flicked her direction.

"Infinity, the state which is inside us, is source of All There Is. Indeed, it may have been by that state, or some aspect of it, you traveled here? Is it possible to return in the same manner?"

Alexa explained that anyone or anything transported through the column of light would go forward in time. "We happen to need to go backward."

Ramakrisna nodded. "My grandfather once mentioned someone his grandfather knew, a saint. His name is SivSatyananda. He is a Master of Masters and an adept in the secrets of sound." The man adjusted his shawl. "Only SivSat would be able to hold the threads of infinity, and assist to transcend boundaries of time." He smiled at Alexa. "Find SivSatyananda."

Alexa stammered, "You think someone can truly help us?"

"Yes, yes." Ramakrisna didn't even seem to doubt the concept.

"Is SivSatyananda alive? From what you said, it sounds as if he would be very old." The ramifications of his assertion began a *boing-boing-boing* inside her head.

"Yes, yes," he said.

"Do you think I might be able to find him?"

Ramakrisna gazed over her head for a moment, then said, "SivSat has been known to locate the deserving."

She couldn't count the number of times Brahmaji also gave almost-answers like that.

The man lingered in silence, with his eyes closed. The fire in the brazier crackled and a log crumbled to dust. Right when Alexa began trying to figure out how to reclaim the crystal in order to leave, Ramakrisna spoke again. "Sound. Sacred sound. That which creates the universe." The swami stopped, eyes still shut.

Alexa held her breath.

"SivSat assembled many pundits," he said, now looking at her, "and wrought great events with sound. This is part of this mystery."

Something tickled in Alexa's memory. "I remember my teacher spoke of a performance of Vedic chanting. The name of a particular chant began with something like 'rudra?' Useful for purifying the environment. Do you mean SivSat brought the pundits together for something similar?"

Ramakrisna inclined his head and leaned forward to hand the crystal to Alexa. "One more thing. An object has been known for more than a thousand years. A crystal lingam, from beyond. It connects all space and time and levels of existence. Enabling transformation of whoever controls it, and others. It has been protected, from those who would misuse it."

Ramakrisna had been watching the fire. He looked in Alexa's eyes. "A small crystal belonging to the lingam is key for locating it. The bearer of that crystal was trusted to protect it and keep it from harm. Until the two would be allowed to reunite." He then sat back and closed his eyes.

Transfixed, Alexa hardly found it in herself to move. She wanted, needed, considered begging for more information about both crystals. In palpable bliss, Ramakrisna didn't appear interested in answering further questions. After a long while of quiet, she rewrapped the crystal and departed the room.

The assistant caught up with her before she exited the house. "Miss?"

"Yes?"

"Please excuse. It is my responsibility to handle matters for Ramakrisnaji." The man paused to collect his thoughts. "The one of which he spoke? The Master of Masters?" He took a deep breath. "The last I heard of SivSatyananda, he was on Earth. He moves around. Very secret, because there are those who would try to stop him. And he disappears, without warning I understand." The man glanced toward the room where Ramakrisna sat, and whispered, "Earth. Go there as soon as possible. That is the best I can recommend. Good luck."

As Alexa stumbled away, she glanced up at the alien stars.

Can I do this?

Chapter 15

While dressing for the conference the next morning Alexa reviewed her options. Selling the crystal, to anyone, no longer seemed the right thing to do. *So close.* On the other hand, considering the less than one hundred dollars in her pack, the idea of traveling to Earth to locate one man among billions made her head ache. Also—*my lucky day*—she had to inform Newcastle about reneging on the deal.

Speeches were already in progress when she arrived at the conference. Alexa took a seat in the middle of a group, between two ladies within the Sufi group. No other seats nearby.

A gentleman on the other side of the room was speaking. "The worst new trends in society began about ten years ago, from my research on Varga." He spoke with a British accent, thus the planet must have at least Latin and Anglo-Saxon cultures. Alexa searched for Corky. It appeared he had not yet shown up.

Newcastle and Lady Penelope's entrance certainly grabbed her attention. They took seats about a third of the way around the arena from her, and Newcastle straight away began listening to the speaker. Penelope scanned the crowd. As soon as she noticed Alexa, she spoke to Newcastle. Alexa switched to studying the red-gold curl she'd been coiling round one finger. At that moment, the headscarves worn by the ladies beside her seemed like a great idea. Newcastle, cool as ever, managed to not follow Penelope's gaze, while Alexa feigned utter fascination with the new speaker.

The aged leader of the TohuMu delegation stiffly rose from her seat. "Too many have forgotten the necessity for the internal path," she said in a clear voice. "These incidents are isolated now, though the direction is clear. We must remind them of their inner Selves, with which they have lost contact."

At that point, Corky burst upon the scene. He strode to behind the Varga group while skimming the crowd. After pausing at sight of Alexa, he continued until spotting Newcastle, then leaned against a column with arms folded, staring at the man and his sister. Penelope must have sensed being observed because she shifted from watching Alexa to scrutinizing the room. Newcastle murmured and she stopped. He spoke again and she turned to watch the speaker. It appeared that a few from Adalans also noticed this whole interchange.

Another man took the floor. Attendees had made references to piracy, but she hadn't truly understood. As he spoke, her own little drama began to seem inconsequential.

"The attacks took the town by complete surprise. At first after the new people arrived, everything seemed normal. They presented themselves as religious emissaries and this community welcomed them." He paused. "Within a couple of weeks, however, distrust among previously tolerant groups began to surface. Teenagers who had never been in trouble began writing hate messages.

"One day, an airship landed nearby. Men in black robes filed out with a hover pallet in their midst." The man swallowed. "An annual fair was going on with everyone attending. From one moment to another, those men changed from supposed clerics to murderers.

"Women, they loaded into one ship. Any able-bodied male still alive after the attack was crammed onto a separate ship." He faltered. "Almost every other soul, young and old. Perished."

The man sat and dropped his head into his hands. A woman beside him took over. "Slogans such as 'Accept the Saint or Die' or 'One World, One Way' or 'The Saint's Priest Knows All' were painted on surfaces still standing."

Another man in the group said, "We learned from interrogations after other, failed, attacks that this group is exclusively disaffected rejects from other societies. Women are meant for their use and males that don't join them are forced into labor. None of the so-called monks captured have been conversant enough in astronomy to let slip even hints about their base location.

"Now that we know their methods, we hope to be better prepared. But this was too quick to muster any kind of response."

Silence reigned in the hall for a good half minute before a kindly looking man rose. "We all know the saint to which those slogans refer." He softly pounded on the chair in front of him, seeming to choose his words carefully. "I have studied the originator's history and cannot believe that man's teachings have devolved this much from the early 2400s."

A man behind Alexa interrupted. "There are rumors of a priesthood taking it over in past decades. My prayers are with those communities hit by this so-called religion. I assume the authorities are tracking them down.

"Nevertheless, whether these pirates are related to this religion or not, isn't an issue we can solve, here and now. The reason my government paid for this trip was in hopes of some practical response to the general increase in negative societal trends."

The man from Varga stood again. "Alas my impression is the authorities have had too few challenges for too many centuries, and budget cuts have reduced their ability to respond."

Ambassador Bridgeth Callaghan took this opportunity to stride to the stage. She waited, to gather everyone's attention. "Would expedited communications aid you?"

The man considered for a moment. "I believe the Varga department I met with before this trip implied they were struggling to cover the territory, which includes another planet in our system. Communications would be a weak point, at those distances."

Bridgeth spread her hands wide. "Then perhaps rapid communications, even at the extreme distances due to the light years between us, might assist us all to respond to this troubling drift in spirit." She turned to take in the entire group.

"Adalans recently discovered a new application for an extraordinary crystal." Bridgeth paused dramatically. "Instant communications, no matter the distance." She stopped long enough for the last statement to sink in. "Would this be of use to you and your governments?"

A man behind Alexa called out, "Also visual? And how clear?"

"Thus far, we have used it for sound." Bridgeth examined around the theater again. "It is about time to stop for lunch. Adalans hoped to present the various crystals at some point. Would this afternoon suit the delegates?"

No one dissented and quite a few responded, "Yes!"

"Good," said Bridgeth. "We will reconvene here after lunch."

As one, people stood and began stretching and moving around. Thus Alexa managed to duck out of the meeting without coming across either Newcastle or Corky. She hurried to Rachel's new room.

As she opened the door and quickly closed it behind her, Rachel cried out, "A.J., I wondered if you'd taken off in space."

Alexa brought up a finger to her lips and waited a few moments. When the crowd including Corky passed beyond the hallway leading to this room, she shook the tension from her shoulders. "I've been working hard for you."

"Or hardly working," responded Rachel. "I know you."

Alexa grinned. Rachel was getting back to her usual self. "There's good news and," trying to figure how to classify the rest, she settled on, "and challenging news."

"Good news first," said Rachel, sitting up in bed expectantly.

"I've been told someone can transport us back to our time."

Rachel did her little screaming, yelpy thing, "Yes, yes, yes," and wrapped her arms around herself. "I will hold my son again."

"The challenging part is finding the man. Considering he's been known to disappear into thin air. Literally."

Rachel fell back on her pillow and made a face as if she couldn't believe the last bit.

Alexa said, "He's a Master of the Universe, I've been informed."

"I don't care what he is, as long as he can do the magic."

"The other challenge is traveling to Earth." Alexa knew the answer, but asked anyway. "You have much money on you?"

"If it's still in my bag, I've got twenty bucks," said Rachel. "Though something tells me it won't be enough, even considering its potential value as an antique."

"Huh. Didn't think of that angle. But yeah, I'm pretty certain we don't have even near enough."

"Any idea on how much we need? Are there frequent space ships?" Rachel looked up to the heavens. "Geez, I can't get used to all this."

"Honestly, I've no idea about costs or schedules. I found out about the way to get back to our time only last night."

"If our old stuff can't raise enough money," said Rachel, "do you think it might be possible to sell the plane? I mean, you were on the way to do that."

Alexa contemplated the possibility. "I wonder if Callaghan really can replace the propeller." She tapped her fingers on the table beside Rachel's bed. "I can't imagine the religious leaders here being collectors of the odd antique plane they happen to find on some small planet. Let me ask Callaghan. Perhaps he'll have some ideas."

When the delegates returned after lunch, a man in a white toga stood on the stage, in the middle of four wooden tables set up in a square around him. On those tables were lumps from the size of a fist to as big as a basketball, each covered by a white cloth. The ambassador introduced the man as a crystal expert.

Over the ensuing hour, Alexa wrote on a palm leaf as fast as she could, more detail than she thought possible about crystals.

Yellow crystals were used for healing.

Red, like a ruby, increased strength and courage.

Green promoted mental clarity.

Purple was for perceiving hidden knowledge.

Orange for breaking inertia

Milky white crystals, like pearls, supported happiness.

Deep blue stones promoted peacefulness.

Clear as a diamond removed negativity; and

Black supposedly absorbed negativity.

When the expert finished, men dressed in the Adalans togas appeared at the top of the theater. On cue they marched down single file, each carrying a cloth-covered item the size of a two-foot cube. They faced out to the crowd and as one whipped off the cloths. Revealed were ten pure crystals, flawless except for golden threads arcing and dipping through the clarity. A sigh escaped from the group.

"This particular crystalline form," announced the expert, "is for communications."

A few people rose from their seats. Everyone leaned forward.

Evidently, the crystal's capability for sending and receiving data increased with the size and number of threads.

"Is that gold?" someone asked.

"The color is an illusion," the expert said. "Each vein is empty space." The man walked to a specimen and picked up a light. "The crystals are all part of the same group. And when you do this," he touched that crystal with a blue light and blue coursed through every other crystal, even feet away, "they all echo it. We have the technologies to specify connections between or among the crystals."

The man who had wondered earlier asked again, "And visuals?"

"We have used it for sound, though video may be possible," responded the expert.

A delegate from the TohuMu group demanded proof, and the ambassador suggested a short break, to prepare for a demonstration.

Chapter 16

Amidst the crowd with everyone buzzing about the presentation, Alexa was lucky enough to locate Murdoch Callaghan standing alone. "Your crystals created quite a stir," she said. "Everyone around me wanted them."

Callaghan chuckled. "Yes, my Bridgeth could have a career in sales if she becomes tired of diplomacy."

Alexa reached for a tart from a table beside them. It tasted nutty sweet, with a swirl of fruit. "Believe it or not," she said, "there may be someone who could help me and my friends get to our time." She took a sip of coconut juice, watching astonishment register on Callaghan's face. "The group from India told me of a man, a master, as my dad insisted should be out there." Then she bent her head to the side, and asked, "To afford tickets on some kind of space ship to Earth—where this man probably is—I wonder if you might have any ideas on someone who would be interested in purchasing an antique plane? Slightly damaged."

Callaghan grinned. "Actually, Jesek told me someone inquired about buying your plane. And if you're referring to the propeller, the new one has been ready for more than a day."

"What a relief about the propeller!" Alexa put down her glass. "Who's interested?"

"A friend of Jesek's, a freighter captain. I believe his name is Pearson."

At that moment, a man came up to Callaghan and muscled in on the conversation. He took hold of Callaghan's hand and shook heartily, speaking loudly about the wonderful Adalans hospitality. Alexa waited a little bit away from the noise.

Pearson. *As on the space station?* She searched around the room for the tall man with long brown hair. When she and Callaghan were alone again after the man departed to run after his wife, she asked, "Is Pearson here?"

"I have not seen him downside." Callaghan began scanning the crowd. "Let's locate Jesek. He will connect the two of you for a deal, and arrange about the propeller."

While waiting, Alexa recognized Newcastle approaching them. She managed to resist an impulse to melt into the crowd and instead bravely turned to face him.

Newcastle, however, was not aiming at her. "Prime Minister Callaghan," he said in an official tone, "I wonder if my family may assist you."

Shocked, Alexa spun to Callaghan. "Prime Minister! You never mentioned that."

"Tis simply a title, for a small population. Not like Prime Minister Churchill for…a country." After almost divulging his shared ancient past with Alexa, Callaghan turned and smoothly asked Newcastle, "How might you help us?"

"Security, for Adalans and the solar system," said Newcastle. "Even among these fine representatives of the highest spiritual attainment, this afternoon I fairly tasted rampant desire, particularly for the last crystal. And where there is desire, among governments there is thought of acquisition and control."

Callaghan sighed. "Aye. I know all about that."

Alexa backed away from what promised to become a long and involved conversation, hoping to make a discreet get-away to locate Jesek. But she should have realized Newcastle would not allow her to escape that easily.

"Miss Alden," announced Lady Penelope, blocking Alexa's path. "I understand we have business to complete."

"Oh. Hello." Alexa bit the inside of her lip. "You know, I don't think we have been formally introduced."

Penelope smiled sickly sweet. "Miss Alexa Jane Alden, may I introduce myself, Lady Penelope Margaret Elizabeth Newcastle, daughter of the Earl of Eastumberland, of New Britain on Varga." She made a mock curtsey. "Now the niceties are accomplished, how would you prefer to receive payment? After delivery of the item, of course."

No way was Alexa going to deal with the woman in front of her. She said, "I believe I would be more comfortable continuing on this subject with your brother." She glanced at Newcastle, still deep in conversation with Callaghan. "I'm certain he and I will meet together soon." Before Penelope could respond, Alexa murmured "bye," and fled.

"Of all the nerve," the blonde trumpeted at her back.

That afternoon, while the delegates witnessed immediate communications via the special crystal, Alexa officially met Captain Pearson over video link. Did he have such sharply chiseled features and direct eyes when he had helped her on the station?

She said, "It's hard to believe you'd be interested in a dowdy old plane."

"I collect all types of aircraft. You should see my 2580 Indigo shuttle XL." The captain flashed a smile.

Alexa's heart lurched. *Mac's smile.* She managed to maintain a neutral face. "Where would one put an Indigo shuttle?"

"My home is on Earth."

"Earth!" She barely restrained herself from jumping up and down. "Where on Earth, if I may ask?"

"I go to my home in North America almost every trip there."

"I thought I recognized an American accent," she said. "Were you born there?"

The captain tilted his head from side to side, weighing his response. "You could say that."

Realizing place of birth had become more complicated over time, with new planets and even space stations, she changed the subject. "Is your ship able to transport a small plane?"

Pearson gave a good-humored chortle. "Oh, yes. Adequate space. One thing, however. I wonder if you would be willing to come here to the station to complete the transaction. I can send a transport for you and the plane."

Alexa had no problem with the request. "Shall we first agree on a price?"

"Of course," said the captain. "I thought something along this line." He pulled a tablet from his green ships coveralls, brought up a screen and held it up to the video camera.

Surprise popped her eyes wide open. "That's about triple what Jesek and Ambassador Bridgeth suggested."

"Considering its rarity, on some planets you could probably receive even more than this." The captain then maybe employed an old sales technique. "Would you prefer to wait for more?"

Alexa gave a quick shake of her head. "We are in a bit of a hurry. Your offer is much appreciated."

"If time is a factor, how about tomorrow morning? Jesek can attach the replacement part tonight."

Marveling at the ease of the deal, she said, "How early can you arrange it?"

Even taking into account overseeing the installation that evening, she still had enough time to locate a couple of extra items that might help distract attention from the real crystal.

Chapter 17

Jesek, Alexa and Donny convened before daybreak to move the plane out of the shed. The three of them had worked the night before, attaching the shiny new aluminum propeller.

In the pre-dawn, Donny held a glow-crystal to give her more light. She verified the tires retained pressure, and the rudder, elevator and ailerons remained firmly attached and moved easily. The oil level? *Okay, enough for the flight.* She also visually investigated whether the fuel tank remained at the point she left it and the line had not accumulated water. All rivets were secure. Brakes and struts checked out.

In the cockpit, gauges and valves indicated appropriately and the lights and flaps worked. After that, she started the engine. It coughed. It smoked. It ran rough. All normal. As the engine warmed up and settled into its usual steady rumble, the knot in her stomach relaxed.

After a wave to the two men, she taxied over to the lawn, all the while addressing a few last-minute tests of instruments and gauges. She took off as daylight was beginning to show itself.

In the air, Alexa became a little misty eyed, almost sensing her grandfather beside her. Instead of proceeding straight to the port, however, she swung by their entry point to the planet. The spot was obvious, a small cove deep enough to accept dolphins. On opposite sides of the inlet towered two columns topped by minaret fretwork that could easily enclose the crystals Callaghan said were there. The white stone columns—of the same white stone as the temple—stood tall and proud. Not knocked down by crashing airplanes.

No clouds appeared. The wind remained calm. No one could even body surf on the waves. No chance of trying her luck in going to Earth.

Alexa banked away to fly toward the mountains, aiming for the lowest one on the eastern edge. As she approached the spaceport, a craft landed without stirring a bit of dust. It appeared capable of holding a couple of planes the size of hers, and had to be Pearson's ship since it was the one thing other than her moving in the bare dawn.

After loading the *Red Arrow* through a side hatchway, she wandered through the ship to the traveling compartment. It was similar to airport waiting rooms for frequent travelers, including an efficient office area, and a kitchen and head facilities. Down the hall, sleeping quarters were also available, said the one attendant-bot.

During the trip to the space station, Alexa allowed herself some playtime, hoping the bot wouldn't tell stories. She vaulted back and forth across the room in the freefall with a silent chuckle on her face, and allowed her hair to float out around her head as far as possible.

At the space station, they were delayed by the arrival of what had to be the biggest cruise liner ever. Well, certainly longer and bigger than had been around on her first trip to the station. Windows traced along the liner's four ridges and a viewing bubble jutted out midway on one side. The mercury vapor engines appeared to be at one end.

Eventually, their own vessel was allowed to move in close enough for connection with the space station via a tube.

Pearson met her at the dock. "Do you have a schedule? We can go directly to the office, or take a tour of the station, or have lunch. Your choice."

In the corridor a few people walked both directions. "A shuttle is scheduled several hours from now," said Alexa. "Why don't we complete the transaction and see how it goes."

The law office of Tuttle, Delio and Kwan suggested by Bridgeth turned out to be a five-minute walk. After introductions Alexa handed the documents to the human clerk.

When the clerk went to another room to process the documents, she asked Pearson, "Do you fly the various crafts in your collection often?"

"As often as I go to Earth," he replied.

"How long does it take to travel there?" Perhaps this was standard knowledge, but she really wanted to know.

"Straight, no stops, less than a week. However, it usually takes longer because most ships will visit stations along the way."

The clerk returned. In minutes, electronic papers were signed, hands shook, money deposited into a bank account, deal done. Upon the breaking of that bond, one of the last with her family, Alexa sat back in her chair. A tiny tremble of her lips might have betrayed her, if she hadn't distracted everyone with busyness. She stood up and headed for the door. *Movement would be good.*

Outside the office, Pearson asked, "May I take you to lunch at a real restaurant, not the kitchen court? They have quite good food for such a small station."

"Sure, love to," said Alexa. She'd seen very little of the station her last trip, and on the way she inquired about a sign pointing to a View Dome.

Pearson said, "The scene is of Adalans and even the other planet in the system since it's relatively nearby now. Would you prefer to stop there first?"

When she nodded yes, he began guiding her with his hand lightly touching midway on her back, as Mac would. Alexa caught her breath. *Mac, wait for me. I just took the first step to return to you.*

Right before they entered the View Dome, a man and woman dressed in formal pajamas exited. They barely stepped to the side before hurrying down the hallway in the direction of the cruise ship.

In the room, the view of Adalans from three hundred miles above the surface could stop a person in their tracks. The planet appeared as those photos of the big blue Earth, though maybe not quite as pretty. A small group at the other end of the room was lively with laughter. When she and Pearson strolled nearby, a matron left the group and bore down upon them.

"Hello! We are so glad to see you!" the woman trilled. "Would you be willing to stand with us as we witness the marriage between these two sweet souls? Tradition is that good luck for a marriage depends on at least seven people attending, and moments ago we lost two friends to a summons about their toddler. All we need is for you to be with us. Oh, you won't decline, surely." Alexa and Pearson never had a chance versus such formidable determination. "Thank you very much," said the matron. "Right this way."

The young couple looked sweet, dressed in their best. The man wore a bright red silky shirt with white trousers and the young woman shimmered in a simple shift of the same red material. They stood in front of a woman in flowing white robes, who held a large brown book opened roughly to the middle. Adalans, huge and shining, beamed on everyone.

The ceremony was in a language unknown to Alexa, though soon the rhythm of two people joining in matrimony became recognizable. Patterns for the ritual appeared similar, crossing boundaries, spanning time. As the girl spoke her vow, Alexa sighed.

Then an icy stillness struck her heart. *That should be me.*

Solely by an iron will power did Alexa not moan out loud. *This day, almost this same hour, I should be with Mac on the beach in front of the minister, saying my marriage vows.*

All sound withdrew to a distance. Her vision narrowed to a point in front of her. Yet she saw herself standing in the View Dome, with no emotion showing. She watched herself close her eyes and soon felt Pearson take her hand, draw it through his hooked arm, and stroll away. Somehow she knew the couple behind them kissed and whirled in a circle, their friends celebrating around them.

Alexa realized she was walking through hallways, though she could not remember how she arrived at the door in front of her. Pearson opened it, turned on the light, led her in, sat her on a desk chair, and closed the door. As he stepped into an adjoining room, Alexa's lower lip trembled. His return released a single tear, which tracked inexorably toward her mouth since all Alexa could manage was staring at the floor with her head bent to the side. When Pearson lowered his tall frame onto his haunches to offer a glass of water, Alexa's heart clenched. A groan like a wounded-animal clawed up through her throat.

How long did she stand there, with his arms around her? How did she come to stand, with this man's arms around her? Mac's arms should be around her. Mac, who had been dead for perhaps nine hundred years.

A moan escaped and Alexa's face crumpled. Her head began to move back and forth, then her body. No tears flowed, even with this. *But my heart is fracturing into a thousand pieces.*

A good deal later the maelstrom abated, leaving Alexa empty. She simply stood, not moving. At length, she took a deep breath and looked up to the man to thank him for his kindness.

At which point, she dropped into one of those intense, small whirlpools of intimacy. A moment beyond time and space.

He bent toward her. She leaned into him, and his lips as they touched hers.

"Oh, no," she gasped. What kind of person am I? Newcastle? Pearson? And I'm supposed to be desolate about losing Mac?

She wrenched away, "I'm sorry." Searching right and left, she babbled, "Thank you. But, I'm sorry. Too much. Thank you. I'm sorry." *Must leave.* "You see, there is someone."

When she glimpsed him, he appeared devastated. "I know. How could I do that?"

"You know?"

"Well." The cogs were turning in his mind. "It's logical."

She managed a nod, amidst the funk inside.

"How can I help you?"

"I should leave," said Alexa. "Lunch cannot happen."

"Of course." He moved to open the door. "Let me take you to the shuttle."

"I can find it." She was desperate to be alone, to be away with the other quiet little desperation inside her to move back into his arms.

"That might be unwise. It is not far, though there are a few turns. I can take you there most quickly." He gestured down the hall to the left.

She'd thought it might be to the right. "Thank you. Please lead on."

In front of the shuttle waiting room, Alexa turned and stuck out her hand. Pearson looked at it, at her, and enveloped her one hand with his two. "If you can, please let me help you."

"If we meet again. Perhaps, then." She shook their three hands up and down. "Thank you. Take care of the *Red Arrow*." Amazed she could look him straight in the eye, Alexa turned and left him behind.

In the waiting area she dropped into a chair and stared across the room, willing herself to equilibrium. At some point a neon sign glowing electric blue came into focus in front of her: Fortune Cruise Lines. Didn't the matron in the View Dome mention that name? By the time Alexa reached the information desk, she'd decided on the best path of action.

The woman greeted her in some language.

"Hello," responded Alexa. "Do you speak standard English?"

"Yes, how may I help you?" the woman replied, reflecting Alexa's American speech pattern. Up close, Alexa noticed the "woman" was also the desk, and a peach-colored mask covered the machine.

"I'd like to purchase three tickets to Earth."

The robot—wobot?—sported a voluptuous physique dressed in a tight-fitting bodice in the same electric blue as the sign. The robot went quiet for a moment, and then asked, "When would you prefer to depart?"

"When does the ship that arrived this morning leave?"

"The *Jasmine* is one of our more exclusive cruise vessels," replied the bot. "Do you have a price range in mind for this journey?"

"What is the cost to Earth for a double room and a single on the *Jasmine*?" The bot's face went blank for a moment. The answer equaled almost half of Alexa's money. But they weren't aiming for the long-term, just traveling to Earth as soon as possible. "Okay, please book those two rooms."

"Your passport data?"

Alexa whimpered, "Uh."

Chapter 18

Galactic ambassadors can arrange almost anything. In this case, Bridgeth organized Adalans passports for the three. By mid-morning the next day, they were on the space station dock, at the cruiser's shuttle, all legal.

Rachel continued feeling weak so she located a quiet spot over to the side while Alexa and Donny maneuvered through customs. At the dock, the liner's tugboatlets were piled high with packages, foodstuffs and metal cylinders, which took turns with humans for shuttles leaving the docking space.

Murdoch Callaghan and Bridgeth had said their goodbyes at the spaceport on the planet. Jesek came up to help and then was called away for some administrative detail for Bridgeth. Even without his help, though, boarding the cruise was turning out to be rather uneventful—considering each of the previous visits to the station left her all but quivering, Alexa allowed herself a satisfied smile. *Perhaps I can get the hang of life in this century, after all.*

A few moments later she glanced over at Rachel, and noticed that journalist, the one with the name of a country in Africa, badgering her. Immediately, Murdoch's food package in Alexa's hands got pushed at Donny.

Rachel looked up as she approached. "Alexa," she said happily, "Zaire says the two of you are good friends."

"Sure, best buddies."

Zaire smiled at Alexa. "I was explaining to Rachel what to expect in deep space, how it's—"

Alexa broke in. "She knows all about that, because she is as knowledgeable as anybody else these days. Therefore there's nothing here for you. You can leave." Rachel's head came up, confused.

Zaire gazed at Alexa, unperturbed. "Rachel says you all are on your way to locate someone to transport you back to your time. A concept I'd love to know more about."

"Rachel." Alexa stopped. After taking a deep breath, she continued. "What we are doing is none of your concern, nor of your readers." She turned to her friend. "Did Zaire disclose to you that he's a journalist and wants to do a story?"

Rachel began to understand. "Ah, he didn't mention that detail."

Zaire brought out the charm. "Others have heard. Other journalists. As soon as you are away from Adalans, you will be out of this planet's protection. Did you know Adalans barred the media from the event downside? It's the reason five or six reporters have not been at your door already." He leaned toward Alexa. "Give me an exclusive. I will tell your story the best."

Alexa declined to comment. Instead she held out her hand for Rachel, who glanced at the man briefly through her eyelashes before leaving. Behind them, Zaire called out, "See you later."

Alexa kept marching. *Not if I can help it.*

On board an hour later, Rachel breezed in from her room across the hall. "Have you checked out the facilities in your bathroom? I can figure out what most of those knobs are for, but a couple of them are a complete mystery to me."

Alexa arranged her stuffed animals from fluffiest to smoothest, while marveling a little at the luxury of it all. It had been a bit of a shock when they boarded to find that she and Rachel were not sharing accommodations.

"Yes. Welcome, Miss Alden," the maître d' bot had said when they stepped from the shuttle into the cruiser. "This morning, a gentleman upgraded all three of your party to individual rooms and each to the best available." When Alexa asked the gentleman's identity she received a letter, on the cruise line's real-paper stationary. To read it, she moved aside from the entryway since four people waited behind them to pass through. Donny busied himself with corralling their luggage and Rachel reminded him the cart-bots would take care of it.

While the ship's outside was utilitarian, the inside turned out to be beyond opulent. Under a starburst crystal chandelier, Alexa leaned against space-blue walls.

The note was short and polite.

Dear Alexa, Please allow me to make your voyage as comfortable as possible. The cost is not a burden. And it is my pleasure to be at your service at any time. Very Sincerely, Pearson

It took awhile to arrive at their rooms. They walked up and down hallways behind a trundling cart-bot; everything was carpeted or covered in a soft material, except for metallic strips along the ceiling and on the floor. Alexa could almost swear she saw certain light fixtures and wallpaper and office doors more than once. Can robots get lost? Short connecting hallways were often bent, as if cresting a hill. Perhaps they were going over a ridge of the ship. Their feet always pointed to the ship's core.

Their corridor was more than a hundred feet long with doors on both sides evenly spaced about twelve feet apart. Their assigned rooms, or cabins as the cart-bot said, were near each other. Two faced each other, with the third down the hall. Donny granted to the girls the two doors across from each other, and opted for the relative privacy of a room a few doors further along.

Floor space in the room was about eight by five feet and the furnishings felt homey. Still, fine-grain wood on the fronts of drawers and closets recessed in the walls was odd in a place that would never have a connection with trees. From the years working for her cousin, Alexa recognized a French polish finish on the wood that required many applications. *Probably now done by robots.*

Multi-hued brocade material covered the bed tucked into an alcove, a box with one side open. Alexa pondered the arrangement. Cushioning covered almost all surfaces inside the box and pockets were available to hold small items. A metal plate about one foot-square, finely engraved with peony flowers, showed on the wall above the pillows. Underneath the plate she found a control panel with four knobs, including an icon appearing to be for oxygen. The compartment even had a window. It was small, with many layers of a glass substance that didn't totally insulate against the freezing vacuum outside. That didn't matter; she wouldn't quibble with a view of planets and stars.

"I wonder if the bed is a safe place," Alexa said. "In case something happens?"

Rachel said, "Yeah. Did you play the safety video?" She leaned into the alcove and ran her hand over the coverlet. "Your brocade is a different color. Mine is burgundy."

"What safety video?"

Rachel reached to turn on the screen recessed in the wall between the door and bed. Then she pointed at a contraption in a custom space between the closet and the bathroom door and muttered, "You have one of those funky little robots, too."

Hunched there was a three-foot tall collection of tubes, the tallest being topped by a half-sphere that looked as if it could be looking at you. On top of one of the shorter tubes and on the bottom of another were contraptions that allowed the bot to grab and manipulate items. The fourth tube appeared flexible.

Alexa gazed at it with distaste. "What on earth is it for?"

Rachel toggled down a list on the screen, and as she chose English, she answered, "Cleaning the room. They're called butler-bots."

Alexa wondered if she could get rid of it.

From the screen's speaker, a voice that could have been explaining the safety features of an airplane at home intoned, "For your comfort, jumps between systems will generally take place during the sleep cycle. Please alert the staff to any special requirements for your comfort during transits."

Rachel asked, "When will we jump? It sounds difficult." The video went on and on about some kind of alarm sequence.

"We have a night cycle and a day," said Alexa, "and during the next night, we will become true interstellar travelers." Rachel shook her head in disbelief.

The video continued, "In case of emergency, please pull straight out on the handle at top middle over the bed. Enter the alcove and allow the door to automatically close and lock."

Rachel wondered, "Do you think this kind of thing is standard on cruise lines?"

"I'm pretty certain I don't want to know if it's standard," said Alexa. She picked up her backpack. "I'm famished. I think it's dinner time."

As the trio took their seats, Alexa recognized the woman from the Adalans space station View Dome sitting at a nearby table. Alas, the woman glanced up from her dinner conversation and Alexa had to acknowledge her friendly recognition. *Uh oh.*

"Why, hello," the woman warbled and gestured with a quick shake of her hand. "I recognize you." Rachel and Donny looked over, curiosity plain on their faces. "You and that very handsome tall man agreed to witness at the wedding of the sweet young couple, on the station." Her tone on the word "very" had gone up a couple of notches.

Alexa's face froze into a smile, willing the woman to cut short the description. It appeared Rachel was calculating five, from two plus two.

While folding her napkin, the woman said, "It seems you are traveling with us. How delightful." She stepped over to stand next to Alexa, who rose to meet her. Alexa had merely a vague memory of the woman's height and presence. Her turban and flowing robes of some hard-to-pinpoint pastel color were the same as on the station. The woman said, "I don't believe I took the time to introduce myself when I cajoled you into helping us. My name is Mrs. Edith Holmes-Fong."

Alexa might have bet her last name would be Smith.

"I am on my way to meet my husband and it seems an eternity. Please let me know if I can assist you. I've become quite familiar with this ship and the cruise line company."

"I am Alexa Jane Alden. Thank you for remembering me."

Rachel shook hands with Mrs. Holmes-Fong. "I'm Rachel, and this is Donny."

Donny stood for the introduction, and asked, "Who got married?"

"Oh, a young couple who boarded at the previous port of call." Mrs. Holmes-Fong tapped her lips. "Or perhaps the one before that. I lose track after a bit. Well, their honeymoon is this cruise and we have not seen them since the wedding." She sighed dramatically. "Of course, that is as it should be."

Rachel looked at Alexa, who gazed up at Mrs. Holmes-Fong, who glanced at her table. "I believe our next course is about to arrive. I should return to my dinner companions. Lovely to meet you properly, my dear." She fluttered her fingers as she turned. "If you enjoy bridge, we play every morning in the forward day room."

As Mrs. Holmes-Fong rejoined her guests, another matron marched toward what must be her claimed table. Following her were seven little dogs on glittering leashes. The dogs lined up side-by-side under the table and waited patiently, showing their manners. The woman forgot hers, considering how she browbeat the robot servitors.

It appeared the woman assumed she was superior over more than robots. A tall man strolled by her table, with a fabulous set of buckteeth. When he tipped his hat her way, the woman turned her head.

Rachel noticed too. "Rudeness, still healthy after all these years."

Alexa chuckled.

Yet, leaving Adalans without speaking to Newcastle must have appeared incredibly bad mannered. She'd left a note for him trying to explain that she couldn't carry through with the transaction. Probably he would simply go back to his expensive life, which would wipe her from his memory. And she would relegate him to her far past.

After dinner, the trio poked around the cruiser.

Taking up much of one ridge of the ship were the main dining room, shops, a multi-purpose room, and workout facilities including a space for games such as handball. In a second side of the ship was an enormous, long hall called the View Gallery. Along one side were windows, opaque at the moment. Someone explained they often afforded views of the stars or nearby space stations or planets. Doors lined the opposite side at about the same interval as if for personal cabins. Rows of chairs faced a large screen at the other end of the room, while stacked benches leaned against the wall with doors.

The exit out the other end of the room led to a fork in the corridor: left to the dining area, and right through a green door marked Staff Only. They dutifully turned left. As the three of them trekked back near their rooms, Donny asked the girls if they would be interested in checking out the bar near the dining room. "Live music tonight."

Rachel wondered if it would be live humans or robots.

Laughing, Alexa declined with, "Thanks though."

In her room, Alexa eyed the butler-bot. What to do with the distaste she felt every time she laid eyes on it? She went into the bathroom to brush her teeth. As she came out she glanced at the bot again, and veered off to put the last of her clothes away. At length, however, she turned to face off with the bot. *This is not going to work.*

A quick test proved the contraption to be not too heavy. She muscled it out of its space and toward the door. In no time, it was out of the room and in the hallway, door locked. After that, she found that sleep came easily.

Next morning, a knock at the door turned out to be Rachel. "You lose something?" She was studying the butler-bot, which seemed almost forlorn in the corridor.

"It's being shunned," said Alexa, as she pulled Rachel in.

"You want breakfast?"

"Sure," said Alexa. "Where's Donny?"

"Sleeping off all he drank last night. Or perhaps sulking because he got turned down."

"Hah. You noticed he's sweet on you."

"Yeah," said Rachel, and stuck out her chest, "for all my charms." After her bravado, she picked up one of Alexa's little stuffed animals, the armadillo. For a few moments she turned it over in her hands, and then spoke in a small, tentative tone. "Would you be okay with... something maybe developing between him and me?" She searched

Alexa's face. A past competition between the two friends for a guy had lost its sting only after Alexa had become securely involved with Mac.

Alexa caught her tongue with her lips. She had tried to avoid telling tales on Donny, since he seemed so penitent. But if romantic feelings were developing, then her friend needed to know about his theft. "He has a past. In fact, Donny stole something from me."

Rachel flinched. "But he's still with us. You bought him a ticket to travel with us."

"True. I guess because he didn't steal it for himself—someone back home hired him to do it. I have the thing now. Also, he's been trying to make up for it all, so I've gotten to the point of tolerating him."

"What did he take?"

"Something I was supposed to give to Mac."

Her friend was trying to decide how to react to the news. "He doesn't seem like a psycho."

Faint praise. "You're right. And it was a business deal, which he is out of at this point."

Rachel pressed her palm to her heart. "He helped when I was sick."

"Just be careful," said Alexa. "Indications are that he may be someone worth knowing, even though he is a 'dude.'" She threw out her hands in whimsy. "And since we arrived, he's shown he is more concerned about us than something that happened back home."

Rachel placed the armadillo on its shelf. "Anyway, you can't give in to that type easily. Whatever happens, you got to make him work for it. Hard."

As Alexa put the finishing touches on making her bed, she said, "Let's go through the View Gallery to the dining area. I want to see some stars." She locked the door, leaving the butler-bot at its lonely outpost.

In one of the corridors, Rachel realized she forgot some information in her room. She stopped a cart-bot delivering food trays into special receptacles beside cabin doors. Alexa found the high whine of the cart-bots bothered her a bit.

"Hi, is breakfast still available?" asked Rachel, as if the robot neither had a purple face nor was working from the top of a chartreuse cart.

The bot mirrored Rachel's speech. "Hi, it is almost over. You should hurry, or you will have to order a meal to your room. And it may take half an hour or more."

"Okay." Rachel turned to Alexa, said, "I'll meet you in the dining room in five minutes," and took off.

At the same moment, a bottle dropped off on the side away from Alexa. The robot looked down and emitted a kind of mechanical concerned sound. Its cart was over-full, so Alexa took the tray out of its hands and stepped back to wait. The robot dipped its head to the side in a parody of curiosity, said, "Thank you," and bent to retrieve the bottle.

Studying the opening near her, Alexa asked, "Does the tray go in this slot here?"

"Yes," the bot replied, from below the cart. And continued with, "however, I will," as Alexa aimed at the slot. It got out, "do that," in time to watch Alexa slide the tray in and close the door on the slot. Almost confused, the bot said, "Thank you, Miss. If you want a job, I can talk to my supervisor."

A robot with a sense of humor! Alexa laughed. "I will find you, if it comes to that."

After breakfast when Alexa and Rachel arrived at the View Gallery, the huge room was completing a play-date for kids. They decided to wait at a window with several parents.

The window, however, could not be a view of space because it was on the wrong side. By standing on tiptoe to see around the adults, Alexa realized the attraction was a room without gravity. Small children bounced off padded walls. A little girl giggled as she turned somersaults up toward the ceiling, and the grownups echoed her. Alexa remembered the rush from her own tumbles on Pearson's transport ship.

"Fun!" said Rachel, as a five-year-old boy dog-paddled by the window, several feet above the ground.

"It is fun, isn't it," agreed the woman beside her. "I haven't done it in more than a week. I plan to come in the morning in a couple of days, during the time for ladies." While saying her last words she began looking past the two of them, with a smile on her face.

"Hi Mom," said a child, from behind Alexa and Rachel. When they turned, there stood a boy of around ten years.

"Hello honey," responded the woman. Facial features and brown wavy hair showed him to be her son. "How did the game go?"

"We lost," said the boy, slumping for effect. "But I scored almost all the goals for our team." He stood tall and grinned proudly.

Rachel stared at him. Alexa sensed her hunger for a hit of boy. "You are a little older than my son," said Rachel, "though I know he would enjoy vying for goals with you."

"You have a son?" asked the woman, pulling hers into the crook of her arm. "Aren't they great. He's not here with you?"

"No he's at home, where I'm headed. It will be so good to see him," replied Rachel, her voice ringing with the confidence of inevitability.

I wish I felt that, thought Alexa.

"Mom, can I have a snack? I'm starving."

The boy's mother scrunched her eyes at him and turned toward the door. Over her shoulder, she asked, "See you in the freefall room?"

"You bet," said Rachel.

On the way to their rooms, Alexa and Rachel counted eight different colors of cart-bots. As they approached their cabins, the fact that the butler-bot was missing from its post beside her door boosted Alexa's mood. Unfortunately, that surge of optimism proved premature because inside, there it was squatting in its cubby.

Chapter 19

The ship arrived at the space station near the wormhole for the Adalans solar system by early afternoon the next day. Some passengers planned to transfer to another cruise line or even to their own ships, so those people were shuttled over to the station first. Later, the afternoon-trippers had an opportunity to explore.

Donny disappeared quickly, leaving Alexa and Rachel to stroll along the hallways and enjoy some window shopping. Huge news screens like on the station above Adalans took up any space between storefronts.

"Are you Alexa Jane Alden?" asked a young woman of Chinese descent. She'd come from behind and began walking beside Alexa as she posed her question.

"Yes," replied Alexa. "Is there a problem?"

"Not at all," said the woman. "I've looked forward to meeting you."

"So have I," said a guy, from beside Rachel.

The Chinese woman complained, "Gavino, I was here first."

All four came to a stop. A shop selling electronics glittered behind the two as they began gesturing at each other across Alexa and Rachel.

"Mae Lin, there are no rules against me interviewing her, too," retorted Gavino.

Alexa's head jerked up at the word "interview." So Zaire did not concoct fiction. "Sorry," said Alexa. "I have rules about not speaking to either of you." She turned around and tripped over a planter of green fronds. *For oxygen? Ambiance? Doesn't matter.* She righted herself and marched away.

It took a couple of beats before the reporters noticed their prey escaping. "Hey," said Mae Lin, as she caught up, "you should tell your story. Get it right for people. Arriving as you did on Adalans, it's unique. Don't you want to be unique?"

"I am unique," retorted Alexa, "same as you. No big news here."

Mae Lin turned to Rachel. "Did you come with her?"

Rachel, eyes big, brought up both palms to wave the reporter away.

"It's so cool having a totally new perspective," said Gavino. "Everything must be radically different."

Alexa almost answered automatically. Rachel, thank heavens, didn't respond either.

"Do you miss home?" pressed Mae Lin.

"Sorry, nothing today my friends." Both journalists turned to identify who was speaking.

It was Lady Penelope; looking fabulous in an up-do of blonde hair and an expensive pajama set, in contrast to Alexa's corkscrew red mop and worn jeans. Instantly, the reporters began shooting questions about Newcastle Space Corporation and a takeover battle. She smiled and replied, "You know I cannot address that now. Perhaps we can talk some other time."

Astoundingly, they drifted away.

"That's some technique," said Alexa. By that time she had no illusion about being on the good side of Newcastle's sister, though it couldn't hurt to give credit where deserved.

"Nothing difficult in it. Constancy in your responses, and the press begins to trust you." Penelope had a sickly sweet look on her face again. "But, that would be difficult for you."

Rachel pulled herself up. "Hey, not true. Anyway, who are you?"

"Someone Miss Alexa made a promise to, then abandoned."

"Well if she did, it was for a good reason," said Rachel.

Penelope took a closer look. "I believe you are the one they carried away on a stretcher." Surprisingly, the blonde softened her tone. "All better?"

﹀

Newcastle strode from where he docked the hired shuttle, searching for his sister. He noticed Donny instead, and lightening fast grabbed the guy's arm. "Hello again."

Donny looked from the grip on his arm to Newcastle's face.

"We never did have an opportunity," said Newcastle, "for me to make it truly worth your while to complete your assigned task."

Donny shrugged off his hold.

"She agreed to sell it to me, you know. She may have developed other ideas in the meantime. Nevertheless you would be doing her a service, helping her lose it." When Donny turned to leave, Newcastle clamped down on his shoulder.

"You do that again, man, and your expensive nose is gonna end up very bloody."

Unconcerned, Newcastle replied, "I solely want to verify you are aware of how much you can benefit by carrying through with your agreement." Newcastle brought out his pad, paged over, and showed him the amount.

The guy took it in and swallowed hard. Tempted, no doubt about it. He even glanced up to verify whether the offer was real. But then, he pressed his lips together and slowly shook his head. "No. They are the closest I have to family now. You are barking up the wrong tree, pal."

As the back of Donny disappeared into the crowds, Newcastle swept at his hair and muttered, "Losing your touch, Iain."

It wasn't long before he caught sight of his sister standing with Alexa and another woman. They were blocking traffic in the middle of the main shopping corridor. And no fight had erupted. That was good news, considering Penelope's rants and raves during their rushed trip to this station. He strode toward them.

"Hello, ladies." The gambit of coming up from behind worked. The redhead visibly jumped. Newcastle moved in close, his body full against Alexa's, a technique that usually got him what he wanted.

"Lord Newcastle," said Alexa, while bringing her hand up to his chest. "How nice to see you."

He smiled brilliantly at her, gazing into her eyes as his oldest brother taught him. "I'm not really partial to the lord stuff. Iain or even Newcastle will do."

"Not Sir Charming?"

Penelope remained deep in conversation with the other woman—who, yes, was nicely endowed. Thus, Penny had no opportunity to interject her usual sarcastic remark about some knight in shining armor. "Afraid not," he said.

"Well then, Iain it is."

Alexa took his arm and began strolling away. He'd noticed this decisive side of her before, and liked it.

"I hope you received the note I left for you," said Alexa.

"What note?"

She stopped, appearing positively stricken. "Callaghan didn't deliver a note from me? He promised to get it to you."

Newcastle reviewed the frantic last hour on Adalans before they arranged for a fast shuttle to catch up with the cruiser at the wormhole station. "I don't believe I crossed paths with the Prime Minister."

"Oh, I am sorry. I certainly didn't want to leave you hanging."

"Why leave? Without completing our agreement?"

Her face telegraphed several emotions: concern, confusion, then deliberation. She took a deep breath. "We left without warning because we've been informed there's a way to get back to our century, but we have to get to Earth quickly."

She broke off, perhaps to check his response. He kept his face impassive.

"And I was informed that I must protect the...item."

"I double-checked the family legend," he said, "and it's wise of you to not publicly specify that item."

"Oh Iain, thank you for understanding."

He stepped back and she released his arm. "If you mean about not selling it to me, then don't thank me," he said. "We had an agreement." His brother would not care how he obtained the crystal. And if Iain didn't bring it home, he might lose everything. The family's message awaiting them at this station made it clear, the struggle against their father's old nemesis had taken a turn for the worse. His brother added a private message: Any amounts lost would come out of Iain's share first.

Still, Alexa's opinion of him was important. Thus outright theft was out of the question, at least at this moment. Perhaps he could make her see the situation sensibly. "You should know, a nasty character was after it then."

She bit her lip. He didn't know which he wanted more—to kiss that lip, or forcibly grab hold of her and locate the blasted thing. *Bet she has it on her.*

Alexa said, "There's more to the situation than whether you or I hold this little crystal."

Newcastle shook his head, unconsciously mimicking Donny. "Somehow, someway, that menace lasted through the centuries. How that was possible, I cannot imagine." He leaned closer and used his most authoritative tone. "Therefore it is imperative that you offload it. Most logically to me."

"I can't," she said, and began backing away from him.

He moved with her. *Time to push.* "Everything points to this being a dangerous situation, making you vulnerable."

She stamped her foot. "Logically, the source of danger might be you!"

Newcastle blew out his breath. "When I said you were not in peril with me, I meant it." The shopping area was emptying as passengers drifted toward the docks. "Alexa…"

"Don't you see," she interrupted, "if I had not found a way to actually accomplish the impossible, I could have followed through on our deal." She looked up at him with those stunning eyes. "Happily so."

He felt his resolve weakening, which needed to stop. "How could anyone do that?"

She smiled sadly. "My father was right."

He couldn't help a look of confusion. "Your father?"

"My Dad. Who years ago disappeared at sea. Lost. Gone. Never a word about what happened." Her voice caught a little at the last.

As much as he might rail against his family's strictures, Newcastle didn't want to imagine losing his father. Still, how could such an old sadness be related to the current situation?

She answered his question. "He didn't die." After a pause, she said, "The same as, I didn't die."

It took him a few heartbeats to realize the implication. "Alexa, your father showed up in Adalans?"

She nodded. "Callaghan pointed out that the fact both my father and I were hijacked to this time might mean we share a responsibility to the crystal."

Unlikely, thought Newcastle.

"My father left Adalans to locate someone who would transport him to me," Alexa threw up both hands, "although it never happened." She took a deep breath, blew it out and gazed over at the public area. "His whereabouts are unknown." She held out her hands in a plea for understanding. "Still, his travels and meetings with holy men and mystic masters brought together all those people to the conference. Including the swami who told me about the one person who can get us home."

Newcastle swiped a hand over his face.

"Is that Corky?" she blurted.

Newcastle grimaced. "In boarding school, that incompetent sap head exhibited everything but the knowledge and instincts he sometimes shows now. Are you certain?"

She shook her head, doubt in her face.

Newcastle returned to his goal. "Must there be a connection between you going back and the crystal?"

"According to this man," she said, nodding, "the bearer of the crystal is responsible for its safety. Above everything."

Newcastle took hold of her shoulders, aware of the warmth of her skin. "At the risk of your own safety?"

She didn't resist his almost embrace. "If I buy into the logic for this trip, I also have to accept the importance of following through

to the best of my ability on the original instruction to give it to…
well, to someone important to me."

Penelope was walking toward them. He gently released Alexa.
"I can't give up, you know. Even if merely to try to keep you safe."

Her eyes became glittery. "Thank you for wanting to do that."
She noticed the hallways were emptying. "I must get to the
cruiser." It felt as if she might reach up to kiss him. Instead, she
laid her palm over his heart. "Goodbye." A small smile, and she
was gone.

Then Penelope stood beside him, watching Alexa weave around
the few remaining people. "You're falling, big brother," she said
softly, before taking hold of his arm. "Remember. Carleene."

Chapter 20

On the short walk to the dock, Alexa kept losing her way. Twice she turned right when she should have turned left and also became mesmerized by a store window's twinkling jewelry. Then she remembered the cruiser could potentially leave her behind.

On track toward the gate, Alexa marveled at how her plan regarding Newcastle worked, with consequences. She intended back there to turn the tables on his past romancing efforts and maneuver him into a willing release from their agreement. He certainly began again on his own manipulations. Funny how words between them often became heated. At last, he seemed to really hear her. Then an emotional backlash swooped around and grabbed at her heart.

How could she seriously declare her love for Mac, when she kept being attracted to Newcastle and that Pearson person? *Good thing I'll never see them again.*

Donny and Rachel waited at the gate, on the lookout for her. Donny had said something about buying clothes other than the "silky stuff" but didn't look to be carrying garment bags. It surprised Alexa that she and Donny shared a preference for their attire from home. Rachel happily wore the loungewear sets, after a little form-fitting modification to make them her own.

"Look at the shoes Penelope helped me find," said her friend, holding up one foot. Uppers that changed colors depending on the angle, on top of a clear, flexible sole with a four-inch heel. "My jeans boots don't work with the PJs." With a sweet smile, she pushed Donny forward a step. "He bought them for me."

As Alexa admired the shoes, the desk announced the last shuttle to their cruiser and they moved to join the group standing in line. Donny dug around in a small shopping bag. "I have something for both of you." He brought out two bracelets with large, flattened beads. Alexa's beads were enameled in white with tiny pink roses.

Rachel's glinted with rhinestones. "Phones," he said.

Alexa stood, mouth slightly ajar. "Wow, thanks." On the flip side of the beads were buttons and little doors on storage compartments.

Donny explained, "I sold mine from home to the owner of the electronics store for an unbelievable amount of money. Seems the market for antiques is huge, especially for 'original' mobile phones." He snickered. "Mine was needing an upgrade."

"Cool," said Rachel, while inspecting the beads. "Instructions?"

"On the phone," he said. "I'll show you."

Rachel glanced at him while floating to a seat on the shuttle. "Wonder if I can sell my mobile, or the newspaper."

A goofy grin spread on Donny's face. "I can help you get the best price, if you want."

As they strapped themselves onto benches facing each other Rachel opted for the seat beside Donny, an action Alexa recognized as anything but random. Donny went rigid; perhaps concerned the situation might change if he brought attention to it. Alexa didn't know if he was correct or not.

Still, Rachel did not award him everything. She kept her attention on Alexa. "Penelope seems nice. Though she doesn't like you."

Alexa was gathering her hair into a low ponytail. "She could use some mood enhancers."

"You might teach her to meditate," said Rachel.

Alexa glanced at Rachel as if she was crazy. "She's about as interested in all that as you are."

"Who is she?"

"She's the sister of the man who joined us and then walked away with me."

Rachel puckered her lips, nodding her memory of him. "Who's he?"

Donny flicked a glance at Alexa, who opened her mouth and then closed it. She hadn't specified to Rachel which group hired Donny. Or that he had been required to call in from the airport.

Tricky. Besides, Alexa had to admit to herself that Donny hadn't known then that the telephone call would result in all this.

Rachel didn't seem to notice the tension. "And why did Penelope go on and on about a crystal you were supposed to sell to them?" Her expression discounted the whole idea. "They are pretty. And when I was sick, believe me, the doctors brought in a bunch of different colors. But I've never known you to pay attention to crystals."

Donny has tried to make amends. "Turns out," said Alexa, "a package Brahmaji gave me has attracted a lot of attention."

Rachel looked at Donny briefly, before asking Alexa, "Your meditation teacher gave you a crystal? Has he ever done that before?"

Alexa shook her head.

"How strange." Rachel glanced at Donny again, then at Alexa. She seemed to be trying to make up her mind about which way to go regarding Donny. Alexa responded with a noncommittal smile. Maybe Rachel decided to figure it all out later, because she turned her attention to the goal of their trip. "How long do you think before we arrive home?"

The shuttle touched the cruiser, attached with a soft cling-clang, and everyone began unbuckling and drifting toward the portal. Alexa played a bit by aiming at the ceiling and bouncing off. "I guess you get used to the weightless experience sooner or later." Alexa pushed off the ceiling before reaching the hatchway where gravity would take over. "I believe this cruise has stops at three or four solar systems. I'm a little hazy about the actual transit time. Though when I bought the tickets it appeared to be weeks."

Onboard they went to dinner first. Afterward when Alexa returned to her cabin, it showed signs of being searched. Her stomach clenched.

Newcastle had sounded adamant about a nasty someone lurking, ready to pounce to claim the prize. With the door caught on the magnet available to hold it open, she checked every place a person or thing might hide. Unless it was pretty darn small, nothing unusual showed its face. Except the butler-bot, crouching in its cubbyhole, eyeing her. Her intuition wanted to push it off a high place. But since such an action would never be possible in that environment, she compromised by escorting the robot out of the room again. Then she locked the door and barricaded it with her bags.

Still, the feeling of being watched persisted. It felt safer with the lights off, so she managed to change in the dark. *No paranoia here.*

When Alexa woke, the clock indicated about eight hours had passed. Light streaming under the door and past her luggage had become cheerily bright. She'd noticed this the previous "morning" and figured the ship changed the lighting as a subtle method to create a sense of day and night for the passengers. She might have even heard soft morning birdsong from the corridor.

The "night" before, they theoretically made a transit through a wormhole. Alexa had noticed nothing dramatic. Except when she was awake enough at one point to recognize something similar to those rare moments during meditation—the bottom falling out and then bliss, vastness of infinity as sweet shelter. It would be nice to have that experience more often.

Then she remembered something else right after: words and phrases, as a radio tuning through the stations. "Wonder if it's real, or more like hearing your own thoughts," she murmured while locking the door to go to breakfast. The butler-bot remained standing in the hall.

Later that morning, Alexa entered the sports area in time to hear Donny yell, "Point," and thrust both hands up, exultation ratcheted to a high pitch.

"Good one, man," responded his opponent.

When after breakfast Donny had smugly agreed to a game of handball, along with a small side bet, Alexa assumed he was an expert. Even so, each time she walked through the area the guy was beating Donny at almost every volley and hardly breaking a sweat.

After another ball zagged when it should have zigged, Donny

conceded. "You are good at putting the ball where you want it," he said, wiping his face with his shirt. From the odor, Donny certainly had worked hard to keep from losing.

"I learned from one of the best," said the guy. "In fact, there he goes."

Alexa followed to where the guy indicated, to see an older man, head shiny where wispy gray hair was unable to cover. Donny replied, "Him? No offense man, but that's hard to believe."

Both players strolled off the court and the man nodded at Alexa. "Don't let appearances deceive you. I am one of several pilots on board. Barnes, there, is the only wormhole pilot. We should have two, but our other one left unexpectedly last system; job offer too generous to refuse, he said. Doesn't matter. That man," and all three leaned toward a window to catch sight of the retreating back of Wormhole Pilot Barnes, "he is the best I've ever seen in setting an intention."

"Intention," said Donny, incredulously. "You mean magic?"

"It can seem like that. But Barnes has an intention of, say, where a handball should land. And it happens. It's a choice. He's way good at handball because as a pilot he uses intention all the time to come out at the intended, correct, other end of a wormhole."

"Yeah, yeah," murmured Donny. "Maybe sometime you wouldn't mind sharing some of those tricks of the trade." Donny pulled a credit chit from his bag, punched it a few times and handed it over. "You won the bet, and the double, and triple or nothing." The guy pocketed the chit and gave a quick salute before striding away.

Alexa and Rachel waited for Donny to shower before heading off for lunch, which ended up taking place at a funny and raucous group table.

When Rachel let slip she'd never been through a wormhole, a well-traveled couple began regaling everyone with stories of the effects of transits. "Once I saw a woman drop into a dead sleep, in mid-sentence, face down in her salad," said the wife. She shrugged. "Me, I get a little dozy."

Her husband said, "All those explanations of, quote, manipulating on the level of quantum space foam, I've boiled down to one thing. Stand in front of an invisible door, mutter hocus-pokus, grab hold of everything, and jump."

"I heard voices," said Alexa.

Everyone at the table, except for Rachel, looked at her a little strange. "Do you normally hear voices, dear?" asked a lady.

Alexa dipped her head. "No, not at all. It was my first jump, too. I'm sure I was mistaken."

"Coming up are several transits in quick order, including two tonight," the man to her right said. "Tell us if you get a good tip on the stock markets."

Alexa heard the man's last words. But she did not see him finish the sentence because the lights in the dining room went out. Totally out. A hush followed for about six seconds. The draft that had been bothering her continued blowing, so the air-conditioning—and thus also the electricity—were still on. Just as suddenly, the lights came back on. Reactions in the room indicated this was not the first occurrence.

"I thought they repaired the lights," complained a woman at a nearby table.

"I understand there should at least be safety lights on the floor, or something," remarked a man nearby.

"Maybe it's the pirates," said the man across from her, trying to sound glib and missing his mark.

After a bit, conversations crept to their previous levels. The lady sitting next to Alexa whispered, "I heard they take the women to… use." Fear passed through the eyes of every female nearby.

"And yell about a saint and his priest," put in a man.

"The whole thing is fabricated by some company wanting to distract attention from a bad investment," said the man with the tales of wormhole transits. "It'll disappear as soon as they clear their books."

Later, while the three friends were enjoying a gooey-crunchy confection on top of ice cream recommended by Donny, he picked up on what seemed to still rankle from the morning. "It amazes me that someone like that," he used his chin to gesture to where Mrs. Holmes-Fong was laughing with an older man, "would be the one to take us through."

Wormhole Pilot Barnes stooped to pick up his dropped napkin. His hair, or what there was of it, bobbed along with his head when he sat up. The man had clear eyes, an intelligent face, and under a long gray collarless shirt over gray pants a rounded belly that implied he enjoyed his meals.

"Intention." Donny looked at Alexa. "You heard. Right?" She nodded.

Rachel asked, "Why a human, instead of some computer?"

"I took a short course on physics that may be related to this," said Alexa, and then worked on dredging up the details. "When a human, say a scientist, puts attention somewhere, say the quantum level, everything is affected, or changed, or modified. Which is considered a pain because it complicates the process of exact measurements. But the man at lunch seemed to say a human mind is able to do more than change measurements. Even move a body and nearby items. Like ships?"

"No mind I know can do that," protested Rachel.

Alexa traced her fingers on the table. "Last night at one point it felt familiar to how it is when I meditate, especially years ago."

Donny turned to her. "Meditation doesn't look like much from the outside." He ducked. "I mean, sorry, but it doesn't."

"Remember the whirl into silence, as we were pulled to Adalans?"

"I remember very little honestly."

"We kind of coned down to a point," said Alexa. "After that, we certainly did make a leap to somewhere else."

Oh no.

Alexa dropped her head into her hands. "Do you think? Is it possible? That I did something to transport us here?"

Chapter 21

"On that day, at that moment," Rachel inquired gently, as they strolled down the corridor, "did you have an intention to go through a wormhole?" While walking to their cabins, Rachel had been jollying Alexa away from her self-doubt. Alexa speechlessly shook her head. "Right," said Rachel. "I didn't think so. Let up on yourself."

By that time, they were approaching their rooms and Alexa automatically checked at her door for the presence of the irritating little butler-bot. Not there. The lack of one, however, no longer led to the assumption it might have permanently disappeared. There it was in the room, stolidly occupying the cubby. "That's it. Enough." Did she imagine the collection of tubes cried as she pulled it out the door? *Hope so.* Door locked, Alexa marched to complain to the ship's maître d' robot.

Very unfortunately, before long Corky appeared at the end of the corridor and then scuttled away.

Alexa's gut reaction was to run the other direction. Instead, she opted to turn before reaching that spot and to accept the walk time about doubling. That Corky had pursued her onto the ship prompted the desire to retch

At the main desk, a couple of people already stood in line, so Alexa leaned against a wall to wait. The man with buckteeth spoke in rapid-fire French and departed. Next, a lady began complaining about too much noise from an adjoining cabin.

Shortly after the woman launched on her story, Corky ambled into the area. When he noticed Alexa, he stopped. This time, though, he didn't turn and run. In fact, after a moment of hesitation he advanced, showing his teeth in what might be intended as a grin, hands outstretched like a zombie. With a wall already at her back, Alexa couldn't retreat.

"Dear lady, we meet again. How marvelous you are also on my ship. Is this not the most exquisite cruise line? I am always happy to be on it, rather than some other, less glamorous. We simply did not have enough time together on Adalans, so now we may become better acquainted, yes? Where do you sit in the dining room? I am searching for the right spot. Perhaps you would enjoy company?"

After a bit, Alexa became fascinated in a clinical manner, wondering when he would run out of inanities.

The man with buckteeth came through the area again and accidentally brushed against Corky, close to knocking him over. "Excusez-moi," he muttered, catching Corky to keep him upright.

Corky, a little dazed at first, became outraged. "Buffoon! Who are you to touch me? How did you obtain permission to board this vessel? Do not ever come near me again, or...I will insist on a duel!"

Before Alexa knew it, her voice rang out. "Duel?" The smell of cologne hit her nose.

Corky cut his eyes to her and to the other people in the area, who all stared at him, stupefied. "A joke." He bent over and raised his hands. "A jest," he said, and emitted, "ha ha ha."

The bucktoothed man turned and left without a word. Good thing he didn't insist on French national pride.

The maître d' bot motioned Alexa forward. She gave Corky a little wave, intending to make clear this was goodbye. Indications were that he understood because he disappeared around a corner.

With the maître d', Alexa decided to try politeness first. "Hello. Is it possible for me to not have a butler-bot in my room?"

The robot in the desk appeared surprised. "There is no other arrangement for servicing your cabin."

"I'd rather clean it myself, than have that contraption staring at me."

The maître d' evidently did not take offense to Alexa having a strong opinion about one of its kind. "If you feel it is staring at you, we can cover its sensor until the actual time. They clean in a jiffy." The last word coming from a robot sounded surreal. Must be some kind of socialization programming.

"I put it out of my room and someone keeps returning it."

"Each is coded to a particular cabin, as is the furniture." The bot did the quizzical gesture with its head to the side. "Have you tried telling it to leave?"

"It can hear me, too?"

"Yes, to be able to respond to a command."

With no warning, the lights went out again and Alexa only heard the last of the robot's sentence. She stood still. Judging by the silence around her, everybody else did as well. Then both people in line moaned, sounding much louder than normal.

As she touched the desk to keep oriented, Alexa heard the maître d' moving items around. Six seconds later, it said, "Here it is," and the lights came on, showing the bot holding a small lamp. "This one runs on batteries." It placed the lamp on the desk. "Please accept our apologies. They tell me they are working on the lights."

Alexa tried another tact. "Does every room have a butler-bot?"

"You joined us from Adalans, correct? I understand Adalans disallows robots. In point of fact, it is quite possible every household on every other settled planet includes a butler-bot. Its price is extremely reasonable, cheaper than a vid screen. If you would prefer, we can show you how to turn it off until it is time to clean."

Alexa pretended to consider the offer. "Thank you. I would, however, truly prefer for it to be elsewhere."

She received assurances the offending butler-bot would be removed. Afterwards, she decided to find some company in the day room, as a hindrance to further attentions from Corky.

Nevertheless, Corky was too quick for her, appearing at a corridor intersection. Alexa considered ignoring him in hopes he would get the hint and go away. An alternative would be to throw something at him.

He spoke to her. "Has it ever happened with you, dear lady, that everything is at stake, for a trifle?"

His tone being the most real she'd heard from him, Alexa responded with a straightforward answer. "It has happened that everything is at stake, yes."

"Your life?"

If Corky meant to focus her attention, he succeeded. Alexa took a deep breath, and then admitted, "Not to my knowledge."

"You possess a crystal. It may be pretty and you may be happy holding it. But is it worth a life?"

The man had an amazing gift for making a girl's hair stand on end. They'd entered the day room mentioned by Mrs. Holmes-Fong. In fact there she was, probably playing bridge. If this conversation would not end at that moment, Alexa insisted it take place with people nearby. She stopped and asked, "Whose life?"

"Someone you know," he said. "Sell it to me. You can be rich beyond your wildest dreams. Any threat to anyone because of this will disappear."

Alexa scanned the room. "Mr. Espinoza, are you implying someone I care about is in danger?" If he knew her at all, he would recognize trouble in her quiet tone.

"If you care about me."

She looked at him closely. The skin around his brown eyes was pinched and a deep wrinkle ran between his eyebrows. Fingers tapped against thumbs. He glanced at her chest: once, twice. Rachel was used to men staring at her chest. Alexa's assets had always been elsewhere.

"You have it with you, I'm certain," he said. "So simple. Please, I beg you."

Alexa stifled an impulse to cross her arms over her breasts. "Corky, I am truly sorry you feel threatened." She licked her lips. "Perhaps you should go to the authorities."

His face fell. The smell of cologne hit her nose. "You do not care," he stated.

She realized the look on her face would probably be as a pious churchgoer and couldn't change it. "I care as any human would care for another. Though, I cannot help you."

His mouth twitched and his hands reached up. To grab her? When he stopped and dropped his hands to his side, her heart started beating again. "Good day," he said.

After he turned the corner, she almost dropped into a fetal position.

Chapter 22

Alexa no longer felt secure alone.

She also needed to investigate around the ship, since the combination safes available to passengers would be obvious and probably too easy to compromise. After a quick knock on her friend's door, she opened it and stuck in her head, "Hey Rachel, take a walk with me, would you?"

Rachel had been napping. "Sure," she yawned. "Want to discover new horizons? Go where no passenger has ever gone before?" She wriggled her eyebrows at Alexa before grabbing her new shoes.

"Sounds good." Alexa would prefer to minimize any knowledge or involvement for Rachel in the crystal drama. What her friend didn't know, she wouldn't have to try to hide. "What did you think about the wormhole transit?"

As they walked, Rachel went on for a bit about the strangeness of it all, then segued to Donny and his strangeness. By nodding periodically, Alexa was able to watch for potential hidey-holes. First she noticed that about every fifty feet or so in the corridors were gaps in the walls of about two and a half inches that traversed all the way around the corridor. The gaps were always in pairs, spaced about three feet apart. Alexa stopped and poked into one.

Rachel asked, "What are you doing?"

"I think I see an earring," fibbed Alexa. What she found was the edge of a door. Logical, if meant to isolate various parts of the ship. Not a good place to leave the crystal, however, since it would be pushed out into the open, or worse, crushed. "Nope. I'm wrong."

In the small dining area, a chandelier caught her attention. She could blend hers into those arranged in the starburst pattern. But when? The room was never empty, of people or robots.

They passed through the shopping area. In a box, buried under merchandise? Too risky. They strolled through the dining room, where Alexa considered the air vents low on the walls. Too easy for some youngster to claim a prize.

Next they walked through the view gallery, where a man lectured on the inner workings of stars. "A star's hydrogen burns first, then helium. Afterward depending on the size of the star, carbon and oxygen burns," he intoned.

No place to hide a crystal there. Alexa and Rachel exited through the doorway leading to the dining area.

Outside of the gallery they hesitated, and for a couple of heartbeats both pondered the green door with the sign Staff Only. Both reached for the handle. Rachel stepped back and gestured for Alexa to go first.

Behind the door was an empty corridor of about forty feet. The floor bent as if going over a hill. A single door at the end was visible from halfway up. Behind the walls on both sides electronics whined, exceeding the high register emitted by cart-bots.

Alexa asked, "You mind staying here to let me know if someone's coming?"

"Guess so," said Rachel. "The door at the end is probably locked."

Alexa nodded. Along the way nothing changed, including the electronics noise. The wall sconces attracted her attention for some reason. She recalled about three or four styles on board and these were the same as along her corridor. At the end, she stopped. Normally she would never think of opening such a private door, same as she'd never have gone beyond the sign saying Staff Only.

But these were not normal times. She'd come this far, probably not to venture here ever again. Alexa tried the handle.

Unlocked.

Heart beating hard, she pushed the door open to a slit to see if anyone inside responded.

No sound.

Holding her breath, she pushed the door a little more and peered around it.

Inside was an unoccupied room, about ten-by-ten feet. An egg-shaped cabinet about five feet tall melded into the left wall—it had to be close to the front of the ship—the open door showing a curved seat of the same material as the walls. Banks of electronics were everywhere. The room had one chair, bolted to the floor in front of the indicators.

Alexa began breathing again, and detected no unusual smell. A few lights twinkled on the displays. It all seemed pretty low key. And despite the relative electronic noise in the hallway, this room was totally silent. "Nice."

"Alexa," Rachel whispered loud.

"Okay, coming." She closed the door and trotted back, then exited the verboten corridor right before the lecturer came out of the view gallery.

After he nodded at them and continued on toward the dining room, Rachel blew out her breath sharply. "I noticed a new store." She started off toward it. "I need a hit of shopping."

That evening Alexa dressed for bed in the dark again, because despite the welcome absence of the butler-bot she still felt watched.

She preferred to sleep right through the two scheduled wormhole transits. The first part of the previous night's episode, the soft bliss, had been lovely. But with Corky providing enough creep-factor for a lifetime there was no need to culture voices out of the void.

No such luck. A couple of hours later she wakened enough to notice the transcending part of the transit. Nice. Then she detected random phrases: "Sell it on Varga." "Three light years till TohuMu." "Location of that big fish." On Earth, in her real life, television in the background was always a bit irritating. This century, even out in space she was pursued by noise. Terrific.

After punching her pillow into the right shape she must have finally fallen asleep. Later, she once more surfaced again to recognize the thick, soft silence. Sweet. Too bad that it ended.

The words, "Many fecund brides for each of the Faithful," slithered through her mind.

After that, Alexa was awake no matter what she did. She needed company. It was too early to wake up Rachel or Donny, but perhaps someone would be in the dining room.

Upon verifying her door was locked, she glanced up at the lights on the wall, glowing low for the night cycle. The wall sconces kept begging for her attention and she couldn't figure out why. As Alexa started out toward the dining room, she noticed that these sconces lay flat up against the wall, all around except for the top. Do they use bulbs now? Different from the other sconces around the ship, these were capable of holding something. Maybe dust, in space. Probably dead bugs if this was a sea cruise on a planet.

With no warning, the lights went out yet again.

The realization she'd been handed an opportunity took an entire second.

Alexa reached down the front of her shirt into her bra. Two seconds gone.

She pulled out what she needed to hide. Three seconds lost.

Reached up to verify the location of the closest sconce. Four seconds.

Jumped, deposited, and raked her wrist on the sconce. Five seconds.

Heard *Ka-ting, tang, TINK* while twisting away to land on her feet. Six seconds.

Lights came on.

She began strolling in her original direction, hoping her clothes weren't awry. She hadn't identified video cameras in the corridors, though assumed the possibility they were around.

Acting as if she forgot something, Alexa ambled back toward her room. A quick up-glance showed nothing unusual in the sconce. Or was it this other one? Nothing showed there either.

Chapter 23

Alexa opted to hang out in the day room. Earlier, she'd been there alone except for the service robots. Recently, people had begun wandering in, often taking what seemed to be their usual places to pick up where they left off the day before. Many read electronic pads or listened to news or entertainment. Some joined friends, bringing with them coffee and breakfast. A few began card games. It was good to be safe in the herd.

"Hello, dear," said Mrs. Holmes-Fong, lacking her usual chirpiness. With a gesture of her hand, she inquired if it was okay to take a nearby chair. "May I join you?"

Alexa hastened to move her dish to the side. "Of course." The woman was a total mess. "Has it been a hard morning?"

"Unfortunately, yes." She massaged her forehead. "I've been sitting with an old friend." After the woman leaned her head against the wall, she said, "In the decades I've known this man, I've never seen or heard of him being sick. Nevertheless, he fell very ill last night." She came forward in her seat and drummed both hands silently on the table. "He turned a corner less than an hour ago, it appears. The doctor is with him."

"Are you traveling with your friend?"

"Oh, no. Neither of us expected to find the other on board." When the servitor-bot wheeled toward them, the woman asked for tea, black. "He helped me out a couple of times when we were young. And I know him to be the best at what he does." She leaned to the side, stretching her back muscles. "The doctor seems to have no diagnosis. Even implying a patently false accusation of overuse of that silly gas." She shook her head, "which I never would believe."

Alexa wondered what "silly gas." She reached over to lightly touch the lady's hand. "I know your friend appreciates your support, Mrs. Holmes-Fong."

"Oh please, call me Edith."

A screech of frustration erupted from the two-year-old girl at the next table, a moment before she threw her glass on the floor. Orange liquid sprayed everywhere, including onto Alexa. The child remained untouched.

As Alexa mopped her face and checked her clothes, Edith watched the girl lead her parents on a chase around several tables. After the youngster was corralled and taken away howling, Edith turned to her. "Those two were the ones who left on the Adalans space station to handle an emergency with that little one, and thus how you and I met." Edith brushed off pulp from Alexa's sleeve. "Are you dry?"

Alexa nodded. "I think so. Luckily the color blends with my hair."

"And such a beautiful red it is, dear," said the woman.

Alexa inclined her head in thanks. The two fell silent for a bit.

Edith spoke first. "Shocking as the youngsters can be these days, it's nothing next to what is beginning to show up for the police, according to my husband. Truly, times have changed since I was a child."

Alexa smirked a little, despite Edith's genuine distress. If she were to risk sharing with the woman about her situation, Edith would probably find it amusing how humans view change as bad no matter the century. She asked, "Your childhood was where?"

"Many places," said Edith, "though all on Earth. We started in England, lived in South Africa for seven years, and then settled in North America."

"Ah. Not in China, or on TohuMu?"

"You refer to my last name, I suppose. It is my husband's name. He is from TohuMu."

"You said he considers much has changed?"

"My dearest Ghengis," Edith smiled fondly, "is a police detective. We've been married for six years, and during this time even I have noticed a change for the worse." She sat silently for a moment. "So different from when we grew up."

"You have siblings?"

For a moment, Edith seemed to shut down. "One sister. I haven't seen her in decades."

"Excuse me, Madam." A young man stood in front of the table, hands clasped. He stared at Alexa and then turned to Edith. "The Captain asked if you would come directly."

"The Captain! Oh, dear." With brow wrinkled and eyes closed, she said, "Thank you. I will go now."

A different man came to a crisp halt beside Alexa and said brusquely, "Miss, you must come with me. Forthwith."

He stood close and spoke loudly. Edith sounded a bit sharp when she responded. "Sergeant, what is the meaning of your tone? This young woman is a friend of mine and I would welcome her support, but why must she come with us?"

"Mrs. Holmes-Fong, excuse me. I did not mean she should go with you. As of this moment, she is under arrest. If she has any desire to remain discreet, she should not resist. And walk with me, at once, to my office."

Chapter 24

Rachel and Donny were already in the office when Alexa entered with the sergeant on her heels. Rachel argued with a tall officer. Considering she wore the teensy hot pink T-shirt and no bra, with black leggings and no shoes, she must have gone to the weightless room this morning. Donny alternately tried to calm her down and stood speechless, enthralled by her chest. The other men in the room also appeared anything but bored. Except for Corky, who leaned against a wall watching the spectacle with arms crossed.

Alexa came to a sudden stop. "Why are you here, Corky?"

"Lord Corcoran," said the sergeant, "do you know this woman?"

When Corky looked at her his eyes were black, not brown, and his glare was like a knife.

"We are acquainted," he said to the officer. "Though I hesitate to admit a connection to a murderer."

Alexa felt herself looking at him stupidly, trying to make sense of the last word.

"Not proven, Lord Corcoran," said the sergeant. "In hand, nonetheless." The officer put Alexa into a chair and turned to address the increasing chaos around Rachel.

Corcoran's face was cold. He'd aged decades.

When Rachel went postal, winding up into one of her routines, the sergeant sounded like he'd about had enough and was on the verge of something unpleasant. Alexa couldn't find the wherewithal to intervene.

Lord Corcoran raised his voice. "Officer, I recommend you search Miss Alden. Look for ties to the pirates, since they are the ones who would want the wormhole pilot dead."

There it was again, the stupid look. Alexa's brain began to wake up when the sergeant turned toward her. Even Rachel lost interest in her drama.

Alexa stuttered, "The. The wormhole pilot is…dead?" She

looked to the sergeant. "Is that the person Mrs. Holmes-Fong was with last night?"

The officer approached, stood over her and pulled her up by taking her elbow. "Details are not your concern. Go with this female officer."

Probably he meant the large woman approaching. Alexa said, "I don't understand how you can have any indication that I, or Rachel, or Donny, would be involved in this. What proof do you have to implicate me or them?"

"For pirates, we do not need proof," said the sergeant, "merely plausible likelihood."

"Even considering that, what would give you a plausible likelihood regarding us?"

"No record of you, any of you, exists in any database, on any planet," said Corcoran. "The single situation outside all databases is the pirate's domain. Quite plausible, isn't it Sergeant?"

"But our papers are from Adalans," said Alexa. "We joined the cruise from there." She turned to Corcoran. "And you saw us."

"Many staff and some officials of Adalans said you showed up a few days before the conference under mysterious circumstances," he replied. "At this point, Ambassador Callaghan's standing in the League of Planets is uncertain, considering she blithely awarded identity papers to pirates."

Alexa screwed her eyebrows in contempt.

"Ensign," said the sergeant, "take Miss Alden into the cell and search thoroughly." The woman nodded and reached for Alexa's arm.

"What do you think you're going to find?"

"Evidence of the substance that killed the poor pilot," said Corcoran. "Considering a vial was found in your room and traces were on your door, it will probably also be on your hands and clothes."

For a moment, all she managed was a blank stare. "And why exactly are you involved with this Corky?"

"I was trying to protect a citizen of Varga. But you were too efficient."

Alexa did not resist as the ensign led her toward a door to the left. Instead, she stared back at Corcoran, trying to process the last information and the dramatic change in him. *Multiple personality disorder?*

"Perhaps she is also carrying a weapon," said Corcoran, as the door was about to close. "She may have camouflaged one. I recommend we all view what is found."

Though the woman appeared intimidating, she proved tactful by taking a stance in front of the door to block the view through the small window. As Alexa took off clothes and jewelry, even the band holding her hair, the ensign gave Alexa a robe, which was a good thing because it was cold.

The ensign was thorough and shook her head when the tests of Alexa's hands and clothes glowed under a light on a stand in the corner of the room.

When the woman asked, "Is there anything else?" Alexa shook her head. The ensign brought out a flat wand, a bit longer than those used by airport agents, at home. "I must run this sensor, Miss."

"How could I possibly be carrying something metal?"

"Not necessarily metal," the ensign said. "Anything that would not naturally be in your body." Alexa's eyes widened. She nodded and stood still. After a pass down from head to toe, and up the back from heal to head, the woman said, "You may redress," and averted her eyes.

A few minutes later, the sergeant also looked unhappy when he viewed the results of the tests of Alexa's hands and clothes. "Positive. You came in contact with the substance."

"That's not conclusive," protested Alexa. "Someone put the stuff in my room, and yes I use the lever to my door."

"You handled the pilot's food tray this morning," said sergeant.

"This morning? No way," said Alexa.

"Is this not you?" The sergeant turned and began a playback on the wall screen. The time and date stamp on the image was from very early that morning, after the two wormhole jumps. Alexa watched herself come into view and smile at the camera. Video-image-Alexa took the tray, looked at the little door to the right of a room door, slid the tray into the cubbyhole, and shut the door.

"I did help a robot, though it was morning before last. I don't remember which corridor."

In the video, the robot's camera eyes remained focused on the door to the room, showing the room number. The view then swiveled to across the hallway. An orange hand reached out and rang the bell. The sergeant stopped the playback.

"But I helped a purple cart-bot," said Alexa. "And that wasn't my room number."

"It is the room number belonging to the wormhole pilot," said the sergeant. "The pilot died of massive heart failure. And tests are indicating this substance in the food caused the failure. You are plainly implicated."

"Alexa, say not one more word," warned Rachel.

Lord Corcoran asked, "Where are the items she had on her?"

The ensign put on the table Alexa's room key, her hair band, the chain with the small gold heart and her engagement ring, then backed off while looking at the sergeant.

Corcoran stated, "That can't be everything."

Alexa narrowed her eyes. "What were you expecting, Corky?" The shortened version of his name seemed to irritate him.

Corcoran turned to the sergeant. "Are you aware of where she goes?"

When the sergeant shook his head, Corcoran said, "To where a pirate who has killed the wormhole pilot would go." On his tablet, he brought up two photos of Alexa. The first one was her entering through a green door marked Staff Only. The second was a photo appearing to show her entering the one door on the hallway.

The sergeant went very serious. "Put her in cuffs and take her to the cell."

"I didn't do anything in that hallway," exclaimed Alexa, "and I didn't go into that room."

The ensign turned Alexa around, not as gently as before. She brought Alexa's hands together behind her back and slipped something over her wrists. Impossible to identify metal or plastic binding her hands. The ensign turned her toward the cell door and propelled her at it.

"I don't understand the problem," said Alexa.

Corcoran asked, "You want us to believe you just happened to choose this room?"

"Sergeant," came a warble from the door to the office, "what is the meaning of the treatment of this young woman? You can stop right where you are, Ensign, until we shed some light on these proceedings."

"Who are you?" challenged Lord Corcoran.

"Young man, I might ask the same of you," replied Edith.

Corky drew himself taller than his actual height. "Lord Corcoran Esteban DeSoto FitzDermot Espinoza, attaché to Prime Minister of Brasileria on Varga."

"How nice for you," replied Edith, and turned her back on him. "Now. Someone has informed me Miss Alden is somehow under suspicion for a serious crime, if there was one. Sergeant, what possible proof do you have for this allegation?"

"The most damaging information is a video of the young lady at the door to the wormhole pilot's room early this morning, interfering with his food tray."

"Does she appear to have the ability to be in more than one place at a time?" asked Edith.

Looking unhappy, the sergeant slightly shook his head.

"Then we have a conundrum. Despite the video provided to you, there are images of her at the same time in a different part of the ship."

Edith was evidently well acquainted with bringing up her desired view on a screen, because she quickly divided it into four segments.

Each segment displayed the early hours of that morning and ran sequential times overlapping the previous video. Alexa vaguely remembered passing several robots in those hallways.

"I believe these are strong enough to cast a good amount of doubt on the first vid," said Edith. "What else brings her under suspicion?"

"It appears she may be connected to the pirates," said the sergeant.

Edith grimaced in disbelief.

"Lord Corcoran reported to me that her citizenship documents were issued recently by the Adalans ambassador, and seem to cover up that these three have no proof of citizenship on any planet. I have observed that people without proper citizenship are generally involved in an illegal situation, as are the pirates."

"Perhaps. Or they have been granted new identities because of service to the greater good in some manner," replied Edith. "Again, an alternative that casts doubt upon the assumption. Anything else?"

"She established a base in the pilot room," said the sergeant, and then in a somber tone, "the Jump Room."

Taken aback, Edith turned to Alexa.

"It wasn't locked," said Alexa.

"Alexahhhhh," whispered Rachel.

Edith pursed her lips. "Did you not notice the space was marked official? Did not everything about the corridor and room indicate it is special purpose and off-limits to passengers?"

Alexa assumed she had a sheepish look on her face, and realized it would probably be worse than the stupid look.

Exactly at that moment an alarm, loud and irritating, sounded in the office and the hallway outside the office. Then an announcement blared. "Attention, all guests and all staff. Make immediate time to the sleeping alcove in your rooms and close the safety door. This is not a drill. Enter your sleeping alcove without delay and close its safety door. This is not a drill." The alert sounded again and the same message began broadcasting, in another language.

Everyone in the office stopped, until the sergeant boomed, "Take your stations. Keep traffic flowing. Make sure passengers have their doors closed. Then go to your own compartments. Move!" Edith was the first out of the door.

During the announcement, Lord Corcoran moved to Alexa. He leaned near and whispered, "Give me the crystal and you may save lives, including your own."

This close, Alexa realized why the eyes were black. Pupils that had dilated completely, overtaking any human color, had become a window onto naked calculation. No light, no warmth, utter coldness.

"What crystal?"

Quicker than a rattlesnake, he snagged her chin. No chance to resist his tightening grip. If the intent was hurt and humiliation: success. Cheeks painfully stretched, tears couldn't be stopped.

"No games," he said with zero emotion. "I have waited enough. Where is it?"

Alexa latched onto a small lick of anger rising from her gut, alongside the terror. Her voice through a squeezed mouth sounded funny. "Don't know what you're talking about."

Abruptly, no air. Windpipe, *crushed?* Need. Air.

She whimpered. She kicked. Alerts screeched. Grip on her throat tightened.

"Make it worth my while. Or you will be a bride, after all." His lips drew back, like a crevasse in ice. "Of legions."

Chapter 25

A large hand clamped onto Corcoran's shoulder, pulling him off balance. Rather than easing her attacker's grip, the opposite happened when Corcoran tried to right himself by leveraging off her jaw. *Hnnnh.*

At last, blessed release. Corky jerked, his eyes darting. A man's face came into Alexa's view. Maybe attached to the hand.

"Having a quiet, personal conversation with Miss Alden?" The bucktooth man with the sea captain's hat on bushy black hair spoke in perfect English. Alexa hadn't realized his height. Tall enough to lift Corky and let him dangle. The bucktooth man asked her, "Did he harm you?"

Alexa took desperate breaths. Somehow, Corky flew through the air and bounced off a wall. One part of her mind watched Corky slide into a heap while another part somewhat recognized bucktooth man's voice.

"Hey." The man reached for the ensign as she rushed toward the door, and indicated Alexa with his head. "Release her bonds." The ensign glanced at him, then searched for her sergeant. The man said, "She will end up as space dust if caught outside a pod."

The woman shook her head, looking for her superior.

"She cannot go anywhere," said the man. "Give her a chance to defend herself." Finally the ensign pulled out a little wand, more in a hurry to get away than to help, because the tall man wouldn't let go of her. She seemed to simply touch what was holding Alexa's hands behind her back. As the ensign then ran from the room Alexa stroked her chin and throat. They would ache for a bit.

Without warning, the ship shifted to the left. A signal sounded again. Some people in the room kept their bodies upright, some didn't, while Alexa caught herself on a nearby table. The ship settled to level quickly, at which point Donny grabbed Rachel's hand and headed for the door.

The man took Alexa's hand, said, "Come with me," and pulled her toward the hall. She wrenched to the side, reached to sweep up her necklace and ring and allowed herself to be hauled out the door. The last thing she saw in the room was Corky climbing off the floor.

The bucktooth man turned in the direction of her room and began loping along, forcing Alexa to run to keep up. Twenty feet down the hall, it hit. "Wait!" Alexa dug in her heels and pulled, which swung the man around. With this, she had a good look of his face. "Captain Pearson!"

He raised an eyebrow.

Too much. "Is everyone and their dog on this cruise?"

He turned to continue down the hallway, pulling her along. "No time to explain," he threw back. Whistles still shrilled and instructions droned in language after language.

From around the left corner at the T-intersection in front of them, Rachel's face appeared. "Alexa. Hurry!"

"Go with them, climb into your pod," said Pearson. She must have appeared uncertain because he clarified, "Your sleeping compartment. Close the door. It will be necessary, if the data are correct." Punctuating his statement, abruptly the ship again shifted to one side, throwing her the other direction. Pearson kept her from falling, gave a firm nudge toward Rachel and headed off in the opposite direction.

Alexa caught up with her friends as they turned into their own corridor. Then the ship shuddered. *We're under fire!* When they approached their rooms, Alexa yelled, "I have to get the crystal."

Rachel glanced at her. "Crystal?"

"The one Brahmaji gave me," shouted Alexa. Alerts blared.

"You don't have it?" bellowed Rachel.

"If I had, I wouldn't now, would I?"

Rachel narrowed her eyes. "No, guess not. Where is it?" Alexa glanced up at the wall sconce beside them. "Wow," said Rachel. "Maybe smart. Definitely crazy."

Alexa checked up and down the hall, waited for a woman to dash into her room and asked, "Donny, lift me up?" He maneuvered behind her and was able to boost her up to where her fingers touched the top of the light fixture, not down into it. Rachel slid in and pushed her up enough for Alexa to reach into the fixture. Empty. "Oh no!" Alexa desperately wriggled. "Try the one on the other side of the door!"

"Are you kidding me?" cried Rachel. "Forget about the smart part."

She and Donny, while holding Alexa, tried to crab-walk to the next light. But Rachel wasn't strong enough. Alexa squirmed down. She took hold of Rachel, turned both of them around, locked eyes with Donny, and they hefted Rachel up.

At the next light, Rachel yelled, "Nothing in here," above some language being broadcast between screaming alarms.

"No no no!" wailed Alexa. "Try across."

A cart-bot was behind Donny. They waited for what seemed an eternity for it to trundle past. Then he stepped backward across the hall, with Alexa following and Rachel sandwiched up high between them.

Rachel ended up with her back to the light. She whipped around and still couldn't reach into the fixture. Alexa realized what was happening and grabbed Donny to dance around so Rachel faced the light. Right as she reached the fixture, another series of pings on the ship's skin sounded and a second later the ship emitted a terrifying sound of metal screeching on metal. During that time, Rachel's hand came out with what Alexa was looking for.

"Two?" said Rachel.

Donny cried, "Two?"

"No, three," yelled Alexa. "Try again."

Donny blared, "Three? There was only one!"

"Two decoys!" shouted Alexa.

Rachel came out with the third, triumph on her face.

"Yes! Let's go!" Alexa pushed on Donny, who guided Rachel's

slide down in his arms while she dropped the three crystals into Alexa's hands.

Rachel grabbed Donny and stepped across the hall to her room, slammed her key into the lock, pushed open the door and jumped toward the bed, towing Donny along.

Alexa turned, switched her prizes to her left hand, and reached for her key. Not in her pocket. A picture of it on the table in the office came to mind and she slapped her forehead with the heel of her hand.

She wasn't aware of Pearson beside her until he took her shoulders and pushed her to the side. After he kicked in the door, it caught on the magnet.

"Thanks," she yelled. "For saving me. Again." She heard her petulance and couldn't stop it. He guided her into the room. "By the way, what are you doing here? Are you following me? Where I come from, that's stalking." Pearson kept moving her toward the bed. "Is it about the kiss? It really was merely an almost-kiss. And I have to tell you, I was in a state that day, about another man. My fiancé, as a matter of fact. Who I was supposed to have married. That day. But. Well. I can't tell you the whole story. But it wasn't necessarily about you."

"Yes, I understand," said Pearson, with far more patience than would seem humanly possible. "No, as nice as it was this is not about any kiss." Now an insistent clanging made it impossible to think. "You must get into the bed. The alert is sounding."

Alexa stood her ground. "What about you? Where are you going?"

Pearson picked her up. "Just get in." He tossed her and pulled on the handle on the top of the bed.

He leaned on the door from the outside, forcing it to close faster. As it shut, Alexa heard air exiting from her space. A low, slow whoosh sounded first. Then the pitch increased higher and higher, as air slipped through a smaller, tinier, and then infinitesimal opening. The sound stopped. Then a click. As she pried the cover off the window providing a view into the room, a precious flow of oxygen began. Some part of her subconscious noted this in its job to protect her body.

Her attention focused on the view into the room. Pearson held onto something beside her pod and was stretched off the floor with his feet pointing toward the door. Alexa's mind tried to figure out how a man as big as Pearson could be in the air. Weightless? No. Her body remained firmly rooted on the bed. Then she noticed jars from the bathroom, the little armadillo, streaking past him out into the hall.

The door slammed shut. A bottle stopped at the slit of light and stuck.

Inside her pod, Alexa's body raised up and off the bed. Reaching over to one of the pockets for gear, she deposited the crystals and then grabbed onto the window ledge with her fingertips to pull into position.

Pearson let go of his handhold, turned around and pushed toward the door, as if he were in a swimming pool. At the door, he stopped, reached down and opened it. The bottle and other stuff from the bottom of the door also drifted around the room.

Before exiting, Pearson looked over his shoulder at her. Hard to figure his expression. Quite blank, actually.

A red light inside her pod caught her attention. Alexa's brain went numb. The light *blinked, blinked, blinked* a warning. Outside the safety of her pod—was vacuum.

Chapter 26

Alexa bounced off the sides of her safety pod, while intellectual impossibilities dueled with spiking emotions. A ringing scared the bejeezus out of her. She reached into the pocket where she kept the telephone overnight and punched buttons on various beads. At last she got it answered. Someone was calling her name from the phone. She said, "If this is a telemarketer, your timing is the worst."

"God, you're okay." Rachel's relief was plain. "I saw the tall guy close your pod. But the door to my room slammed shut and we can't see a thing. What happened? Is he all right?"

"You are not going to believe this. I can't believe it. It is vacuum out there. As in, no air. And he wasn't affected. At all." No sound from the other end of the line.

"Where is he?" asked Rachel.

"He left. A couple of cart-bots have gone by. Nothing else."

"So," said Rachel, "he doesn't need air." Moments of silence passed between them. "Robot?"

"Guess so."

Donny laughed in the background. Rachel said, "He looked normal. Must put in a lot of effort to do that. He certainly seems to be keeping it a secret. Cool."

"No! It is not cool," said Alexa. "I kissed him." Alexa brought her hand to her forehead in disbelief and started a slow roll backwards onto the ceiling. "I kissed a robot."

"You kissed him? You mean, passionately? How did you have time?"

"No. On the Adalans space station. He's the captain who bought the airplane."

"Ah, it was the day of your wedding," said Rachel. "I realized it then, but didn't want to remind you."

"Yes, it was that day. The whole thing blindsided me while we were witnessing a wedding in the Viewing Dome, and later

Pearson was extremely supportive. Then we kissed. Well, barely kissed. Though I still felt I'd cheated on Mac."

"How was it?" asked Rachel.

"How was what?"

"The kiss and everything leading up to it. It must have been phenomenal," Rachel pronounced each syllable of the last word distinctly, "for you to be this shocked now. And for him to have followed you here." Her tone went analytical. "Could a robot feel so much that it would follow a human?"

Alexa was trying to figure the whole thing out. "I am way into clueless territory." She added, "I accused him of stalking me."

"Stalking you? On the Adalans space station?"

"No. A few minutes ago. Right before he threw me onto the bed." Alexa blew out her breath. The gales of laughter coming over the phone were just too much.

It all stopped when an explosion rippled through the ship. Alexa checked around her pod. "All my systems are still producing life support. How about for you two?"

"We're okay," said Rachel. She sounded nervous. "Donny says there's a huge ugly wreck of a ship nearby on our side."

Alexa turned to see out her window to the stars, and saw stars. She strained to see the sides of their ship. No view of anything. "I feel so helpless."

"Anything happening in the corridor?"

Alexa moved back to the pod window looking into the room. "No change there I can see."

The lights flickered. Came back on, flickered a second time and then failed. This time, little lights along the hallway floor switched on, as they were supposed to, and produced gloom. As she heard a moan over the phone, Alexa said, "Wait, something stopped at the door."

The sound she'd been hearing, a Click-whiiiiiiiiiinnne–Click-whiiiiiiiiiinnne-Click-whiiiiiiiiiinnne, must be the cart-bot in front of her.

The bot turned into her room, which was odd since she'd never seen this type do that. As the robot entered, it lost contact with the floor. The humanoid form on top reached out and began pushing and pulling itself around, systematically poking around in drawers and closets.

"What's happening?" pressed Rachel.

The bot stopped at the pod and peered in at Alexa looking out.

Alexa said, "A cart-bot is in my room, looking in at me." The shadowy figure gave her the willies. "The same color as the cart-bot in the video showing me in front of the wrong room number." She held up her phone with the camera in the biggest bead showing the face to Rachel.

"Yuk. What's it doing now?"

"Reaching for something at the bottom of the pod door." A click on the door mechanism sounded. "Hey, stop that." She let go of the phone and hit the button to lock the door. Her body, leveraged by the hitting motion, bounced away. "Leave my door alone you crazy robot," she yelled, while rebounding off the mattress.

The mechanism sounded again. The door held shut. When Alexa was able to bring herself to the window, the robot was looking to both sides of the pod. "Rachel," she shouted at the phone floating near her head, "is there some kind of control out there to override me locking the pod from inside?"

The robot face came up to the window. "Where is the crystal?"

Alexa heard the question, but couldn't for sure tell where it came from. She glanced at the mobile. Not from there.

"Where is the crystal?" repeated the bot, in a flat, even monotone.

"Who are you?" Alexa entreated.

"Where is the crystal?"

Absolutely the spookiest sound and question Alexa had ever heard. Completely lacking in emotion. No doubt, the bot would space her, given the slightest reason. "I don't know what you mean," Alexa yelled, trying to distract it. "Whatever you're looking for, could it be in my room?"

The lock light beside her head went out. Alexa hit the lock button again and the light came on as she bounced away. She cushioned each rebound to bring her body under control, and then turned toward the inside window, barely in time to notice the light go out again. She aimed at the lock button while trying to hold her body in place by gripping the window frame with her fingers.

Too late. The air seal ruptured with a squish and her oxygen began leaking out.

Heart pounding, Alexa braced her feet on the bed. She reached down between her bent legs to pull on the door handle, which hit the bed level to her feet. As she pulled, she slid toward the door instead of it closing.

By shuffling back a quarter-inch at a time, she was able to bring it almost closed. But the door stopped, metal hitting metal, less than a millimeter short of safety. Enough to slow the air leak, but not stop it. The engaged lock mechanism blocked her efforts and if she reached to disengage the lock, the breach would widen and she'd lose more air.

Rachel's voice came from the phone, bobbing somewhere near her head. "What's happening? Are you okay?"

"I'm losing oxygen," Alexa yelped.

A chime sounded in the distance while the door slipped away from her. She felt herself slide on her feet as the cart-bot pulled from outside. She was losing the tug of war.

Some part of her heard Rachel say, "It's on."

"What?"

"The oxygen is on. We're on our way."

Inside her, the bottom dropped out. Meditating? No. Lack of oxygen? No. Wormhole transit? Perhaps. Because next she heard a whisper in her head. "Follow them."

Despite all that, hands grabbed her and she flew at the wall opposite the pod. She bounced, and the weightless pinball effect started up again. The next trajectory was interrupted when suddenly, painfully she slammed onto the carpet. Hello gravity.

Immediately, orange hands began searching her. Rachel burst into the room, screaming New York cabbie obscenities.

It took a few moments after the collision with the floor before Alexa got her breath. When she looked up, Rachel was holding onto the cart-bot's head from behind, with it wheeling one direction and the other, trying to dislodge her.

Donny danced around the scene, trying to get in a punch. He took a hit on the chin from Rachel's heel when the bot turned one way. Next, the bot ran over Donny's foot when it came back around. Her friend dropped, but he was not out. From Donny's position on the floor, he searched for something. The second time the bot's backside came around, he reached out and jabbed low.

The cart-bot came to a dead standstill.

Rachel's momentum kept her swinging and she ended up sitting astride the cart-bot, facing the garish orange torso of the unmoving robot. For good measure, she punched its jaw. "Ow. It's hard."

"What took you so long?" asked Alexa from her prone position on the floor against a wall.

"Don't know," said Rachel. "We both kind of blacked out for a bit, between the bed and the door." She looked at the robot face in front of her, over at the bed, and down at Alexa. "You okay?"

The chiming began again and Alexa experienced the same sensation, a swirling into a cone, to slip into silence. When she opened her eyes, Rachel was slightly moving while slumped into the arms of the robot. Donny's head leaned on the wall, his jaw slack and mouth open.

"What the hell is that?" mumbled Rachel.

She was answered by an announcement over the public address system. "All guests, please remain in your pods. We apologize for the unannounced jumps. All staff, report to position Tango Charlie. All guests, please remain in your pods until further notice. We are planning more jumps."

Rachel climbed down off the bot and went over to Donny. His opened eyes remained unfocused. She took his hand and tugged, urging him to stand.

Alexa sat up and then slowly stood up.

Rachel started toward the door, but glanced back.

Studying what was left of her bed, the murderous robot silent in the middle of the room and the damaged door to the cabin, Alexa said, "I don't want to stay in my pod."

"Yeah. I can understand." Rachel looked at Donny. "How about if you go to his room?" She felt in the breast pocket of his shirt and pulled out a key. Alexa accepted it, collected her things from the bed and followed her friends into the hall.

As Rachel opened the door to her room, Donny mumbled something about Rachel needing to kiss his chin to make it better. "We'll see." She flashed a grin at Alexa and closed her door. During the time that Alexa fumbled with the key for Donny's room, a blue cart-bot sped by. Its normal high-pitched whine preceded its arrival and lingered after it passed. The empty room was heaven and the bed appeared reasonably tidy. *Oh, thank you.*

Alas, the cabin's butler-bot stood there. She draped one of Donny's T-shirts from the corner of his bed over the bot, and it was almost better. But not enough. She moved the bot into the bathroom, closed the flimsy door and barricaded it with Donny's duffel bag. Then she felt safe.

Alexa climbed on the bed, shut the pod door and sealed it. *I keep locking myself into safety, and it keeps not working.* She was beyond bushed. On the cool sheets, sleep proved elusive. Instead, hot tears welled up and leaked over onto the pillowcase. Curling into a ball, she brought the comforter over her.

Visuals of the last hour, then of the last two weeks, tumbled.

Tears slid, slow at first. *I miss my home, my life.*

Then they cycled into racking sobs. *Mac. Mac. I miss you, Mac.*

After some time, hard to tell how long, some comfort began to accumulate inside. Or at least some of the misery leaked out with the tears. She used a corner of the top sheet to dry her eyes and face.

A stray thought flitted through. "How were we making jumps with the wormhole pilot dead?" Despite all the weighty subjects, at some point, sleep must have happened.

Chapter 27

A bell woke up Alexa. Soon afterward, she realized that instead of a warning it was one of the usual ones communicating with the staff. When she tentatively opened the pod's door, the air in the room smelled as usual. Voices from the cabin next door were detectable, also the high-pitched whine of a cart-bot as it whizzed down the corridor. The normal sound in the pipes of a flushed toilet nearby rebounded through the room.

With that, nature began requiring her attention. She could not face using Donny's bathroom. Warnings of more jumps or no, she would venture into the corridor to her own room to use her own facilities.

At the door a key lay on the floor. She picked it up and waited at the entrance to allow passage for a yellow cart-bot wheeling by. Judging by the items on the cart, perhaps it was doling out cleaning supplies to the butler-bots in various cabins.

"Excuse me," she asked, "are more jumps still possible?"

"No, Madam. The alert was lifted three-point-four-two hours ago."

Alexa thanked the bot, asked for sheets to replace those on Donny's bed and dashed in to allow the butler-bot out of the bathroom. On the way to her room, she noticed that the Do Not Disturb light glowed on Rachel's door, as well as an indicator on the cubby beside the door requesting a food tray to be carried away.

Food would be nice.

When Alexa tried the key on her repaired door, it worked. Big relief, her space lacked one orange cart-bot. The room and bed were in a complete shambles, however, and way beyond the state when she'd left. While trying to make sense of it all, she noticed a folded note in the middle of the bed, on top of the tossed sheets. It read: *Not certain what happened here. At least I could arrange to have your door repaired.   Pearson*

No mention of the cart-bot, and who might have searched the room.

As Alexa showered and dressed, she tried to figure out her attachment to Mac and how it could exist with the emotions inspired by Pearson. There was no denying a certain rush when she laid eyes on the note. Newcastle aside, she was also attracted to Pearson. Hard not to be, when a handsome man kept coming to her rescue and took care of her in such a conscientious manner.

How to blend the fact of Pearson-as-robot with the undeniable experience of him? His touch had been warm and pliant, not at all like when the cart-bot snatched her from the pod. But a robot is a machine, right? At home, would she ever feel this way about, say, her car, or a smart phone, or a computer dressed up in a human suit? Then? Never. But now, evidently yes.

No real answer being available, she opted for what she could understand—straightening up the room. Slowly, carefully she decreased the chaos around her. Interesting, in the process of establishing order a feeling of watching herself began to grow. Physical movements flowed, tiny sounds reverberated in her chest, sheets were acutely smooth, her hairbrush prickly, and the one remaining stuffed animal silken. She'd asked Brahmaji about it in her early teens, and that wise man had explained the perception as a peep into expanded states of consciousness.

Half an hour later as she entered the dining room, she was almost bowled over by how packed it was, the boisterous noise from her fellow passengers.

The maître d' robot found it a challenge to locate a place for her. At a table far off to the side one chair remained, since the others were crowded around nearby tables. As she settled, conversation snippets about how each person experienced the scare floated around her. The word "pirate" came up, as well as remarks about the view of Sirius being as never seen before.

Something else not seen before, at least for her, the extent of how separate she felt from everything around her. Ordering food seemed to take place at a distance. Her eyes perused the menu, her finger pointed, and her voice thanked the servitor when the food arrived. Her mouth tasted the food and her nose smelled the aromas of everything around her. She was fully present and nowhere else, though also uninvolved.

She noticed when Edith entered the dining room. The woman, looking not much improved, eased herself into a seat at a table that must include acquaintances because they all greeted her.

Corky crept in. At first he seemed afraid someone would accost him. When it didn't happen, he relaxed and began searching for a place to sit. Their eyes didn't exactly meet, though he certainly noticed her and went immobile before pelting from the area. He seemed like he did when back on Adalans, instead of that scary version in the police office. No doubt, the guy had at *least two* personalities.

Shortly, Pearson strolled in. He'd abandoned the fake teeth. And reverted to the Adalans space station look of a green jumpsuit and shoulder-length straight brown hair pulled back into a single braid.

It wasn't her intellect reacting to the sight of him, because she'd never seen her Mac look just so. More it was a gut reaction, a longing for Mac so intense that Alexa had to turn her mind away from it or begin to cry on the spot. Perhaps the draw to Pearson was due to the similarities.

That line of logic was interrupted by a raucous yell from the other side of the room. A man at the head of a large table including a family with children stood up and began waving both arms. It was Pearson's attention the man wanted to attract. He insisted Pearson come over to their table.

Just about everyone there stood up to shake hands or kiss Pearson on the cheek. A little girl about three years old reached out to be held by him. When he took her, the girl cupped his face in her small hands and gave him a big smack of a kiss on the nose. He laughed out loud and jostled her up and down. She seemed to love it. Her mother reached for her and the little girl allowed herself to be transferred to her home arms. A chair was brought for Pearson at the head of the table beside the man. Someone gave him a plate piled high and he took a mouthful before nodding his head in agreement to a comment from someone sitting down the table. *He eats?*

Alexa's own plate was bare. With nothing else requiring her attention she decided to tour the View Gallery, to find out why everyone was excited about the star Sirius.

One side of the gallery divulged a panorama of the solar system, including light brighter than the noonday sun, with a bluish tinge. Sirius, twice as massive as Earth's sun and more than twenty times brighter, glistened off to the right. Far to the left, its companion star, a white dwarf, twinkled.

Alexa slowed her steps at the middle of the gallery where benches offered a seat with a view. Inside herself, the hush expanded to a roar.

Donny had said the star's name was connected to Shiva. From a college course on world cultures, she remembered Shiva to be one of the Hindu gods, termed by the professor as an "expression of nature." Shiva was all about silence. That seemed to fit her current situation. More than silence, the professor said Shiva was also the one that destroyed or transformed.

With the last thought, all pretense of reality inside her fell away.

Emptiness bloomed in her consciousness, as the bud of a black rose. Infinity, terrible and cold, spread through her being. The awareness seemed to connect to the blue light, within her and of her. The hall remained for its human inhabitants warm and hospitable, a contrast making the emptiness inside her that much more devastating.

Alexa sat, immersed in this new depth of stillness. Inner perceptions teeter-tottered from starkness to intense bliss. People came and went. Sirius remained constant, to the right of center in the picture window.

A thought arose in her head about once in ten minutes. One of the mental bubbles was about noticing how the crystal next to her heart had become almost hot. It had never changed temperature before.

After a while Rachel and Donny entered the gallery and stood at the window, gazing at the star. They perched at the edge closest to the entrance, Rachel right up to the railing and Donny standing behind her with his arms wrapped around. As Alexa watched, Rachel leaned her head back onto Donny's chest and he bent to kiss her cheek.

Rachel turned in his arms and brought out from a pocket her funny pen. She took his hand and wrote on the back of it. This was not uncommon, Rachel writing on her beloved's hand, her name complete with flourishes and hearts. She handed the pen to Donny who dutifully also branded her as his. This change between her two friends felt right. And it had nothing to do with her.

Alexa felt irretrievable. Would she ever again be part of the world?

Some time passed as Alexa watched inside herself. She had no idea of how she appeared to others. A clue presented itself, when a man walked into her line of vision and smiled at her, gently inquiring with his facial features if she was all right.

Sheik Farooqui had been at the conference on Adalans. If he'd been in her own time, with his white hair and beard, she'd think him in his mid-eighties. He still stood straight and tall, though he probably moved slower than as a young man. Those brown eyes took in everything around him, both actual and implied.

Alexa returned his smile and said, "We met on Adalans, didn't we?" When he gestured toward an empty bench nearby, she agreed. After he settled, she asked, "I trust the recent drama treated you kindly?"

He nodded slowly. "Yes, we were well protected. And you are well? You are almost shining, yet you appeared sad when I first saw you."

Alexa smiled her embarrassment. "I didn't realize my face is a billboard." He seemed confused, so she clarified, "I exhibit my emotions so publicly."

He chuckled quietly. "No need to be concerned. I am certain that to others you simply appear peaceful."

"You headed up the Sufi contingent on Adalans, correct?"

"Yes. My group is returning home. I have a further meeting on Earth and I was able to obtain passage on this luxurious cruiser." His eyes were smiling.

Alexa's late aunt always said a person whose eyes smile along with the rest of his face would be a candidate for trust.

He spoke. "Do I remember that you were asking about the feasibility of traveling through time? A fascinating concept to be thinking about in a practical manner. Did your search locate a viable method?"

"Perhaps so." She was unwilling even with this good man to divulge much information. "We are on a quest to verify."

Sharing silence, the two gazed at Sirius for a bit.

Alexa began talking without realizing she intended to. "I wonder if your faith has an insight into an internal perception, something in consciousness? I have heard of Sufi mysticism, though I admit to not much knowledge."

"It is possible. Can it be described?"

"You might think it sounds weird."

"I have lived long. Not much would astonish me." He did look wise.

"Well, I have a friend, who is finding an internal state to be," Alexa searched for the best words, "a cross between bleak and blissful." She watched him to see how he reacted.

"Oh. Yes. Such a divergence could be rather unsettling."

"I...my friend experiences deep silence inside. In fact beyond that, to possible vacuum. Even while eyes perceive and the mouth speaks."

He sat for a moment, pondering. "Yes. Such states may be quite strange at first. But if from God, they may result in true knowledge."

"Is there anything in Sufism, or Islam, relating to this? The closest I would know from Christianity is, 'The Kingdom of Heaven is within.'"

"That, in itself, is a wonderful statement," the man said. "How about this, from the Quran." He quoted:

My servant draws near to Me, until I Love him,
I Become the eye with which he sees,
the ear with which he hears,
the mouth with which he speaks,
the hands with which he feels,
the feet with which he walks.

Alexa allowed a flowing sense of awe at how these simple words fit. Her smile spread as her eyes shut. They sat quietly together, soaking up the wisdom.

It was not long before a young man approached the sheik and explained, with great deference, that the imam was needed at a meeting.

"Excuse me, Miss…" The sheik was obviously searching his memory for her name.

"Alden. Alexa Jane Alden."

"Miss Alden. This is my assistant and it is his responsibility to make sure I am where I should be. I do not want to complicate his mission." His tone took on extra warmth. "I think your friend will do fine, because such incidents generally come to those who have been prepared for them." He smiled as he stood up.

"Thank you for your kindness, sir. I know my friend will deeply appreciate your insight." She watched him walk away with his assistant. *At least someone who should know can verify I probably am not crazy.*

Chapter 28

After some time the episode waned. What took its place was her normal, day-to-day consciousness: total engagement in the task at hand, feeling the hardness of the bench under her behind, wandering mind. *Bingo.* A conversation between two men became fascinating.

Right after a robot wheeled through to announce that passengers would soon arrive to exercise their animals, the men passed by Alexa on their way to the window. The young one spoke to his older companion. "Every time I've come through here since the jumps after the attack, it's been this view of Sirius."

They were son and father, judging by their similarities. "I thought we were trying to transit to our next destination," the older man replied. "We shouldn't be jumping many times around any star, no matter the striking view."

"Seems to me we're kind of stuck, though no one is saying that."

For Alexa, something Callaghan said about the crystals in Scotland long ago surfaced in her mind. "The wee one appeared insignificant, though it was a great honor to protect it. Because the Dog Ear would always take the holder to the old Dog, the Ceres Crystal."

Could it be that her Dog Ear tracked to the nearest Ceres, which sounded so similar to Sirius? The ramifications of the thought did a fine job of erasing all the expanded consciousness from earlier. If the crystal could track, could it take them back in time? Likely not, since that had not happened. She wondered where the big Ceres might be in the current century. Or if it still existed.

Since so few people used the door at the far side of the gallery, she noticed whenever it opened. This time when its hinges squealed, Edith stuck her head and torso into the gallery and glared at Sirius. Why would she have such a strong opinion about this star?

Then Pearson appeared behind Edith, and also slightly entered the room to peek around her, studying the star. Pearson whispered and the older woman nodded. He backed out of the gallery, followed by Edith. Before the door closed, Alexa noticed that she turned to follow Pearson to the right. Toward the green door with a sign declaring it to be only for staff.

Alexa had to know how and when did Pearson and Edith become this friendly? It took no time to reach the Staff Only door. Peering into the corridor she caught the last movement of the door at the end, the one to the Jump Room.

But hours ago she had almost landed in jail for breaking such security.

Alexa launched herself down the corridor. At the door she stopped, a little girl admonished not to touch the candy jar. All the while, she strained to hear. A masculine laugh from within cinched it. She pushed on the door and peeped around enough to see inside. There was Pearson standing behind a seated Edith, reaching his arms around her.

"Pearson, you are so fast," said Edith.

Alexa's intake of breath was more audible than she intended.

Edith noticed her first. "Alexa! How did you get in here?"

Alexa pushed into the room a bit further. "I, uh, was in the Gallery and, uh, saw the two of you." She put one foot into the room. "I wondered what was going on." Pearson glanced at Alexa during her humiliating response and then faced back to above his hands, which were right in front of Edith.

The woman said, not unkindly, "Dear, this is probably not the best place for you." Pearson must have said something because she looked at him and whispered, "Do you think so?" He nodded and she relented. "Yes then, come in. Please lock the door behind you." When Alexa reached the desk Edith asked, "Have you seen how fast Captain Pearson can type? It's super human."

Indeed, Pearson's fingers were a blur. He turned his head toward Alexa while continuing to produce pages of characters. "I can imagine," said Alexa. A look of trepidation crossed his face. *Does he think I would out him?* "The Captain is pretty super."

Edith glanced at Alexa. "Pearson is showing me an equation that might explain why we have not been able to jump away from Sirius." She turned to the screen and leaned forward to look at some part of it more closely.

"A man in the gallery," said Alexa, "mentioned he'd noticed the ship remained in the same spot after the recent jumps."

Edith sighed resignedly. "Thus, my hope that none of the passengers noticed our predicament is for naught."

"A small question." Alexa switched from one foot to the other. "Who is doing the wormhole jumps? I thought they said in the police office the wormhole pilot died."

Edith straightened, turned in her chair and looked squarely at Alexa with a face including guilt and concern. Pearson stood up and also faced Alexa. The two of them glanced at each other. Edith, with her facial features, asked Pearson if something would be okay. When Pearson nodded, she took a big breath and said, "I am also a wormhole pilot."

With that, Edith's assumption of command in the police office became more understandable. "That's great news," said Alexa. "You saved us from the pirates."

"I am retired," the woman said. "And it's looking as if I've lost my touch. Thus, perhaps it's not great news."

Pearson put in, "I verified every action of yours has been correct."

"Still, we remain here." She turned to Alexa, "By the way, it is important that no one knows it is me doing the jumps. If my dear friend was murdered because he might transit the ship out of danger, the captain wants those responsible to not know who next to target."

"Thus you wondered why I showed up here," said Alexa. "I hope I can put your mind at ease. I am not with whomever hurt the pilot. In fact, I was attacked in my room."

"It appeared a fight happened there," said Pearson.

"It was you who slipped my room key under the door?"

"Yes. I was informed you took refuge in that room."

In the most casual manner she could muster, Alexa took the

opportunity to inquire, "Have you two known each other long?"

Edith absentmindedly replied, "What? No, not long. We met officially a day after the cruiser departed Adalans." She glanced at Pearson. Then, like the social butterfly she'd seemed on the Adalans space station, she said, "Here was this tall man with funny hair, fabulous teeth and an odd gate. I stepped into his path and introduced myself."

The monitor attracted her attention, and her role as the wormhole pilot took over. "Pearson, is this correct?" She pointed to a spot in the equation. "It appears we are jumping each time." Pearson affirmed with a nod. The woman drew her eyebrows together at the equation.

She turned her gaze to Alexa. "Shortly, I recognized him as the man who was with you, when the two of you kindly witnessed the wedding on the Adalans space station. He explained his radical change in appearance with a story about trying to not be noticed by a prior customer of his, one with which the last deal did not go well." Pearson laughed. "Come to think of it, I never saw him with you, dear," Edith said. "Though when he came to me concerned you might not be treated fairly by the ship's sometimes overzealous security officer, it did not seem out of character."

Alexa reflexively glanced at Pearson.

Edith continued. "During these days, it's become clear how knowledgeable Pearson is about the math and science behind wormhole travel. And when he saved so many people in the fight against the pirates, well I must say," she said with great flourish, "I have been consistently impressed with this man."

Pearson moved his head side to side in low-key embarrassment. Perhaps he needed to change the subject because he turned to Alexa and asked, "Who attacked you?"

"In my room?" She pulled her gaze away from Edith. "An orange cart-bot. The same color as the bot's hand in the bogus video of me supposedly tampering with the pilot's food."

"There was no robot in your room when I arrived."

"Donny turned it off before we left," she responded. "It must have been able to turn itself on, or some other bot or a human did so."

Alexa wanted to know out more about wormhole jumps. She said to Edith, "The experience of going into a wormhole is fascinating."

"Cruise ships try to jump when most everyone is asleep," replied the woman. "I understand some people prefer to schedule their bedtime with a jump, since it puts them right into slumber. Is that what happens?"

"Actually, it feels like the deepest point of meditation."

"Well I can tell you, as the pilot, the experience is quite transcendental," the woman said. "Which makes sense, because the pilot takes the ship into a state between two normal space/time geometry points."

Alexa asked, "Could the jump ending here at Sirius have been a one-way jump point? Only in, no out jump?"

"We wondered, also," said Edith. "One of Pearson's equations looks to disprove that hypothesis. And as this equation shows, when I try to leave Sirius the jumps do happen. At the end, however, we have gone nowhere."

"Did you intend to come here?"

"No, I wanted the jump to Earth's solar system, which transit is the most familiar to me. We ended up here."

The conversation having flowed to what Alexa truly wanted to know, she didn't consider how odd her questions might sound in the current day and age. "How does a pilot take a ship through a wormhole? How does it work?"

Edith considered Alexa, as if her intelligence was questionable. "You seem a well-educated young woman."

She'd exposed her ignorance of this century. *Mental head slap.* "There is a very good and long story behind why I don't know this. I'd be happy to tell you all about it some time. But my intuition is screaming that time is something we don't have."

Edith glanced again at Pearson before launching into an

explanation. "Holes, which are concentrated areas of what was originally called dark energy, generally have a default destination. Although there is more involved, a certain thought—a sound—in the pilot's mind when in front of the hole takes the pilot and the ship to the destination. In a more technical explanation, the thought or sound resonates with the super strings of the quantum space.

"The pilot sits in a cabinet, which makes the ship intimate to the pilot, as close as his or her clothes. Since it's the same substance as the ship's hull, the whole ship is carried through with the pilot. The pilot having the intention, even of the default destination, makes the transit more smooth."

Alexa asked, "Therefore, you had an intention for the Earth wormhole, and we ended up here. How can that happen?"

"The hole we entered is classified as unstable and unpredictable." Edith turned to check a dial on the board in front of her before adjusting a knob. "Most pilots would bypass it, especially with passengers aboard. I would think even pirates would avoid it. On the other hand, it occurs to me they attacked us where and when they did because that transit was available to them if something went wrong. Whatever the case, its unpredictability might account for coming here instead of the Sol solar system."

Alexa asked, "Could Sirius be the default destination for this wormhole?"

"Perhaps, though it hasn't always been the case. I remember stories about this particular wild card sending ships all over the place. No stories of ships not being able to jump somewhere else later. Therefore, when we ended up at Sirius instead of Sol, I was not particularly worried. That we cannot seem to leave Sirius is strange. Not something I've ever heard of."

"Why didn't the pirates follow us?"

"Perhaps they tried. I jumped our ship again quickly in an attempt to evade them. It's lucky they haven't shown up."

"Thus," said Alexa, "we jumped to an unplanned location and cannot seem to leave."

"That sums it up," said Edith, settling her shoulders.

Alexa debated with the tip of her tongue slightly out her lips, and said, "I may have an idea on why both things happened."

Edith blinked. "Pray tell."

"Another long story. I have with me an item that I've been told is a homing device to a crystal. The reason I have it with me is part of the longer story I mentioned. The name of the crystal, where this device always tries to go, is Ceres." Alexa waited, to give the woman time to notice the pronunciation. It took one second.

"Sounds similar to Sirius, though I believe Ceres was a Roman goddess for agriculture," said Edith.

"Scotland has a town named Ceres, and that country has a legend about the crystal," said Alexa.

"Do you think this item you have is powerful enough to waylay a cruiser?"

Alexa shrugged. "I honestly don't know. This item, and the actions it inspires in others, has consistently been a surprise. It was entrusted to me to deliver to someone else, which I am trying to accomplish. And going to Earth is part of that effort. Please believe me that it is absolutely my desire to help you transport us all to the Sol system."

A red light next to the knob Edith had adjusted began to blink. She glanced at it and scowled. "Someone scanned this wormhole. Pilots do that before entering, to avoid collisions."

"Okay," said Alexa. "This is what I think might help." Antsy would be the word for how she felt. She wanted to move. At once. "Perhaps we, together, could make this little homing device take us to Ceres on Earth, instead of Sirius. The last time I saw Ceres, it was on Earth. Perhaps your intention to go to Earth and me seeing Ceres in my mind, would get us to it."

Edith considered the proposal for what seemed hours. A sense of impending danger beat in Alexa's chest.

Edith glanced at Pearson, again asking for his opinion. He said, "I cannot see how it could hurt. And it might make the difference."

Alexa's intuition proved itself. The snout of a big, ugly wreck of a ship began to exit the wormhole.

"Do you by chance have the item with you?" snapped Edith, now very much the wormhole pilot. Alexa nodded yes. The woman hit a button on the console. "Captain, take us into position to go through the wormhole, and we will do it this time."

"In two minutes," barked the man on the other end of the intercom.

Edith turned to Pearson. "Would you handle what you can?" He nodded while taking a seat at the console.

On her way to the cabinet, Edith took Alexa's hand. Chimes sounded in the distance, announcing to everyone on the ship to prepare for a wormhole jump.

Inside, there was enough room for Edith to sit in the curved chair and for Alexa to kneel at her feet. The pilot shut and secured the hatch and clicked on a soft, low light. In the womb, she punched something into a monitor beside her, settled herself, closed her eyes, drew a deep breath and let it out.

Alexa quietly extracted the crystal from her bra. Cradling it, she reached up and laid her hands onto Edith's lap. The woman opened her eyes at Alexa's touch and raised an eyebrow at the sight of their fate being tied to such a small object. But then she took Alexa's hands in her own. Alexa shut her eyes, waited a moment and began meditating.

Shortly, the man spoke low over the speaker. "We will be at the jump point in, counting: Five, four." A screech of metal on metal intruded. "Three, two." An impact faintly rippled through the cabinet. "One. Now."

How Edith reacted, Alexa didn't ask. She simply tried to do her job. As she sank into whatever silence was available to her, she remembered Ceres—sitting there on its cushion beside Brahmaji the last time she saw him and the crystal. Her own consciousness began whirling. Down the cone her awareness slid, slowly, slowly, toward infinity.

Chapter 29

"Do you think we went through?" asked Alexa.

After listening to sounds from the ship, Edith mimed a hopeful anxiety and reached to toggle open the cabinet.

As Alexa fell backwards out of the box, she yelled, "Pearson, did we make it?"

"Yes," he shouted, and both women cheered. Unfortunately, he followed with, "But the pirate ship must have been touching ours because they were dragged along."

Alexa felt herself pulled up from the floor by strong hands and pushed toward the exit. "Go, now, run," commanded Pearson. "You too, Madam. Run as fast as you can. They will target the Jump Room first."

The ship jinked down and to the left, which threw Alexa backward. "What's that?" she shouted, climbing up off the floor.

Pearson yanked open the door and pushed her through. "The captain is maneuvering to give us time. Go."

While running, Alexa reached into her shirt and deposited the crystal beside her heart. Edith puffed behind her and Pearson brought up the rear, making sure no one straggled. Over the bridge, and through the corridor, to the door to safety they ran.

When they exited the green door, Pearson slammed the safety latch to separate the two parts of the cruiser. Barely in time because the front of the ship where they'd been, received a direct hit from the pirates. The blast threw all three to the floor.

"Turn in there," gasped Edith as she climbed onto her knees. "Safety-pods in the gallery."

Alexa hauled open the door, to the din of barking dogs of all sizes. Owners were climbing up from the floor, where they'd collapsed either from the recent hit or the almost unannounced wormhole jump or the evasive maneuver. Their canines were yap, yap, yapping at them to hurry. A few humans had tabbed open a pod or two along the wall across from the window, urging other owners and dogs to pile in.

"Wait," said Pearson, catching Alexa and turning her to him. "You were attacked by a robot." He swept her up in his arms. "No one has seen you yet." He tucked her face toward his chest, while Edith stripped off her own jacket, threw it over Alexa's head and led them into the gallery. Alexa snuck a quick peek, to identify only one robot engaged with its doggy charges. It might work.

Edith stopped at a pod. "We'll leave the floor space to the dogs." She entered a closet and lifted her foot to climb.

"Madam, allow me," said Pearson and stepped aside for her to back out. He reached in, and on an upper tier of benches deposited Alexa, who quickly found her balance. Pearson then lifted up the top five chairs in a stack beside the door, leaving one in place, and hefted the five high onto another stack before bounding up to find his own seat. Edith reentered, closed the door and engaged the lock, which caused oxygen to begin pouring in.

Alexa drew a breath.

As Edith settled onto the chair beside the door, she commented, "Though I've been almost bored in space many times, I have to say this journey has been rather too fascinating."

In agreement the cruiser jinked again, which threw the lady and her chair to the right. With everything in the closet tightly packed, the three people reaching out with arms and legs worked to steady the contents. Nothing tumbled, either human or furniture. Barks and howls sounded from adjoining rooms, though no sharp yelps indicating an unhappy squashed dog.

"I concur," said Pearson. Pings and louder hits prompted them to pause, waiting for a larger ripple of impact through the ship. But none came. "It is possible we might have a savior, hopefully in the guise of a well-armed war ship because I put out a distress call at sight of the pirate ship."

Another set of pings from debris hitting the hull sounded. Shortly after that, a voice—sounding remarkably calm considering the circumstances—made an announcement over the public address system. "If you are in a safe environment, please remain there. If not, please find a safety pod. Most of the ship is secure for the moment and assistance looks to be almost here. Still, the danger is not over."

Pearson sighed deeply, a totally human expression. "I should go help."

"Young man," remarked Edith, raising one eyebrow, "there is no rule that you must put yourself in harm's way at every opportunity." Such a look from her grandfather would have stopped Alexa in her tracks.

"Madam, my training is useful in these situations. It would be lacking on my part to not offer my services. Plus I can let them know you are safe." He ended with an earnest gaze at her.

Edith seemed to find Pearson's response a bit much. "Very well," the woman said after a moment. "Do please be careful and return when you can. Three quick knocks, then two, then one, will let us know it's you." She stood up to allow Pearson to climb down, unlock the door, scoot out and quickly shut it behind him.

Alexa and Edith sat without talking for a bit, monitoring the sequence of shrapnel hitting the hull. After another maneuver, the ship settled. Then as if picking up on a long-held conversation, Edith said, "Something's up with him, though I can't quite put my finger on it."

Alexa caught her lips between her teeth. She certainly wouldn't try to explain it all to Edith.

When the ship betrayed no signs of being attack for almost five minutes, Edith whispered, "I would love a whiskey and soda."

Chuckling, Alexa stretched her arms wide to brace the benches behind her and reached her legs across to the stack on the opposite side of the closet. "I'd go for an entire bar of chocolate. Dark chocolate."

"Oh yes," agreed the woman. "If you like chocolate, I make a marvelous sour cream chocolate cake, a recipe from my mother."

Alexa said, "Wonder if the kitchen would let us do that. I'd be happy to help."

"I'd take that cake, with a cup of good strong tea," said Edith.

"Or a smoothie. With frozen bananas and fresh raspberries and strawberries. And double vanilla ice cream." The other woman groaned. *Something other than dire circumstances, yeah, good.*

The moment between them had just settled down before the cruiser took another evasive move, throwing everything to the left. Both women scrambled to keep chairs and benches from tumbling. Once it was evident no furniture avalanche was imminent, Alexa began chuckling and Edith smiled. Soon something like chortles developed for both of them, and Alexa couldn't stop an edge of desperation. Then a long, low howl came from the compartment beside them, and she burst into laughter, Edith right along with her. Several decibels of yipping from the safety pod on the other side reduced them both to helpless guffaws. Alexa struggled to keep from falling off the bench. Both women ended up holding their sides.

Finally they ran out of breath. As Alexa worked through her hiccups, Edith wiped tears from her face. Soon only momentary smiles flitted across their faces, while rearranging themselves and listening to the nearby hound sounds.

Edith was the first to speak. "When were you attacked by a robot?"

After recounting the ordeal, Alexa said, "I'm not entirely sure why it wanted the crystal, or why people have been so intent on stealing it."

This caught Edith's attention. "People? As in numerous?"

Alexa nodded.

"For the little crystal? Don't get me wrong. I had my doubts on whether it helped." The woman gazed at her shoes for a few moments, then waggled her head. "But perhaps it did."

Something jogged the ship, like being sideswiped by a large object. Metal screeched and the gravity faltered for a moment, prompting worried yelps and barks from the canines on both sides. Thankfully, the force resumed its reassuring pull toward the floor.

Edith, bless her, wasn't fazed and joined Alexa in an indulgent smile at the sounds coming from the adjoining rooms. Then she glanced up at Alexa with a shrewd look of speculation. "Forgive me, dear, but you must have some idea about the value of this crystal. You are in possession of it, and had a theory about what it might do."

Alexa switched her gaze from Edith to the wall in front of her and swallowed. "All I know is that it is a key or locator for Ceres. Someone told me the bigger one was capable of structuring profound changes, on many levels."

The complexity of who could know which details had become overwhelming.

Before her father disappeared in the Caribbean, Alexa was able to ask herself a yes/no question and the most immediate response inside her mind would be correct. For fun during those years she proved it to herself many times. "Can I trust this woman?" came into her mind before she even intended to form the query. Yes, came the immediate reply inside her.

Okay, leap of faith. "The whole story is complicated and not terribly believable."

"That kind of story suits me fine," said Edith.

Not surprising, upon hearing the story, Edith was reluctant to believe that Alexa came from the twenty-first century. But once they got past that hurdle, the woman asked, "Is your little crystal from Atlantis? If I remember correctly, Adalans was all about crystals."

"That might be logical, though someone on Adalans said it probably wasn't from there."

"How did you come to have it?"

"It was given to me on Earth before we were transported, to deliver to my fiancé."

"Fiancé?" Edith appeared taken aback. "You mean Pearson?"

"Not Pearson."

"Forgive me dear," said the woman, "I thought the two of you connected in some manner."

"No," said Alexa, shaking her head. When Edith appeared to not believe her, Alexa tried again. "I am engaged to Armstrong MacPhearson, from my own time. And I intend to marry Mac. Right after I hand him this silly crystal."

Edith smiled, at once tolerant and skeptical. "All right, dear."

After a bit of quiet, Alexa caught her head from dropping toward her chest. She opted to lean it on the wall.

Edith remarked, "How?" As if something was impossible.

Alexa snapped open her eyes, to find the woman contemplating her.

"How do you think you can accomplish the feat of going back in time?" asked the woman. "Will you look for the same situation that brought you forward?"

"We understand doing that won't work," said Alexa. She hesitated. *More trust.* "This is private. But it comes down to finding a man known as SivSatyananda, who was last seen on Earth."

As Alexa watched, a guarded look manifested on Edith's face, right before the woman became absorbed in a study of her hands.

About five minutes passed before the woman spoke again. "Did you wonder if you could trust me, before telling me your story?"

"Well, yes," said Alexa. "Not because of you, more because of the situation."

"Why did you trust me?"

Alexa tried, and failed, to come up with an explanation of her decision process she would be willing to share. "Instinct." A dog barked and its human made a shushing sound.

"Yes, that's also the best reason I have for me to trust you."

This time, it was Alexa's turn to raise her eyebrows.

After a moment, Edith said, "Me being on this cruise is not an accident."

Alexa's pulse quickened. *Good grief, does she also want the crystal?*

"My husband sent me on a tour to see if I might detect," Edith brought her eyebrows together, "a current of ill-will regarding a new Head of Planet." Alexa scrunched her forehead in confusion, so Edith explained. "The leader of the most recently discovered habitable planet has received threats. More than would be usual, and from an anonymous though credible source."

Alexa gestured with her hand, to say please continue.

"The group's speedy success at locating their planet has dominated much of the news lately,"—as in, of course you know about this—"nevertheless, few people realize the Head of Planet, a Mr. P.N. Sharma, is only a public figurehead for someone else. Even fewer know whom.

"My husband and I found it curious the group wanted to keep the identity of 'this person' secret, and that they were able to do so was nothing short of astonishing. Their concerns were explained, however, when specific threats began to surface, in ways that cannot be ignored."

"Beyond watching the news," said Alexa, "how is it your husband and you know about this?"

"My husband is a ranking detective in the Earth portion of the League of Planets," replied Edith.

"So," Alexa said, inviting more explanation.

"It is his job to keep 'this person' alive and safe. A task made rather difficult considering sometimes this man disappears for varying amounts of time. Actually disappears. As in, not figuratively."

"Huh, even in my time satellites were able to track finer and finer detail," said Alexa.

"The location of everyone and everything," said Edith, "can be pinpointed at a moment's notice. A fact resented in many circles."

Both women were startled when three knocks, two knocks and then one sounded at the door. From the main room, dogs barked, happy to be let out. When Edith opened the door, a grinning Pearson stood there. "A small fleet is on its way to escort us to the space station above Earth. The pirates slipped away unfortunately, though not before taking a severe beating."

Chapter 30

It took longer than Alexa would have thought for the cruiser to power to Earth's main space station, almost three days. This gave her time to research newly discovered planets, their governing councils, and the locations of key people. She also arranged for a flight to Earth for the three of them.

Pearson made himself scarce. Except for the time he appeared next to her in the dining room, to explain that the blue cart-bot had been instructed to follow her to provide protection.

Rachel and Donny spent their time together.

Alexa and Edith lunched with each other once, during which they traded contact information, at least what Alexa could offer— her telephone number. Edith said, "I do hope you will be successful in your quest, my dear. But in case."

The lights went out again a couple of times, to groans from everyone.

Arrival at Earth's space station occurred during their night shift. The next morning, Alexa made a special trip to the viewing deck. She stood close to the window and gazed at the huge blue and white marble hanging in space. A lump rose in her throat. In reality, she'd been absent from her beautiful planet only a few weeks. Still, it did feel like hundreds of years.

This space station was a great collection of spheres in different sizes: some gigantic, others hardly larger than a house. People-size and machine-size tubes connected them. Exterior windows seemed random, as were access points into the station.

Some ships docked outside the two biggest spheres, a far bit away from huge openings through which other ships zipped in and out. Liners and tiny fly-abouts whirled busily around the station before zooming away. Some craft appeared to aim at the Moon, others headed straight "up" out of the solar disk toward the wormhole. Most made directly toward Earth.

Their own sizable cruiser seemed a mere blip as it drew closer and closer to one of the larger spheres and passed through a huge orifice into an immense hanger.

Later in her room Alexa was packing her small roll-on with it propped open on the bed, when two quick knocks sounded at her door. A few moments earlier, Rachel had come by to verify their plans including what to wear onto the station.

"Come in, Rachel," she said over her shoulder. The door opened slowly.

"Hello," a man said. "How are you?"

Alexa spun to find Pearson, looking handsome. "Hello there. I'm good, thank you. Happy to see Earth. And wondering what to do next. After packing, of course." He remained at the door. "Come in, please." She thought to offer him tea from her breakfast. *Useless to him.* Instead she cleaned off the one seat in the room and gestured toward it. "What are your plans?"

"My transport from Adalans, the one carrying your plane, arrived two days ago. I will join it for the time being."

Alexa smiled at the thought of the plane. Then to fill the awkwardness, she said, "Thank you for the protection during these days."

Pearson inclined his head. "You are welcome."

"It worked, on the whole. My room was searched once, I think. Small telltale signs were evident when I returned from lunch one day. And our dear Corky seemed to be nearby a lot." *I am prattling.* "But because of my blue-cart protector, there was no actual trouble."

"Good."

She pointed to the door. "Would you mind if I shut this?"

Pearson looked to the portal then back at her and briefly nodded.

"Thanks." After closing the door, she considered where to sit. The bed wasn't appropriate, so she dropped into a cross-legged position on the floor, against the wall. She took hold of a red-gold curl and began wrapping it around her forefinger. "Also, thank you for protecting me from detection by robots before the three of us squeezed into the storage closet."

"You are welcome."

Alexa tried to figure out how to ask her questions. "A few days ago during the first attack, when you put me into this pod. And you stayed outside the oxygen environment and were able to function normally." Pearson's expression became guarded, then he looked down and over toward the door. "The logical conclusion is." Alexa smoothed her sleeves. "That, you are." No doubt about it, she found it exceedingly difficult to define this person sitting in front of her as a machine.

Pearson did it for her. "A robot."

Alexa opened her mouth to respond, and closed it again when she found she didn't want to confirm the reality with words.

He opened his hands in front of him. "I was made for a special purpose."

A wry smile flitted across her face. "As we all are, in my understanding."

His face mirrored a smile back to her. And she felt a flutter of attraction. *How can I feel that? And also be true to Mac?* Pained and confused, she leaned forward and blurted, "Are there many robots similar to you? Do I need to wonder whether every new person I meet is human? Or not?" *Could I have been any more crass?*

Pearson took it in stride. "All indications are that I am unique. However, your concern is not uncommon. To the point that on some planets I am illegal. If certain authorities knew how to identify me, I would be hunted down, captured and disassembled."

Alexa fell against the wall. "That's. Just. Shocking."

Pearson made a hand gesture of acceptance. "Humans prefer to know what they are dealing with. Besides, the potential for danger from a robot gone rogue, and undetected, is quite real."

She cringed and admitted, "You need to be aware that Rachel and Donny know about you. I asked them to keep your secret. They said they wouldn't mention it to anyone."

Pearson angled his head, indicating his gratitude.

"I don't believe Edith knows," said Alexa. "Still, right after you left the closet she said 'something is up' with you."

He laughed. "I generally am able to tell whether I would be in danger from any specific person, and that is not the case with the genteel Mrs. Holmes-Fong."

They both smiled—tiny, polite. Bells sounded in the distance.

Pearson asked, "What are you planning, for your time on Earth?"

Again the issue of whom to trust. Since Pearson had protected her time and again, it would seem trusting him would be a safe bet. Wait, said her internal sense. "I will visit some," *how to put this*, "old haunts, including where I lived the last time I was on Earth. And search for certain people."

Pearson nodded. "I am much familiar with Earth and have many contacts who are happy to help while keeping their questions to a minimum. I would be happy to be of assistance."

"All your attention has been pretty remarkable." She gave a tiny shake of her head. "In fact, I don't understand why you've been this generous with your time and resources." She gazed up at him. "Why have you been so supportive of me, a stranger?"

"We are not strangers."

Alexa narrowed her eyes. "We were before you purchased the airplane. Yet you went out of your way to pay an extraordinary price for it, and added much more toward the cost of this cruise."

He peered at her quizzically. "Can you not guess?"

With no idea, she spread her hands.

Pearson developed the thinking look and spoke slowly. "I have emotion programs. Quite sophisticated programs."

Alexa nodded hesitantly, indicating him to continue.

"But I am not always certain every emotion traversing my circuits is due to programming."

Alexa screwed her eyebrows, trying to understand.

"In other words, despite the theoretical limits for machines it may be possible for human-like spontaneity of feelings to develop."

Alexa sat up straight. "Do you mean you are attracted to me?"

Pearson was quiet for a moment. "When I first saw you, every aspect of my structure began to sing." His face softened. "And it continues."

Tears came to Alexa's eyes. "That is the sweetest thing I have ever heard." *But I am promised to Mac.* She drew a deep breath. "You should know that I have a quest I must pursue." She looked at her hands. "And I have promises I must keep, or at least try my utmost to fulfill them."

"And if you would allow me to help you, in every manner I can, I will be content."

Transfixed, her eyes locked with Pearson's.

A cough over the public address system interrupted the moment and both of them switched their focus to a point in the middle of the room, waiting for what would come next. The ship's captain spoke, loud and clear, "Ladies and gentlemen, I am deeply pleased to announce we are docked at Earth's main space station. Representatives from each country and planet as well as from our cruise line, wait at the gate to assist everyone with travel details. This fine ship deserves a good rest and repair. Thank you all for your fortitude during these trying times."

Alexa scrambled up from the floor. They both reached for her bag and his hand closed over hers. A wave traveled up her arm, through her chest and to her gut. After catching her breath, Alexa glanced up to find Pearson staring at her with what looked to be the same intensity she was experiencing. She swallowed and switched her gaze to their hands—his enveloping hers. He must have thought she had a problem with the situation, which the rational part of her did though the primal part of her did not, because he slowly let go and pulled away. The primal part of her missed his touch, while her mind wondered how such animal magnetism could be shared with a machine. What is the term? Cognitive dissonance? *Yeah, that's it.*

"We should get you to the dock," he said.

Outside the ship's door, Rachel and Donny waited for her, chatting with the ship's captain. Various groups on the dock spoke with their various administrators, judging from the similarities of clothing and hand gestures.

"Hey, Alexa," said Rachel. "There's a dance contest going on in the station, using music from the twentieth century."

"You're kidding, that century? What an incredible coincidence."

"I thought we'd check it out, after I see if I can sell the *Times*." Rachel held up the plastic bag that still held the newspaper. "Maybe closer to Earth, the value would be higher."

Alexa was nodding in agreement when Donny walked to the group after saying goodbye to the guy with whom he played handball. "They say people are dressing in costumes for this dance contest. You think we might manage?"

Donny continued to favor his old clothes. Alexa recognized his under-shirt as one he wore the morning they took off from Florida.

She wore a new blouse, and her cargo pants because they always proved useful, particularly when traveling. All of Rachel's attire was from the current century. "Except for our fashionista here, I bet we'd fit right in."

During this time, Pearson had been shaking hands with the captain, who turned to Alexa and bent from the waist slightly. "Mrs. Holmes-Fong told me of your assistance. Thank you. It made all the difference." As the captain left he reached over to pat Pearson's arm, "See you again, my friend." Pearson gave a mock salute.

A moment later, a high-pitched squeal came from across the deck. "Captain Pearson! You're here!" A lovely lady, dressed in coveralls and carrying a wrench, stopped and waved with her empty hand. "It's been too long since you've been with us."

Pearson smiled. "Hello Twinda. Good to see you."

"I will find you." To Alexa, the words sounded fraught with meaning. Hardly a minute later, a blonde cooed from the door of a nearby ship, "Pearson. My, you have been away for far too much time."

Pearson smiled and waved. "Good to see you, Camille."

The woman grabbed hold of her arms. "We could meet together, for lunch. I'll look for you." A man stuck his head over her shoulder. He took in their group amid other passengers on the dock, and pulled back into the ship, taking the woman with him.

Donny glanced over at Pearson, and said, "Popular."

Pearson shrugged and turned his attention to Alexa's luggage.

Intent on the impending contest, Rachel asked, "Alexa, didn't you take some dance lessons at home?"

The group made it across the deck to a door leading into what looked to be the customs area. "Pearson!" shrieked yet another woman, a redhead of the bottle persuasion. "You left last time before we could meet again. We must get together this trip."

"I may not be here long, Sandy, before shuttling to Earth."

"Okay. But do let's try!" And she departed.

Alexa and Rachel stared at Pearson. Donny watched the backside of the woman longingly. With a look, Alexa questioned Pearson about all the attention.

"I have a few friends here," murmured Pearson.

"Yeah, obvious," remarked Rachel. "Pretty ladies." From across the hangar yet another female called his name. "I don't suppose this has anything to do with, you know."

Sandy walked nearby again. This time she came up to Pearson and plastered her body against his to the point his arm would fall around her shoulders. Gazing up, she said, "Promise you will save some time for me."

Pearson looked down and patted her shoulder. "We will see, Sandy."

As the woman sashayed away, with an embarrassed smile Pearson whispered, "I had an opportunity to arrange for a certain physical ability." He finished with a blank look into the space right in front of him.

Rachel seemed to get a point that Alexa felt had gone over her head. A knowing smile appeared on Rachel's face. She flicked her eyes toward Pearson. Donny chuckled too. Then he noticed Rachel looking at Pearson and he stifled in mid laugh.

Alexa sensed a small, confused look on her face.

Donny drew Rachel, who'd doubled over laughing, into the next hall. As the door closed, Rachel said, "But think. Such direct attention on exactly the right spot. Yesssssss."

Alexa whipped her head toward Pearson, and whispered, "Oh."

He was studying the deck at his feet, pulling on his earlobe in a distracted manner.

"So," said Alexa, in a deceptively even tone, "there's a good reason for being so popular with the ladies."

Pearson spread his hands in supplication. "I have been around for a long time."

"And do they make you sing inside, too?" Alexa clipped each word. "Meanwhile, I think we can handle things from here. It's been swell meeting you." She picked up her bag, ignoring the wheels so she could put her attention on its weight, instead of her anger.

She snapped, "Bye," and did not look back before striding through the door.

Chapter 31

On the other side of the portal, Alexa walked smack into the arms of Corky.

The cad enveloped her in his arms, causing her to let go of her bag, and cooed, "Hello." Other passengers streamed around them toward lines forming at the end of the room. She struggled and he said loudly, "It has been too long, dearest, since we've talked. Let's move over for these kind people. Mr. Arbuckle, how are you? I agree. It was a wonderful save from those pirates."

Some part of her brain registered that this seemed to be the Corky she'd first known.

Despite being not much taller, Corky managed to pin her to him and keep her face against his jacket, which disallowed calling out to anyone nearby. Soon he backed her into a corner and planted his mouth on hers, all but sucking the breath from her lungs. No passion, merely the business of keeping her quiet. His breath was terrible. One hand held her in place and the other methodically searched. He stopped at a pocket on her cargo pants and crowed, "Yes."

As she made an effort to yell, he leaned in enough to free up the other hand for covering her mouth. "Don't misunderstand, Miss Alden," he said, one inch away. "This is not personal. I'm glad you do not have to die." He brought up the gold wrapper. "However, I must have this."

Alexa detected a quaver in the background of the last statement and recognized his cologne, a cloyingly sweet-spicy smell. She popped her eyes wide and struggled, staring at the wrapper.

"Nevertheless, there is someone nearby who would not mind doing any necessary work." Corky cut his eyes over toward a door where a Mafia thug stood. "Stand here for ten minutes not moving a muscle, and you may live through the day," he whispered. "Open your mouth, wave your hand or take a step, and your top half will say goodbye to your bottom half. Is that clear?"

Alexa gave a small, terrified nod, and almost fell after Corky released her, but managed to stand against the wall considering his admonition to not move. Corky got away via the dock. Mafia guy remained, appearing to gaze off into space.

Much of her time in purgatory was taken up with watching two security men investigate and confiscate her roll-on. Alexa spent these minutes moving her eyes between Mafia guy and the security men and wondering why Corky assumed she would have his prize on her. If not already in the midst of a crisis, she might have freaked out about the concept.

After Security departed with her bag, Alexa tried to see through two windows to the dock outside their ship, whenever doors opened and shut. A delivery van arrived and departed, still she found no one she might trust to extricate her from this predicament.

She didn't notice when Mafia guy left, because Rachel and Donny began striding across the hall and she was frantically trying to figure out how to keep them out of the line of fire. The requisite time must have passed, however, because the goon was gone right before they stopped in front of her.

"What are you doing here?" demanded Rachel. "We've been looking all over for you. Mrs. Holmes-Fong's husband is here. He cleared us through customs and she wants to introduce us all."

Alexa grabbed her hand and tugged. "Let's get away from here. Now."

"But you have to show them your bag," said Rachel.

"Not necessary. The bag will wait. Let's go." Her friends clearly thought she was crazy, though they acquiesced. Donny led through the lines and out of the crowded hall.

Alexa needed a safe place. Any place without a large bozo thinking to split her in half with some god-forsaken ray gun. She aimed at the first ladies restroom she noticed, dragging Rachel along. Some little sane part of her mind appreciated the architect who designed individual rooms.

"What's going on?" asked Rachel, after Alexa slammed the door and locked it. Safely inside the room, Alexa began to shake. Rachel, shocked at first, enveloped her in a hug.

Alexa wailed, "I'm not cut out for this. I'm not the right person for this job. Someone made a mistake."

"What do you mean? Is it Pearson?"

"No, not Pearson." Alexa blew out a breath. "It's the crystal. Having the crystal just got really scary."

Rachel narrowed her eyes, in question.

"Corky caught me right after I entered the hall," said Alexa. "He searched every pocket of mine and would have moved on to other more intimate places if he hadn't found the package he wanted."

Rachel looked concerned. "He took the crystal?"

"No, one of the decoys. But that wasn't the worst of it. He threatened me with this honest-to-god hooligan. Corky said this guy would 'slice me in half' if I moved or yelled or anything." She looked Rachel in the eyes. "He was still watching me when the two of you began walking across the hall. You could have been hurt." Alexa began kneading her forehead. "There is more to this crystal than I imagined."

"Where is it?"

"I sent it off the ship. It's waiting for me somewhere." The water Alexa splashed on her face was cold.

"Good. Smart." Rachel patted her own cheek. "So Corky thinks he has what he wants, right? Maybe you're in the clear."

Alexa used the air dryer. "I hope so." Before leaving the room, she checked both directions.

By the time they reached the big hallway, Donny was talking to an earnest young salesperson. They both stared at a small container on the otherwise empty table between them. "I wonder what 'wonder' the little box is supposed to produce," murmured Rachel, and motioned for Donny to follow them.

As they walked, music could be heard. Alexa kept searching for

Mafia-guy, though she couldn't help feeling a little better with all those familiar sounds from her own time.

Rachel began nodding her head to the music. When Donny caught up and a familiar driving beat washed over them, it was clear that for him all thoughts of doing anything else vanished.

A few stores before the big hall, Alexa noticed her bank. "I need some money. Wait for me?" Both of them nodded. Inside, a scarlet-colored robot teller was embedded in the desk. "Hello," said Alexa. "This is the office for this bank on the station, correct?"

"Yes, Madam."

"Have you received a shipment from the *Jasmine*, a recently docked cruiser?"

"Yes, we did. May I help you?"

"There was a package I kept at the bank on the ship, and asked for it to be transferred to you upon arrival. My name is Alexa Jane Alden." She gave her thumbprint and looked into another identification device. "Might someone please bring the package here? I want to take it with me."

The teller consulted her internal data for a moment, producing a look of stasis. "The package will arrive momentarily."

Later, as the trio entered the big hall, happy chaos reigned. On one side, a food court was busy with crowds. Smells of pizza, spicy burritos and something stir-fried with chilies filled the air. Families congregated in a nearby area with a few live animals. The children petted rabbits, dogs and cats, and some small tribble-looking creatures that must have originated on one of the new planets. The biggest was a mother goat, being milked. Rachel strode directly to the area, with Alexa tagging along. Donny followed for a bit.

Opposite the food was the dance contest. Some of the costumes missed the target century, and in some cases didn't allow for much movement. Still, all couples were smiling, jumping, swirling, laughing, sliding, swinging or grooving with great gusto. Judges watched from a gallery that ringed the area about fifteen feet up. Periodically, a lighted sign would blink a number in red. When couples recognized their number, meaning they were eliminated, they drifted away. Those remaining would pick up on each new tune and keep on dancing.

Donny returned with identical numbers for him and Rachel and began dragging her toward the dance floor.

"You okay?" mouthed Rachel. When Alexa nodded, Rachel held up her bag to ask if Alexa would mind watching it.

Alexa took the bag and waved her on toward the dancing. It was an act; she was kind of nervous being left alone. She opted to back up against the wall near a group of teenagers while scanning all around.

The music sounded as good as the original recordings of hits from the last half of the twentieth century and first part of the twenty-first. That could be possible if they'd been preserved appropriately with each new technology through the years, Alexa surmised. She caught the eye of the girl next to her, who had ringed her eyes in black to emulate the Goth style. "Do dance contests happen frequently?"

"Not ever. That I can remember," the youngster replied in a cadence that would have pegged her a hip teenager back home.

"How do you know the attire and dances?"

"The contest was announced a couple of days ago, so we had time to research." The girl briefly mimed a 1960's dance step. "We practiced last night. I had to radically change some of my clothes. And it's so worth it."

"Are animals usually here on the station?"

"Never. That I've noticed. We recently returned from a vacation on Earth, where I was around animals, or I'd be over there with the little kiddies." She glanced at the petting zoo. One of the other teens turned toward them and the girl asked her, "All this food, for free, and the dancing and the animals, it's never happened before. Right?" Her friend nodded in agreement. "But I love it. Couldn't resist coming."

"That would make two of us," sounded a deep masculine voice

from behind Alexa. Judging by the widening eyes of the two girls, Alexa figured the man must be either well known or very attractive.

Chapter 32

When she turned, Alexa realized he was both: Turner Bishop, a man easy to recognize since the gossip magazines featured him on the big news screens all the time.

Bishop said, "I believe that in the century for this music it was acceptable to ask a lady to dance." He flashed a galaxy-wattage smile and held out his hand for Alexa's.

"And she might accept," said another man, "if she hadn't already promised the dance to someone else."

Alexa about fell over when she recognized the source of that statement. "Iain?"

The girls aimed their cameras at the two handsome men.

"I told you I would make it," responded Newcastle, as he slid his arm around her. "Sorry, Bishop. This dance is mine." Newcastle nodded at the fuming man as he turned Alexa away from the group and shot over his shoulder, "See you day after tomorrow at the conference."

When Alexa glanced, Bishop was gone. The girls were excitedly talking to their friends and pointing toward the door.

Newcastle didn't even hesitate before swinging out onto the dance floor while holding her right hand. He guided her up close into position in front of him and placed his hand in the small of her back. With scarcely a pause, he picked up on the beat of the current song, a pop version of a song from the 1940s.

"Bishop is a good businessman," remarked Newcastle, as he stepped left. "And he's enjoyed a lot of extraordinary breaks." He swung her out. She dipped with the swing and extended it with her left hand, before flowing back into his arms. No doubt, he was an expert. Matching his pace was exhilarating.

"Nevertheless, the man is quite erratic in his behavior." With a twirl, Newcastle emphasized his next point, "at unpredictable times." He spun her twice quickly, brought her back in front of him and slid into a turn, round and round for them both, exactly keeping time to the beat.

Alexa was almost dizzy. "What are you doing here?"

"Not giving up on you," he replied, marking time before spinning her out, then in under his arm and guiding her around his back to return to position in front of him. He was excellent at leading. She would have had to *try* to miss steps. "And other things."

They danced through that song and began another. Newcastle favored a style that included a good deal of body contact.

"Is everyone on the station at this event?" She was breathless after a particularly challenging series of steps.

"Ready? Keep your legs straight. I'll get you through this." Before she even agreed, he brought her hands to her hips, picked her up vertically, twirled once like a baton, and brought her safely to her feet. By that time, she absolutely felt dizzy. He brought her against his body.

"No," he answered. "The number of this crowd is perhaps four hundred. At least a thousand people live on the station, while thousands more transit through on any given day." He took them through a final swing. "I happen to be fascinated with this era." The song came to an end. "Have been all my life."

They stood in the lull facing each other, him breathing hard too. "Something to drink? Or perhaps we should locate Bishop for your next dance."

It simply wasn't possible to resist smiling at his deliciously facetious tone.

"All right, this way," he said. After pulling her hand through his arm he headed off the dance floor. People they passed tracked their steps. Taking Iain's photo? Seemed so. Then before they reached the bar, a real human jumped out of the crowd and began bobbing and weaving. Stunned, it was a bit before Alexa realized the man's black glasses included a camera.

Newcastle held up his hand. "Joco, Joco," he intoned. "Such an adventure. To see you again, and again. And again."

"Hey, Newcastle. Doing my job, you know?" Glancing at Alexa pointedly, he leered, "And trying to keep you honest." He solemnly nodded. "Such a pretty lady." Dashing away, he muttered, "Thanks for the 'toes.'"

Newcastle and Alexa watched the lanky man lope away. She asked, "Paparazzi?"

"That gentleman began following me when I was twelve years old, and has made a fortune."

After a small sip of some kind of soft drink beverage, Alexa said, "Joco." Newcastle nodded.

"Did he say he was trying to keep you honest?"

"Well, yes." He went quiet for a bit. "I am engaged." Newcastle seemed to be kind of tongue-tied. "To be married." He glanced at her. "Have been for awhile." Suave, debonair, galactic Newcastle suddenly appeared entranced by his high-quality brown suede boots.

"Oh," she whispered. *Fair enough.* He's engaged. I'm engaged. Nothing can develop between us, which simplifies matters. Pearson has his harem. And I am going back to Mac. Good. Settled. "Congratulations." Since there was nothing to talk about, between them, about them, Alexa opted to change the subject. "So you're not here for business?"

"In fact, I am," he said, looking relieved she didn't demand explanations about his announcement. "I'm here to pick up a cruiser to deliver to Adalans."

Alexa peered onto the dance floor, searching for Rachel and Donny.

Newcastle said quietly, "I found out more to convince you to be careful."

"Tell me something I don't already know," came her tart reply.

From behind them, Donny moaned, "You are not gonna believe this. They eliminated us. And we were dancing way better than anyone else." Rachel, standing behind Donny, lifted and dropped her shoulders. She scanned the area, looking for something.

"I'm sorry," said Alexa. "Your newspaper is where I left it, on the table over there." She pointed. "I can see the white bag." Rachel trotted over and Donny followed her.

Not five seconds passed before Newcastle suddenly grabbed her and pulled her to the floor, him landing on top.

"What are you doing?" she cried. "Get off me!"

Newcastle flicked his eyes to the chair nearby and her nose registered a burning smell. The chair sported a hole, an inch in diameter, angling from the back down through the seat. Heat radiated off it. On another chair right beside them, a tiny red light moved around on it a moment before it also developed a hole and the same smell.

It took about half a minute for the people nearby to realize someone was shooting. No one was hit, except for another two chairs and a table, all in the vicinity of Alexa and Newcastle. The smell, and a chair spontaneously combusting, did it. Everyone scrambled.

"See, I told you," Newcastle said.

He'd saved her, though his hands began doing an efficient job of pinning her down and searching all of her. Alexa stared him in the eyes. "Jerk."

Rachel was crying out, "Alexa? Are you okay? Alexa!"

Donny bellowed at Rachel, "Stay down!"

"Perhaps, but not on purpose," Newcastle replied in her ear. His hand stopped over her heart, gently massaged and located the crystal. It was only a matter of time before he took it.

Alexa looked away first. "What are you going to do?"

"I don't suppose you'd be willing to hand it to me?" Again, they locked gazes.

Alexa began wiggling and he looked at her like she'd lost her mind, until he realized she was trying to reach the pocket on her calf. It wasn't easy with Newcastle remaining square on top of her, or possibly shielding her, hard to tell. But finally she brought up a crystal and offered it on her flat palm.

Newcastle momentarily appeared confused, then he took a closer look. "I assume this is a fake, since I would not expect you to give in this easily."

Her smile at him was twisted.

Newcastle's eyebrows came together. "Why don't you keep this one and give me the real one?"

"Because I have a job to do."

He pressed his lips, reluctant.

Alexa said, "All you need is something to please a bunch of people who lost it a thousand years ago, probably because they misused it."

Newcastle took the decoy and turned it all around. "I need the real one."

"Your family is doing fine without the real one."

He sighed. "It's close enough. Maybe it could work."

Donny arrived, having pulled himself along the floor on his belly, intent as a marine. "Off," he commanded. "Now."

"Not yet," Newcastle murmured. "Not safe."

Whistles shrieked as the police entered the hall. Newcastle shifted, and stowed her gift into his pocket.

"Lord Iain," said a policeman, looming near them. "How is it you're involved?"

Newcastle climbed up and pointedly stared at the chair. As Rachel came to stand by Donny, bag in hand, another policeman noted the chair's condition, its position and the probable line of fire. Then he examined the other chairs and the table.

"Perhaps an instance of over-active jealousy," Newcastle replied, as he began dusting off his trouser legs. "It's unfortunate this young woman was in the vicinity. I have time to go with you to file a report before I must join a business meeting. However, I believe this lady has a flight to catch. Might you let her go?"

The officer seemed reluctant. "You don't think she was involved?"

"I assume I was the target. I can't see how anyone would want to harm such a pretty lady, do you?"

The policeman smiled tightly and said, "If this is happening in such a public place, I am nervous about you being exposed."

"We are meeting at Hotel Cairo, in this sphere," explained Newcastle.

The officer nodded, as if that made everything acceptable, then turned to his assistant. "Please escort this young woman to her flight."

Alexa had clambered up while Newcastle was speaking, trying to remain in his or someone else's protective shadow. She turned to Donny and Rachel. "It appears these gentlemen have everything under control."

"I wish that were the case," the policeman replied. "Trends have changed here, lately. Have a good trip, Miss."

Soon the group stood in front of a wall of monitors, with Alexa staying close to the man's protective body mass.

"Which is your flight?" asked the policeman. "I should take you there and return to my post."

"We can take it from here," said Alexa.

"My commanding officer would bust me if I did not make sure you arrived at your gate."

She searched her memory for details on the flight she'd booked for them. In reality, it was a day later. She settled on the one listed on the monitor to Earth leaving soonest. "This one. Where is it located?"

"That gate is perhaps thirty minutes by tram."

Rachel put in, "Alexa, I think the lady changed our reservations to this one. Isn't this flight right down this tube?"

"It doesn't leave for hours more."

"I know. We wanted to do some shopping," said Alexa. "And Rachel wants to see if she can sell an antique." Rachel looked confused. "Your newspaper."

Rachel mouthed, "Oh," and nodded.

"Then," said the young man, "may I escort you to the gate?"

"Sure. Let's all go."

In another five minutes, the policeman was happily returning to duty and the three of them sat at an empty gate that appeared relatively safe, as far as Alexa could tell. "I'm hungry."

"You're kidding," said Rachel. "After everything that just happened?"

"Being frisked, threatened with bodily violence, shot at, and groped, can make a girl want some comfort food."

"Who groped you?"

"Newcastle. He was willing to accept my last decoy."

"He wanted the crystal, too?" Looked like Rachel couldn't believe it.

"His family wants it," said Alexa. "Now he has something that can make them happy."

They located a decent restaurant near their gate. Alexa was relishing the first bite of a crusty mac and cheese entree when a smooth, masculine voice intervened.

"Well, hello" said Turner Bishop. "What a pleasure to see you again, under more congenial circumstances."

Chapter 33

A little more than an hour later, at the intersection of several corridors in the middle of nowhere, Alexa whispered, "How did my life become some intense horror flick?"

Not fifteen feet away, a hit man with less than a full set of teeth was holding Donny by the hair on his head and aiming a god-forsaken ray gun at his private parts. Donny, though larger and probably stronger than the weasel, stood motionless. If the gun had been to his head, he might have struggled. But the man pegged Donny right when he took aim.

Rachel exhibited a momentary instinct to attack, instead muttered "bastard," and sprinted down the hallway behind Alexa.

Alexa held her position, a wall and a corner away from the attacker and Donny. Everything except the man's face was hidden behind Donny or the corner. A third passage joined the scene between them. In all directions, no hint of humanity or robots. Their voices reverberated through the corridors.

"What say, princess?" snaggletooth demanded. "The crystal? Or his balls."

Alexa cringed. After a couple of beats she asked, "What crystal?"

"Don't get cute with me," said the rat. "This guy will be singing in the high registers if you don't hand it over."

No! She had to give Donny credit. He didn't start blubbering to her to hand over the blankety-blank piece of glass. "Listen, you're late. Someone already took it from me."

"You go get it," the thief snarled. "Of course, that gives me more time to make little changes to your friend."

"Detective Holmes-Fong is nearby."

"Too far away to help you, or this guy," replied pointy nose.

Technically Edith and her husband were close, but they'd begun strolling in the opposite direction from Alexa twenty minutes ago. That was after she parted from them outside the restaurant.

Edith and Ghengis had seen Rachel, who had been out and about in the corridors after Bishop gave her the name of an antique store that would buy her newspaper. Bishop had flashed one of his toothy smiles and instructed Rachel to, "Tell the manager I sent you."

Alexa was about to try a cocktail ordered by Bishop when Edith poked her head in at the door of the restaurant. When she hailed with her usual high-pitched, "Yooh hooh," Bishop's lips thinned.

After a bit of coaxing from Alexa, and no assist from Bishop, Edith and her husband joined the table and ordered for themselves. During the meal, Bishop and Detective Holmes-Fong seemed overly polite to each other. To the point that it wasn't surprising when Bishop excused himself and left. She never could find the cocktail later.

Alexa asked the detective, "Do the two of you know each other?"

In his upper crust accent, the short Chinese man with a huge gray mustache and blue eyes had replied cryptically. "We've almost interacted a suspicious number of times."

Now Alexa was in this corridor dealing with a sleaze bag. From the direction of Donny and no-teeth, she heard a click—perhaps the equal of pulling back the hammer of a Saturday night special.

"Hand it over, or he weeps," the guy said, having heard far too many old holovids.

Donny was nearly crying.

"Wait," urged Alexa. She eased her left hand into view, turning it so the back of the hand showed, and wiggled it in the light. "Wouldn't a diamond be easier to turn into cash?" Mac had saved for a year to buy the engagement ring.

"I'm paid for the crystal, sweetheart. That or nothing."

A man from behind needle-nose said, "I would take her offer if I were you."

The rat took the voice seriously. He yanked Donny around to

cover him from that angle.

The new arrival said, "If I made it here to help, odds are others are on their way, too."

Alexa recognized the voice. Newcastle. *Here? How?*

"Time to slink to your hole, Grunger," said Newcastle.

"This has nothing to do with you. And the name's Granger."

Alexa risked a better peek, to find Newcastle bringing up a small laser. "I will not drill you this time Grunger, if you take her offer and let the man go. At once."

Alexa had worked the ring off her hand. She tossed it into the corridor across from them all. It bounced twice and then slid to a stop against a wall about twenty feet away. Forthwith, the scum wrenched Donny around, stepped both of them across to the intersecting hallway and whipped into cover around the corner. Next thing Alexa knew, Donny was flailing back across the corridor, trying to keep from landing on his face. Snake-nose must have scooped up the ring because all that remained was the echo of running steps.

Rachel almost flew to Donny.

As he strode over to Alexa, Newcastle asked, "Did he come near you?"

Either she was in shock, or used to being attacked and threatened, or in denial. Whatever. Alexa shook her head, already missing the connection to Mac through the ring. "I am not giving you the crystal," she stated. "And if you try searching me again, I will…do something."

His effort to not smile at her lame threat was almost successful.

"How is it you were here, or nearby," insisted Alexa. "And why did what's-his-name follow your instructions?"

"Rachel found me."

"She knew where to find you, that quick?"

Bullheaded, Newcastle retorted, "She pays attention and found me at the hotel. I have a shortcut this way to my office because I happen to know the area is free of the contagion that first got it quarantined. Most people won't go near it and don't want to deal with robots that traverse through it. Why were you here, besides rank ignorance?"

Alexa knotted her brows. "What was the contagion? No, wait. Don't tell me. I have enough going on." She traced in her memory to why they came this direction. "Rachel was given directions to a shop here, by the store Bishop sent her to. They declined to buy her newspaper."

"Bishop! He found you again? Has he worked his magic yet?"

Alexa issued a tolerating-type smile.

"Which store?"

Rachel and Donny appeared next to them —two people moving as one. Rachel responded, "Sheffield's."

"Bishop owns the store. If they sent you here, they were instructed to do so."

Alexa began to wonder if Bishop could somehow be connected to Corky, but couldn't figure out how that would necessarily be the case. Why would someone like Bishop want the crystal?

Newcastle said to Alexa, "If you would give it to me, people would stop chasing you and pursue me instead."

"Nice try, but the thug wouldn't take that excuse."

Chapter 34

In the lull, Donny touched Alexa's shoulder and whispered, "Thank you."

Alexa was saying, "I'm glad he accepted the exchange," when a door in the distance squealed and clanged shut.

Soon Pearson turned a corner far down the hallway, at an all-out run. The group watched as he barreled toward them and came to a smooth stop. Breathing hard. Alexa suppressed a smile. *Nice touch.*

Pearson did a slight double take when he recognized Newcastle and said, with no inflection, "Newcastle."

Newcastle replied, "Pearson."

Then Pearson turned to Alexa. "My sources warn that the pirates are almost here. We have bare minutes to get away from the station before the authorities lock everything down."

Newcastle protested, "It takes a while to warm up any craft before taking off. Even one of your freighters, Pearson, as good as they are."

"We have been preparing for this," Pearson replied.

Everyone turned to Alexa. Did she need to debate? "Okay. Let's go." In the moments before they all took off, Alexa sensed Newcastle's discomfort. She turned to him. "What will you do?"

He stuck out his chin. "Fight the good fight." After glancing at Pearson, he said to Alexa, "You should leave, though."

Before she turned the first corner, Alexa glanced back. Newcastle stood there, watching them.

Soon the group erupted through a set of double doors into a large common area that Alexa hadn't seen before. They slowed to a walk through what would have been considered a town square on Earth. Since Pearson kept to merely a brisk pace, Alexa forced herself to not run.

Adults and children sat at tables, a group of elderly lounged in a garden area, and travelers moved along to their flights; each person blissfully unaware of the danger approaching. A sunbeam shone through a window, evoking in her an intense desire to sit with one of those groups and pretend all the danger was an illusion; that reality was simple living.

Rachel stopped in front of a bank of monitors. "Wow, look at that."

The name Lord Corcoran Esteban DeSoto FitzDermot Espinoza blinked in six-inch letters. "Today, found dead, of an apparent brain hemorrhage, at the age of thirty-two," the talking head intoned. Alexa and Rachel glanced at each other in disbelief. The newscaster said, "A recently discharged laser was fou—"

A blaring siren drowned out the rest of the newscast. People jumped and searched around, wondering about the earsplitting beats.

An official provided explanation over a loudspeaker. "Attention, attention. It is highly probable an attack is imminent. Please rapidly proceed to your security areas. Volunteer response squads, report immediately to your stations. This is not a test. Repeat. This is not a test." Shock registered on each face Alexa took time to see, though no fear. Instead, everyone quickly collected his or her children and belongings. Able-bodied men and women transported those needing help.

Across the common area, Turner Bishop banged through a set of doors, just like she and her friends had a moment earlier. Except, trailing after him was a group of men, more big and bulky than would be required at any time. Bishop's glare at her made the idea of some little safe hole very attractive. Whether or not Bishop wanted the crystal, there was no doubt she was his focus.

Alexa caught Pearson's sleeve, jerked her head at Bishop's group, and swerved away from where their paths would intersect. Pearson, as fast as ever in comprehension, took a rabbit-quick maneuver to a side door. She yelled, "Rachel, Donny, this way." Before she raced through the door, Alexa took one more look at Bishop. The angelic face he wore during their meal was replaced with something mean and ugly, and disturbingly familiar.

The hallways all looked the same.

Alexa called out, "Pearson, do you have a map of the station?"

Three doorways and two longish corridors later, he brought them out onto a flight deck that was totally utilitarian, no trappings to cater to tourists.

Controlled chaos ruled in the hangar. Alarms sounded, some at a distance, one right close. Everything in the air was landing, as tugboatlets shifted vessels to make more room. People and robots cleaned all excess items off to the side. A massive door outside the sphere's skin looked to be slowly moving to close off the hanger. Could they make it out of the huge docking space before it closed?

Pearson touched a bracelet and a door on the side of a nearby freighter opened. Without slowing, he raced toward it and the three of them followed close on his heels.

"Hey!" yelled a stout man at a standing desk near the door they'd sprinted through. "Pearson, what the hell do you think you're doing? I ordered your crew off that freighter." As the door to their craft closed, the man's tone ratcheted up a notch. "Don't even think of taking off from here."

When they entered the bridge, the same man was threatening over the intercom all kinds of bodily harm if Pearson did not come out and explain himself. A bank of screens showed different parts of the ship, including one compartment that contained the *Red Arrow*!

Another screen showed how the stout man threw his clipboard onto the desk and tugged on a communication line, while ordering his helpers around.

As a whoosh of hydraulics announced their ship cutting loose, Bishop and his bruisers rocketed through the double doors. Pearson's ship glided away from its position and headed toward the shrinking hole, to open space. Bishop, pictured big and bad on the monitor, was furious in a coldly frightening manner, exactly like Corcoran looked when he was practically strangling her. Alexa again fought an urge to search for some safe closet.

A moment later, Bishop's face changed to confusion. The man

glanced right and left, took in the men around him and appeared to have no idea who they were. He shook his head, turned and started toward the door. One of the tough-guys caught his arm. Alexa didn't see how Bishop responded because the screen was taken over by the face of the stout man.

"Captain Pearson, you are in direct disobedience of my orders to stand down and return to the Dock Captain's post. Be forewarned, you will be disciplined to the full extent of the law, up to and including being barred from landing at this station."

"Yes, Dock Captain," Pearson replied. "We are very sorry to not follow your directive, sir. Nevertheless, we must go to Earth. It is a life and death matter. I assure you, I will pay any fines deemed appropriate."

"Don't think your money will get you out of this one, sonny," the dock captain responded. "I'm on your ass." Both audio and video went blank. The crew around her called out the freighter's status as it changed. An engine drive engaged.

One of the beads on her bracelet began its funny ringing sound. As the hole to space got smaller and smaller, Alexa located an ear bud inside a bead and inserted it into her ear. "Hello?"

"Alexa? It's Edith."

Alexa remembered about the impounded bag, the one containing her computer with all those precious photos of Mac. Her heart plummeted to the deck.

"I am so glad I remembered your number," said Edith. "Where are you?"

"Believe it or not, Pearson is trying to get us to Earth."

"Thank goodness. Ghengis informed me. A moment, please," she muffled the phone, then returned. "The person you're looking for?" She paused.

"Yes, that person," said Alexa.

"Unfortunately, Ghengis doesn't know a location at this moment. However, you need to know time is short. *That person* will become unavailable, possibly for decades, in less than twenty-four hours."

Chapter 35

In a corner office of The Herald building in New Delhi, India, the principal newscaster for *The India Herald* studied a bank of screens at her desk. The gossamer silk sari of Varshana Vagwhatar moved along with the bingle-bangle sound of her gold bracelets. She worked on an article destined, she assumed, to earn another award.

Focused on her work, Varshana barely heard the voice claiming her attention.

"It is time," the voice repeated.

She glanced around. "What?"

"It is time to fulfill your promise," said the voice.

"Promise?" She pushed back her chair and rotated to view every corner. No source for the voice could be located. "What is this? Who are you?"

"A business partner," the voice replied.

At this point, she realized the words were not sounding in the room, but in her head. "How dare you take such liberties." Varshana searched to verify some trick wasn't being played. Nothing out of place, as usual.

Out of the blue, it dawned on her. "No. You must be kidding. That agreement was years and years ago. You cannot be serious, after all this time."

The voice replied, "Years during which I delivered data specifically useful to you. Was it not satisfying when you exposed the dark side of the prime minister to all the worlds?"

Varshana continued her part of the conversation out loud. "The people had to know."

"As with all your other exclusives, was it not also a great boost to your ratings? And of course, your fame."

For a few moments, Varshana rested her chin on her left thumb, tapping her lips. She made a counter-offer. "I have an assistant."

"Time does not allow, even assuming he would make the same choice as you." A moment passed. "This is an opportunity to complete your part of the bargain."

Varshana sat up straight and tossed her head. "Not possible," she pronounced, using the tone that always cleared her path. "This is not convenient for me. I have a deadline."

"Convenience was not part of the agreement."

Without realizing, Varshana switched to thinking her responses. "You can't do this. You can't get away with it."

"I do it any time I deem appropriate, for far longer than you could guess."

"I will do an exposé on you. Your filthy business will be stopped."

"How will you explain that you carry on conversations with someone else in your mind? And even if you convince people, how will you justify the chip in your brain? I intend to keep all interactions private, but the chip is now known to certain authorities—who I assume you would want to remain in good standing with."

Varshana rapped a stylus on her desk. After a moment she said, "I will have it taken out."

"You will lose every byte of data I provided."

"I will find you and destroy you," she thought back, resisting alarm. "I have many powerful friends."

"And you have many powerful enemies, who will need little urging on my part to destroy you."

She reverted to speaking out loud. "I will not be used in this manner."

"Do you have secrets?"

The question stopped Varshana. She tried to not picture any one of the actions she always assumed would remain known only to her.

"I will have no problem divulging them to those who would harm you most." The statement was delivered as fact, with no emotion. "I will not even have to utilize my assets."

Her agile mind, usually able to find a path around any obstacle, came up against a wall. "What must I do?"

"You have one hour. You may find it useful to be in a private place when I return," replied the voice.

"I strictly forbid use of my position with *The Herald*."

"I will use what I consider appropriate, including the position at *The Herald* that I created for you," said the voice.

"You created! How dare you. I have been the one working day and night for years for this position. I demand my standing remain at its high status. I offer no compromise on this."

"Whether you offer or not is inconsequential. If I decide so, you will become a pawn of the Priest, or a bride." A moment, and the voice began again. "If you cooperate and this exercise is fully successful, you will be released from your contract."

Varshana's throat tightened with apprehension. "But the information would continue, surely."

Before she completed the sentence, Varshana already felt emptiness in and around her. Further argument would be with the air. Her mouth settled into a line and she punched the com-button.

Chapter 36

The group's rickety teardrop-shaped taxi stopped at Mandala House, in a genteel shabby neighborhood in the far suburbs of New Delhi. The vehicle must have been old, because its hovering ability had certainly not protected them from the road's potholes during the previous six hours.

As Pearson announced, "This is it," Alexa brought her attention from the herd of Brahmin cattle ambling by. Protection of sacred animals remained common in India, even this close to a big city; hence the smell of livestock cascading through her open window. On the other hand, diesel and gasoline fumes were unknown.

Cities had become a mix of architectures, some Alexa recognized and others stretching her imagination. One elegant house appeared to be an open pavilion. From his front-seat vantage Pearson had assured Alexa it would have an energy field to keep its occupants secure.

The driver produced a receipt for their ride from Jahnsi. "Two hundred thousand rupeani." Screens in the front and back seat, which had been blaring in various languages, showed 150,000 rupeani. Pearson erupted in Hindi and the driver yelled back at him. A quick back and forth ensued, then they both nodded while Pearson ran his chit through the reader.

During the few steps from the curb to the gate, Rachel stretched. "That was the most brutal ride I have ever experienced."

"Roads were better in the city," said Donny. "Maybe they try harder to control monsoon runoff here, though I understand the season was bad this year."

Outside the gate, two policemen brandishing lasers stopped the group. One spoke, first in Hindi then in English. "Do you have an appointment?"

Alexa said, "No appointment, Officer. But Detective Holmes-Fong with the League of Planets recommended I come here."

They certainly recognized the name. "This is not a good time. Please return next week."

"I'm sorry, sir. But we won't be here next week," said Alexa. "Pearson, would you mind contacting the detective to give these officers the full story?"

Pearson played along brilliantly, bringing out his mobile. The two policemen began to consider whether it was a good idea to continue harassing her and risk attracting the wrong attention from a superior. Using their phones, they communicated with a supervisor in the embassy. "Someone will be here shortly."

After a few minutes, out the ornately carved front door strode a young man. Over tan trousers, he wore an unadorned collarless top of a sharply pressed fine white material that fell to the knees. Some women Alexa had seen during the drive wore the silky pajama sets commonly worn by galactics, other women sailed along in saris. Generally, women wore a long tunic over pants with a matching scarf. Also seen were headscarves, even covering much of the face, probably used by the female Muslim population.

The young man approached the gate. He did not invite them in, opting instead to speak from the other side. "What do you want?"

Alexa evoked the most charm she could muster. "Is Dr. P.N. Sharma in, please?"

The young man's demeanor became guarded. "Why do you ask for Dr. Sharma?"

"Detective Holmes-Fong suggested he might help me locate a person."

"I'm surprised the detective did that. You see, what you ask is not possible." The young man's voice broke. "You are an hour too late. Dr. Sharma is dead."

Alexa's mouth fell open and she blinked a few times. "I. I'm sorry."

The young man's lower lip trembled. "It happened as he left his house after lunch." He shook his head and switched his gaze to the space in front of him. "It is incomprehensible."

While leaving the embassy in a different cab, they were almost sideswiped by a vehicle that in their own time would have been the ubiquitous white van. The vehicle, emblazoned with *The India Herald* on all sides, came to a sharp stop in front of the embassy. Their own driver yelled and gestured at the van's driver, who completely ignored him.

A couple of minutes later, after their cab turned a second time to evade an indolent cow, Pearson asked, "Where do you want to go?"

Alexa shrugged. "It seemed from my research that Dr. Sharma would be the one person in the organization who could help us."

Rachel look worried. "Is it possible his death is related to us?"

"I hope not," said Alexa. "Not only would that be awful, it would mean someone knows, or can guess, where we are going and who we plan to see."

For a moment, it appeared Pearson might join the conversation. Instead, he glanced out the cab's window. The cabby hit the brakes to avoid a scooter with two men cutting through traffic. Donny muttered, "Ow," and rubbed his head where it had connected with the driver's seat in front of him.

The screen in the back seat switched at a fast speed from what looked to be advertisements, to news about the current strike by train and airplane employees, to interviews with beautiful people. A graphic came up with flowery letters spelling "Kumbh Mela" and a video began, with a reporter standing on a high ground to show a vast stretch of humanity behind him. The names Allahabad and Prayag scrolled underneath. Alexa watched for a few moments, her eyebrows together. She asked her internal question: could he be there? The answer: *Yes.*

"Pearson, would you ask the driver if the Kumbh Mela is going on now? In Allahabad?"

Pearson nodded, let forth again with a stream of Hindi, then switched to a different dialect. After a short reply from the driver, Pearson turned around to her. "Yes."

"What's the best way to get there?"

He asked, and translated, "Airplane is the fastest, though the driver prefers the train. Neither would be certain because of the strike." The driver spoke for a moment. "He says he would be willing to drive us there." Pearson asked him another question. "An eight hour trip, which in this traffic is optimistic, I assume."

"We have only a little more than nine hours left," warned Rachel.

Alexa explained. "The Kumbh Mela is a conference of spiritual luminaries like the man we are searching for. He could easily be there. In fact, if he is anywhere in India it's almost for sure he would be there."

"I've heard of those events," said Donny. He switched to the fake Indian accent he began using when in the spaceport in Jahnsi he bought the red and orange tapestry Nehru cap he now wore. Donny bobbled his head side-to-side and said, "Millions of people will attend."

Alexa deadpanned a look at him, then got to business. "I know it's a stretch but this is the one thing I can think of. Anybody else have an idea?" Everyone's face was blank. "Okay." She turned to the driver. "Airport please, sir."

Fate seemed to be on their side. One last plane for the day would depart at 5:05 that afternoon and four seats were available. It would fly only as far as Agra, though that city was in the correct direction and the agent said there was a small chance some pilot would decide to fly to Allahabad and the Kumbh Mela.

Pearson chimed in, "Alexa, I brought your plane in the shuttle. If we go to the spaceport it would take about two hours to fly to Allahabad."

Rachel closed her eyes and moaned. "More hours of mammoth potholes. I don't know if I could stand it again." The vote tipped in favor of the flight.

They had eight hours to travel three hundred miles to Allahabad.

In Agra, city of the Taj Mahal, the robot in the counter delivered the bad news. "I am sorry, Madam. The sole flight leaving this evening is to New Delhi."

"For this airline?" asked Alexa.

"No Madam, for all airlines."

Alexa understood the benefit of programming to keep a robot from adding, "because the silly humans have a problem with how efficient we are." Although the strike had developed suddenly, more than one person mentioned that humans were upset about how robots monopolized many jobs.

"Is there a train to Allahabad?"

"If I may, I should point out I am an airline information specialist," replied the robot. "However, I am capable of accessing train schedules. A moment, please." The blue-tinged androgynous face went blank, then reanimated. "There is one train in that direction, scheduled to arrive here at two a.m. and proceed to Varanasi. You might take that train and another to your desired destination. The one other train available is to Jahnsi."

"When does it leave?"

"In less than hour."

"Okay," said Alexa. "We'll come back here shortly."

On her way to their agreed meeting place Alexa stopped in front of a store window with gorgeous saris, many covered in intricate embroidery and sparkles. The blues and reds and sunset colors were a feast for the eyes.

Thus she was taken by surprise when a middle-aged Indian man spoke to her. "Excuse me. Are you the woman *The India Herald* is looking for? Miss Alexa Jane Alden?" He appeared a bit embarrassed. "You look remarkably similar to the photograph on the news. If you are that woman, would you share your winnings with my family? The station said you might be willing to do so."

Alexa stared at the man, trying to figure out what he was talking about. She opened her mouth to say yes, her name is Alexa, when Pearson stopped her.

"Hello, sir," he said to the man. "No, she is not that woman, though I agree there is a strong resemblance. Good luck in finding her. I hope if you do, she will share much of the prize with you." Pearson turned her around and steered her away. "Good night," he said to the man. As they walked away, he whispered, "Here, put on this sari."

"Why? What's going on? By the way, it seems Jahnsi is our only hope. Can you arrange for train tickets?"

"Hey Alexa," said Donny as he jogged up to them.

Pearson shushed him and asked him to not use her name.

"Oh, okay," replied Donny. "You're right." He glanced around and found they were relatively alone in the wide corridor. "A woman looking a lot like you." Donny nodded as he began to understand how to handle the situation. "Yeah, the spitting image of you, is all over the news. The lady newscaster is saying *The India Herald* wants to give you everything you deserve." During this time, Pearson had walked them all toward a ladies restroom, past one of those huge news screens showing a picture of Alexa.

Inside a restroom stall, Alexa carefully unfolded the silk. Luckily, a friend had once showed her how to put on a sari. Simple, the woman said. *Hah.*

After deciding to wear her own blouse, Alexa managed fairly easily to wrap the material around the lower half of her body once. Then anchored the topside of the length of silk in the waist of her cargo pants. Next the hard part: fold, fold, fold, fold the material in the front. Stick this bulk into her trousers and pray it would remain in place.

Then wrap the end of the yardage once, and twice, round her torso, angling upward each time, and for good measure in this circumstance over her head. Exhausted and dressed to the eyeballs, Alexa began to wonder if she should even think of leaving the stall, much less traveling to Allahabad.

A friendly voice called out, "Alexa, you anywhere in here?"

"Rachel?"

"Yeah. It's me. We've got to go, honey. Are you ready?"

Alexa moaned, "Go how?" as she fumbled open the door. On the first step, the folds slid from her trousers and down underfoot, tripping her. She reached in and around two layers, grabbed and hiked up the front of the garment, then smashed the folds more securely down into the front of her trousers. A final jerk on the end of the silk up and over her head made it so she could see only about three feet in front.

Alexa didn't want to even glimpse the smile Rachel was probably trying to hold back.

Chapter 37

The super-fast train from Agra to the Jahnsi spaceport wouldn't show up for another fifteen minutes, so they settled themselves in the empty waiting room. The road to Jahnsi was closed because a bridge had become damaged by a recent flood. Therefore, train employees agreed to keep a limited schedule instead of joining the general strike.

When the sari slid off her head on their way to the waiting room, two more people approached Alexa about being the woman on the news. The second time Alexa had to resort to acting crazy to drive the person away. She'd noticed other people taking photos of her and her friends. Were they sending them to the news station? Who was this newscaster?

"I need more protection," said Alexa, as she settled into a seat.

"Here," said a guy. "Wear this over your hair."

Rachel looked up. "Zaire, you found us."

"That's me, Zaire Chevalier at your service. And in this case, really at your service. If Varshana Vagwhatar is after you this much, you are in trouble. She has been known to go to extremes for a story, but this stunt is beyond anything she's done before."

Alexa considered the item Zaire dropped into her lap, a headscarf that could also hide much of the face. An extra benefit was that she could place it over her head and thus it would stay on.

"But you're in luck," he said, "I will help you elude Varshana." He paused for two beats. "If you give me an exclusive."

Alexa did not hesitate. She laid the scarf over her hair and adjusted the extra material to fall over her face.

"You'd better ditch what you're wearing too," Zaire said to Alexa. "All over the news is you in living color, trying to hide behind that sari."

Alexa ducked behind a bank of chairs and began unwrapping the silk. She'd wear her regular clothes and the head covering.

Luckily, she had on a long-sleeve shirt and long pants. She'd appear unusual, though not beyond reason.

Rachel asked, "How'd you find us?"

"Been tailing you best I could since Adalans. It hasn't been easy." He looked over at Alexa and caught her eye. "All those 'toes of you and Newcastle on Earth's space station let me know I was on the right track."

Alexa stopped from adjusting her clothes. "Toes?"

Zaire carefully enunciated, "pho-to-graphs," and said, "I would have caught up with you all on the space station, but the pirate scare came up."

"A scare? I thought they were about to attack," said Rachel.

"Never happened." He spread his hands and looked at the group. "Now, it's easy to find you. Because of Vagwhatar." He smiled at Rachel. "Miss me?"

Donny rushed up. "Hey guys, we are all over the news screens. Different pictures of each of us." He looked at Zaire. "Who're you?"

"The knight in shining armor."

Both Donny and Pearson responded with, "Uhnn."

Donny handed Rachel a headscarf similar to the one Alexa had on. "You gotta wear this."

Rachel studied the cloth in her hands. "No way."

"I'll take it," said Alexa, "in case I need to change. And henceforth, I'm not with you all." She turned on her heel and walked to the farthest end of the waiting room. Pearson watched her every step, and thenceforth pretty much ignored the conversation around him.

It turned out that Rachel wearing Alexa's castoff sari did a pretty good imitation of an Indian princess. She asked for help in donning the sari from the washroom attendant, who was delighted to help. Rachel must have found eyeliner in her bag, which still contained her ever more battered copy of the *Times*, because her eyes were rimmed in the same manner as other women they'd passed during the day. Donny ditched the Nehru cap and thus managed to blend into the background.

In this manner, they boarded the train. Alexa searched through the cars until she located a family, and nodded shyly at the mother as she sat on the bench seat right behind them.

Pearson sat about four rows behind and across from Alexa and put on a look disallowing any soul to come near him. Rachel settled on a bench in the middle of the next car in front, with Donny beside her. Then Zaire moved to sit on the other side of her. It was hard to know for certain what Donny said, but it was probably something like, "Beat it," because Zaire abruptly veered off to the seat across the aisle.

With luck, the one-hour ride to the Jhansi spaceport would pass without incident. Which was the case, until the train began to slow sooner than it should have.

A few people in her car began collecting their belongings. She glanced at Pearson, who sat on the side away from the station they were pulling into. His eyes were closed. *Wonder if he sleeps.* Perhaps she'd ask him, before they found SivSatyananda and left Pearson behind for their journey home.

Alexa gazed out at the platform. Few lights shone in the station, or nearby. They might be in the middle of nowhere or near a small town, it was hard to tell. She yawned and felt an impulse to slide down on the seat enough to lean her head against the window to catch a nap.

But then her window coasted past three huge guys. They certainly seemed out of place, big and bad enough to make anybody in any place cater to their whims. No need to check in with her internal question. Her gut said to run, immediately.

After catching Pearson's attention, she jerked her head toward the next car with Rachel and Donny. She smiled sweetly at the woman and her family who had been her protectors and slid past the youngest child standing in the aisle.

Pearson followed into the space between the cars. Alexa had

to shout for him to hear above the train noise. "Three men are waiting for us, about to board the train."

Without comment, he opened the door on the side opposite the platform, made certain Alexa could exit, then left to alert Rachel and Donny. The train had slowed, but it was still moving. Didn't matter. Alexa jumped out and down about three feet onto a rocky slope. On impact, her clothes and the scarf protected her, kind of. She climbed up and sprinted through the dark over two deserted tracks, to hide behind a wagon.

By the time she glanced back, Pearson and Donny were on the ground jogging along with the train to assist Rachel who was encumbered by the sari. After Rachel was on the ground and running too, Zaire appeared in the doorway and jumped. Alexa sighed when she realized the journalist was not going to relent in his intention to tag along. At least he didn't seem to be aiming for the crystal.

Once her group knew her location, Alexa turned and ran as far as possible from the train. Rachel ditched the silk, leaving her wearing the sari's colorful cropped top and her trousers.

Outside the train yard and behind some shrubs, the group congregated, as a few dogs barked. Breathing hard, everyone watched to see if they were followed. The train lurched, rolled forward and slowly picked up speed. After it passed from their line of vision, the platform was empty. Each person in the group then peered behind them through the blackness. Alexa didn't want to be jumped by some goons from out of the shadows.

Pearson spoke low, "We need to find someone with a vehicle."

Alexa whispered, "They're going to arrive there before us, you know."

He nodded, took out his mobile, and soon was instructing someone to, "move the plane without delay." After stipulating other details Pearson finished with, "be prepared to receive visitors with weapons. Keep them occupied until I contact you." He disconnected and glanced around.

Donny leaned in toward Pearson. "There are some lights over there and a car is in front of the house. You know the languages. I'll wait with the girls."

Zaire said, "I know them too. And my face hasn't been all over the news. This place may appear to be the middle of nowhere, but almost everyone has a news feed."

It was plain that both Pearson and Donny would not be willing to include Zaire in their plans. Alexa weighed in before an argument began. "How about if Zaire goes and Donny is with him? Pearson, Rachel and I would need you if those guys do come around."

"Speaking of those guys," said Zaire. "What guys? Is that why you left the train?"

Again, Pearson and Donny truly wanted Zaire to disappear. Alexa decided to explain briefly. "I saw them. My gut said they were sent to stop us."

Zaire shook his head in disbelief. "If so, Vagwhatar has gone way off her gray. You must be hot stuff." His tone went earnest. "I'll be nice to you, I promise, if you'll give me your story instead of her."

Alexa clarified, "Gray?"

Zaire made a face, like duh, and pointed to his head. "Brain."

Alexa fixed him with a stare. "Do you want to be included?" She emphasized the last bit, "Or not?"

Zaire answered with a chipper, "Okay." He looked at Donny. "You got my back?"

Donny raised his eyebrows in disbelief.

With great portent before he left, Zaire said to Rachel, "We will return for you."

Rachel snorted, "Ah, all right. That's good."

Later in the rattletrap passing for a taxi, Alexa reviewed her decision to cut and run from the train. If the men had been simply waiting for the next train, she'd complicated their lives considerably. Alas, she might never know if her decision was correct or not.

When the car fell into another deep rut, Alexa's head bounced up to the roof, again. Then she fell onto Pearson's lap, again. At first, the contact had been overwhelmingly intimate and decidedly distracting. But it had happened so many times, she was pretty sure neither of them noticed anymore.

Two seats in the front of the vehicle and room for three in the back resulted in Alexa sitting half on Pearson's lap and half on the middle console. Another bump, and the half of her backside on the console let it be known she would be bruised the next day.

The next day, however, she might be home. The thought kept her going.

Back in the village when the car slowly pulled up to their hiding place, with Zaire in the front passenger seat and Donny in the backseat, two boys ran along beside it. From the way the driver spoke to them, it was clear that they were his sons. They'd tagged along to see their father off and to check out the men and now women wanting a ride this late at night. Rachel smiled at them both, then at their father and ruffled the hair on each of the boys' heads. The two drew together and giggled a bit at such attention, while their father beamed.

Over the silk top, Rachel put on a long white shirt that Donny snagged for her. Before climbing into the backseat she argued with Donny when he insisted on sitting in the middle between her and Zaire. Alexa continued wearing the scarf, without the part covering much of her face.

They made progress through the night via a tortuous road winding around back lanes, to bypass the main thoroughfare that included a washed-out bridge. The vehicle would move forward a few yards and bounce through a Grand Canyon. It seemed to take a week, though in reality they arrived at the spaceport just thirty minutes later than if they'd stayed on the train.

Pearson pulled out his phone. From the conversation, it sounded like his men had accomplished everything he requested and more. He finished with, "Please have someone file a flight plan to Allahabad under my name for the aircraft. The Jahnsi Tower knows me." Then he spoke in some dialect to the driver, who nodded and turned a corner. "I directed the driver to take this side road outside the airport perimeter, to a spot not easily noticed."

Where they stopped, a man waited inside the fence. Pearson must have been generous when he paid, because the driver almost dissolved in tears before speeding away.

"Welcome, Captain," the man said, between snips of the fence. "The craft is about a hundred feet from here, under a tarp. It's fueled up and ready to go. We also completed a standard checklist on the plane."

Pearson acknowledged this with, "Thank you, Lieutenant."

Alexa pushed through the fence first, with Rachel and Donny following on her heels. Pearson caught up and walked with his officer on one side of him and Alexa on the other. In the shadows, two men were peeling back the cover from her grandfather's Cessna. When the red and silver appeared, greyed-out because of the darkness, her heart ached. That last day in Florida seemed another lifetime.

"And, sir," the lieutenant said to Pearson as they approached the activity, "the men you warned us about? When they attacked, it was brief fire. They've retreated to about fifty yards away from the freighter. We didn't contact the tower, since you seemed to want privacy."

Pearson nodded. "Please track them until we leave. My next contact may be at any time."

Chapter 38

Outside the plane Alexa rotated the propeller a couple of times by hand, checked the tires, fuel cap and oil levels. She climbed in, scooted through the back seat to the front, settled into the pilot seat, and then turned on the engine to warm it up while verifying each gauge and control. Such a relief to hear the engine's rumble.

Zaire sat in back of her, beside Rachel in the middle. Donny manned the door.

Pearson was finishing a conversation outside the plane with his lieutenant when a flash of light came from their left and glanced off the runway. Alexa tried to understand the burning smell. Then lights also began bursting from the right side.

Pearson wrenched open the door and Donny leaned over onto Rachel. As Pearson moved around to the co-pilot seat, Donny slammed the door and yelled, "Go!"

"Clear. Ready." Alexa punched the engine and the plane jumped forward. Laser trails followed them further than she would have expected. While putting on her headset Alexa yelled, "Do we have permission from the tower to take off? What is the protocol?"

Pearson powered on a pad sitting on the dash, checked some numbers, and turned two knobs nestled one inside the other on the control panel. The tower was protesting the fact they didn't first announce their taxi to the runway. He spoke into his headset, "Jahnsi Tower, November5337Victor is ready for departure." Off microphone he said, "Go. Traffic is light at this time of night." Then he spoke into the headset again. "Jahnsi Tower, someone is firing at us, in perimeter area delta-five. Repeat, weapon fire, in perimeter area delta-five."

Alexa paused at the runway. "Do we have permission to take off? Was that another laser flash?"

Then she heard in her headset, "Is this Captain Pearson? What weapon fire?"

"Yes, Jahnsi Tower, this is Pearson. We do not know. They came out of nowhere. They are catching up with us."

"November5337Victor, this is highly irregular. But you are cleared for takeoff, runway three-six. Straight out departure approved. Officials are approaching perimeter area delta-five to investigate weapon fire."

Relieved, Alexa angled into position and took off. It was eleven p.m., and they had two and a half hours before SivSatyananda would leave. After a few moments in the air, Alexa asked, "Do we know the flight path to Allahabad?"

Pearson pulled up an aviation map on the pad. "My crew prepared it for you." She looked it over and handed it back to him.

The roar of the engine began to have its effect on almost everyone. Zaire fell asleep in nothing flat; head back, snoring intermittently. Donny began fighting off his nods at about the same time. Rachel could hardly keep her eyes open. Before she gave in to sleep, she asked, "Alexa, how tired are you?"

"Not sleepy. Pearson will talk to me to keep me awake, right?" He nodded his assent.

Pearson had agreed to monitor the autopilot. The next thing she heard was him saying, "Alexa, wake up. You should take it back."

A dark shape swooped over at high speed. Their little plane shook and dipped in the vortices left in that craft's wake.

"What the hell," said Alexa. The excessive turbulence tripped off the autopilot. She brought her plane to wings level and checked bearings. "Everyone, cinch up your seat belts."

The dark shape turned and came for another pass. As it approached the shape became identifiable as a shuttle, not some underworld bat thing.

"You're not going to hit us," muttered Alexa, "because you'd go down also. Two can play this game." It was as if her grandfather sat by her, coaching her as he always did. She kept the plane steady on course, not giving an inch.

The shuttle veered away, trailing a wake that could have accomplished its seeming goal if Alexa had panicked. Their plane bucked wildly for what seemed a stomach-churning eternity.

Alexa asked, "How close are we to Allahabad?"

Pearson said, "Within hailing distance."

"Good. Get them on the radio."

Pearson consulted the pad and rotated two knobs. "Ready."

Alexa called into her headset, "May Day, May Day, May Day. Allahabad. Allahabad Tower. This is November5337Victor, five miles east, at thirty-five hundred feet, declaring an emergency."

"November5337Victor, this is Allahabad Tower. We copy your May Day. State the nature of your emergency. Do you require assistance?"

"Allahabad Tower, this is November5337Victor. I have a shuttle buzzing me, perhaps trying to force me to land. Did you register our near mid-air collision on your radar? Are you in contact with this aircraft? A shuttle. Over."

The shuttle was on the left, coming at them fast.

"November5337Victor, this is Allahabad Tower. One craft in the area is not talking to us. We continue to hail it."

The shuttle aimed directly at the plane's nose. It seemed to hesitate, if that was possible. Then from Alexa's vantage it appeared the shuttle even put on speed. At the last possible second and a distance too close for safety the shuttle slid up and streaked past their nose, entangling the plane in its wash. Reacting on sheer reflex, Alexa rolled the plane to the right along with the wash, completing a full turn before coming back level. The back end of the shuttle disappeared behind them, flying low, perhaps to circumvent radar.

Alexa took a breath and realized she hadn't noticed a conscious thought until it was all done. But Rachel noticed, and understood. She reached forward and touched Alexa's shoulder. "Good job."

Alexa felt as if she might go into shock, if given the opportunity. Undeniably and automatically, she'd taken the right actions. Her grandfather had accomplished his stated mission of training her well, if at the expense of his own killer heart attack during this very maneuver in the skies over Florida.

After enough time to verify no collision was imminent, the Tower voice came on again. "November5337Victor, what is your status? Do you require assistance?"

By this time, the lights of Allahabad and the airport west of the city were visible.

"Negative, Tower, we're okay," said Alexa. "Standby for intentions." Off microphone, she asked, "What time is it and how long to drive from the airport to the event?"

Pearson checked. It was thirteen minutes past midnight. No way.

All Alexa's good feelings from conquering the doubt vanished. "Not enough time." She hit the dashboard once. "I should have figured this out before I fell asleep."

"Let's fly by the event," said Rachel. "Where is it?"

"Along the Ganges," put in Zaire, "where two rivers meet."

Alexa took time to control her emotions. "Allahabad Tower this is November5337Victor, requesting a transition from west to east through your airspace, at thirty-five hundred feet. We will continue to our destination."

Chapter 39

It was easy to locate the Ganges, India's mother river flowing from the Himalayas to the ocean. Alexa followed the wide, black ribbon, rimmed by city lights. Northwest of where another dark line merged with the Ganges from the west, a vast space lay, relatively devoid of light. It must be land because it showed numerous small fires.

Zaire leaned from the backseat. "That area, there," he pointed to where Alexa was looking. "That's the Kumbh Mela. Across the Ganges is a tent city. Are you aware an entrance pass is required?"

Alexa responded, "Considering millions of people attended even in…in past years, I'm not surprised."

"It is late at night," put in Pearson. "Not having passes is perhaps less of a problem."

"Hope so," said Alexa. She eyed the strands of lights bobbing between east and west banks, twinkling as a many-strand diamond necklace. The strands illuminated pontoon bridges. Also from east to west, a hundred feet or more above the entire Kumbh Mela area, spanned a cement overpass for vehicles.

Across from the event and north of the tent city, a long gray line traced a good length of the river. Almost for sure a beach. Periodic lights at the water's edge illuminated the area enough to show the beach as almost deserted.

"What time is it?"

Pearson responded. "Twenty-four minutes past midnight."

"Are there any boats on the river around this area?"

Zaire spoke. "Yes. In fact, many would be available during one of the special dipping times. Not too many are rowing tonight probably."

"Will they understand we're coming in to land?"

"Fly low once," said Zaire. "Let them know you're around. This aircraft is an ancient antique. And how you know how to fly it, I must find out some time. Fly low over them and they should get the hint."

Rachel piped up, "Do you think he's there? Is it worth the gamble of landing on the beach?"

Four people stared at Alexa. No debate inside her head was necessary. An excitement had been building in her since she first saw the site. "I think he's there. It's risky. But it's the only chance we have to arrive in time."

Alexa headed down for a first pass, flying low enough to see men and women pointing at them and running around. The beach looked clear except for a small shack at the far south end of the beach. It became obvious the people understood when some of the men began moving items off to the side.

"That's a good sign," said Alexa. "We'll land on the beach. It is long enough and looks flat enough, given it's all good sand." She banked to fly north into the wind. "Everybody make sure they're strapped in."

To Alexa's considerable relief, the landing was much smoother than their previous one on Adalans. Her ease morphed into unease, however, when she spied a boat aiming at their shore, a motor providing it a pretty good speed. The vessel changed course to intercept them as she turned the plane around to power to the south end of their landing strip to be closer to the Kumbh Mela. Boats lined the shore, pulled onto the sand.

"Zaire, we could really use your help."

Since they had landed, Zaire had been craning to see out both windows. "How?"

"Who do you think that is, there, coming toward us?"

"Easy. It's Varshana Vagwhatar. She must have figured out your intended destination hours ago and would have gotten here, one way or another."

Alexa nodded in agreement and turned to Donny. "Do you still have the cap you were wearing earlier today?"

Donny puckered his lips, and murmured, "Yeah," as he eased it out of his pocket.

The plane rolled to a stop.

"Zaire would you wear that cap. Pearson would you and Zaire go find two women, one who would be willing to wear," Alexa reached in her bag and brought out the scarf Donny bought for Rachel, "ask her to wear this." Alexa looked pointedly at the vessel bearing down on their position. It was about two minutes from arrival. "And arrange for someone to take you, and them, on a chase." They agreed at once.

"Rachel, Donny," both looked at her, "we are going to slink, even crawl if necessary, over to another boat and see if we can elude that woman." They all piled out of the plane as the propeller stopped. While she jogged low over to the shore, Pearson handed over money to a man on the beach and then joined Zaire.

Five minutes later, the three of them hid low out of sight. Two men were rowing them across the Ganges, because no other motor craft were available.

The water slapped at the wooden sides and Alexa wondered if the Ganges had been cleaned up over the recent hundreds of years. It smelled wet and pure, possibly helped by the scent of flowers in the air.

Two crafts with outboard engines passed in front of them, and later behind. The men rowing their own boat responded brilliantly, as in they did nothing special. After a second pass of the chase and then developing silence, Alexa released her breath. *Perhaps this will work.*

If any place could support the good guys, this was one of them. For as many as twenty-four hundred years, the Kumbh Mela had been held at the confluence of the Holy Ganges, the deep blue Yamuna River and the Saraswati, a third invisible river that partly gave the spot its special nature. Would all this specialness be helpful in their earnest efforts to locate the Master SivSatyananda, and beg for his help in transporting them home? "I hope so," she whispered.

Probably only minutes remained before SivSat departed.

As their vessel crunched on the sandy shore, Donny handed over payment. Alexa leaped into the water and waded out. Donny jumped and reached to help Rachel, who responded "I can do this by myself," though she did take his hand. The three of them dashed up the bank.

Alexa asked the first person she saw, "SivSatyananda?" The woman looked at her in confusion. Alexa repeated, "SivSatyananda? Do you know where is SivSat?" The woman smiled and nodded, and pointed to the right half of the area. The trio sprinted in that direction.

Alexa didn't realize her scarf had slipped off her hair until a group of people pointed at her and cried out in unison, "Alexa Jane Alden!" One of the men came at her and stood in her path. "It is you," he said, spreading his arms. "The news station said you might come here." Another man joined him. They were using up precious time. "Will you share your prize with us?"

"Yes. But first, we must find SivSatyananda. Do you know where he is?"

"Yes, yes," said the man, rocking his head from side to side. "I will take you to him."

Almost the entire group followed along, she couldn't stop them. At every turn another person called out, "Alexa Jane Alden," and joined the procession. Alexa tried to run, to keep them at the fastest possible pace. People would dash in front of her grinning, then fall in with the group. They passed sadhus, men who would shock her grandfather to the core since they wore no clothes at all. Men who renounced everything, including clothes and cooking food. The group also passed robots. These were simple formats with hardly any human-type features, though with enough sense of self-preservation to bolt out of the way of the crowd bearing down upon them.

A large tent came into sight ahead of them. No side flaps, thousands of people inside and more streaming in and out. They were aiming at that tent. People beside her sang out, "SivSat, SivSat, SivSat." Those they passed gestured to the tent. This happened over and over again.

Alexa glimpsed inside the tent, sort of. Everyone seemed to be facing away from the river. *He must be sitting there, looking out over the Ganges.* Alexa caught Rachel and Donny's attention, pointed and redoubled her effort to run, moving past a couple of men who had paced her from the beginning. Side by side, the three drew forward and flat-out dashed toward the tent. Racing against time. Soon. Soon.

Alexa, Rachel and Donny were almost to the tent's entrance, where they could get a view of the stage.

They reached the main entrance.

A great cry arose. It must have been every single person roaring at the same moment. People began spilling out of the tent. All kinds of languages swirled around them. Some yelled in English, "Miracle. It's a miracle."

A salmon, swimming against the surge, Alexa kept wading forward. Then entered and peeled off to the side, where she found a box to stand on, to see down to the front.

An ornate stage was there, covered in rich saffron and red. And a bench.

Empty. The bench was empty.

Chapter 40

She heard someone mention "illusion," and his companion replied, "No, it was real."

Another man said to a friend as he passed by. "It was a miracle. I saw it with my own eyes."

Amidst the emptiness inside her, Alexa found an ability to speak. "What miracle? Where is SivSatyananda?"

"He disappeared, into thin air. I tell you, honestly, into thin air, right in front of us."

"Disappeared?" Disappointment threatened to drown her. "Where did he go?"

"He did not tell us. He said he must leave, to accomplish a great deed."

His friend came over. "Alexa Jane Alden, are you not? You have been on the news. Will you share your prize with us?"

Alexa had about lost all patience with this particular question. She managed a weak smile. "If I actually receive a great prize, I would be happy to share it with you all."

"Ah, good," said the man, bobbing his head side to side. "Very good karma."

Alexa stepped off the box to join Rachel and Donny. They stood there for some time, staring at the milling crowd. Alexa's gaze focused for a moment when Pearson dashed in the front entrance, whipping his head both directions, searching for them. He walked up and quietly took position beside her.

"Alexa Jane Alden? Are you Miss Alden?" yet another man asked. This one wore a saffron orange robe. You never know, a Brahmin might want a share of the theoretical prize, too.

Alexa sighed. *Dear God in Heaven, when will this stop?* Instead of screaming at the man, she opted to simply answer his question, "Yes."

"SivSat asked me to find you, if I could."

Alexa had been prepared to deny having any treasure to share, thus it took a moment for her to understand what he said. She peered at him more carefully. "SivSatyananda was looking for me?"

"Yes," said the monk. "Time was running out for him to depart. He asked some of us to keep watch for you."

"He was looking for me?" She wailed, "Why didn't he wait? We were so close."

"The moment for his departure was determined by the stars. Still, SivSat asked his personal secretary to help you if possible."

Both Rachel and Donny came in close for the conversation. "How," entreated Rachel. "How can he help us?"

"You can ask him. He is waiting for you near your plane."

As one they turned for the exit. Alexa yelled, "thank you," over her shoulder and ran.

They pelted up the beach from the motorized boat, to find no one near the plane, or anywhere in sight. The fact no people were around was astonishing. The plane being unusual, you would think someone would hang out nearby to see what might happen. Still, the area was deserted.

The group stopped near the plane and looked every which direction, searching for anybody, a single soul. A dog slept, curled in a ball up against the shack she'd noticed from the air. The dilapidated structure squatted between the beach and fields of flowers perfuming the air. No door was visible but she had to know what, or who, might be inside. Without a word, she took off and sprinted, with Rachel, Donny and Pearson following. Around the corner, the door was ajar. Whether this was normal, or not, she could not know.

At the opening, Alexa stopped and peered in. Donny came up right behind her, muttering under his breath, "I can't believe how deserted it is around here."

A lamp shone in the back left corner, and a man sat cross-legged on a few burlap bags on a large crate near the lamp. He wore a robe of saffron orange. Alexa strode halfway across the space and stopped.

The monk spoke first. "I asked the kind boatmen if we might have some privacy."

"Hello, sir. I am Alexa Jane Alden. Are you looking for me?"

The monk smiled. "Very good. Yes, I have been waiting for you, Miss Alden."

Alexa recognized his consciousness, the profound depth of his understanding of life. She'd experienced this as a child near a preacher her grandmother followed. And she'd noticed it over and over again, listening to Brahmaji. The impulse to sit at the man's feet and wait until he spoke almost won out over everything else.

"We barely missed seeing SivSat," she said.

"Yes, we could tell time was becoming short."

Alexa felt prickles on her neck. "You knew we were coming?"

"The sound of the plane is quite distinctive."

"How could you know it was us, that we wanted to see SivSat?"

"He knew. And asked us to assist, if we can."

Rachel spoke up. "You say, 'If you can.' What does that mean?"

"What do you want?"

How to ask for the impossible? It seemed outrageous. Despite all she and Rachel and Donny went through to arrive at this place and moment, it was difficult to say the words: Technological marvel? Magical transportation? "A miracle," replied Alexa. "We desire a miracle."

Wordlessly, he indicated she should continue.

"We are from many years ago, about nine hundred and fifty years ago." She waited for him to scoff. He didn't. "We want to go home, to our time, to our lives there. I mean, then. To our lives then." He was quiet for a bit. Alexa realized she did not know how to address him. "May we know your title, sir?"

Again that smile: full, easy, no irony, no rush, all the time in the world. "I am not so important as to use a title. I assist SivSatyananda in any manner I can. You may address me as he does, Trotaka. It is an ancient name and I aspire to be as the one of old."

"Thank you, Trotaka, sir," Alexa said. "Thank you for your attention and your help, if you can."

He peeked around Alexa to take in the whole group. "There are four of you."

Pearson had held back behind the trio. He jerked his head up. "It is not necessary to consider me in this situation."

Trotaka nodded in understanding. "All right, there are three of you." His face showed a slight concern. "I wonder if SivSat knew of three." He shifted on the burlap bags. "Yes, I can help you to return." All three of them perked up. He took a deep breath and opened his hands, in supplication. "But, I am capable of taking only one person with me to SivSatyananda."

Chapter 41

Trotaka spoke more quickly, perhaps noticing the hope on their faces crumbling. "SivSatyananda is capable of transporting more than one person. Me, I am able to take only one, and at most can make one trip in such a fashion." In their shocked silence, he waited a bit. "I am sorry."

Alexa was trying to take it all in when she heard a sob.

"What do you mean, one," Rachel cried out. "That means the others must stay here? Now?"

"I do not know when SivSat will return," said Trotaka. "And it is only SivSat who could transport you all to your time."

Donny released Rachel's shoulders and stepped forward. "If you're able to help Alexa, then isn't there at least one other person to help Rachel?"

"I am sorry," the monk said. "I am the only one. It takes a certain awareness to go beyond physical boundaries. I never expect it when SivSat assumes I fit the need. And I suspect the only reason I can do this and take another person with me is because we are here, at the Kumbh Mela. All these seekers together in one place create a great consciousness, which lends what is necessary for the process."

Pearson moved forward. "Sir, we do not know how much time before unfriendly parties may try to stop the process." He turned and touched Alexa's arm, intending to bring her forward to Trotaka.

"There is one more thing you must know," said the monk. "When you return, you will remember nothing of your journey to this time. And," he smiled, "only those items that came with you will return with you. In particular, this may affect what you will be wearing when you arrive home."

Alexa considered her outfit. She wore the pants from the day in Florida, since the pockets were always so useful. Alas, her blouse was new. Luckily, the bra she wore was from home.

Rachel cried, her face into Donny's chest, surrounded by his arms.

Alexa thought of the silly little pen, the one with the space dude on it, which Rachel loved to use because her son, Sammy, gave it to her. She thought of the pictures of Sammy in Rachel's old cellphone. Sammy, who would pay the price of not having his mother help him grow up.

"Alexa," murmured Pearson, "time is running short."

Alexa didn't make a conscious decision. Her brain did not trace clear steps of logic. She simply found herself speaking, saying words the meaning of which she knew only after they were uttered. "Rachel," she whispered. "Come quickly. You need to go with Trotaka."

Pearson opened his mouth to protest. Alexa gazed up at him evenly and shook her head, while reaching her hand to Rachel. She had to act before the strangeness in her stomach took over, and she grabbed the opportunity for herself.

Despite streaks of tears, Rachel's face practically radiated light when she realized Alexa's intent. Donny gently rolled her from his arms and toward Alexa.

Rachel moved forward, gave Alexa a quick hug as she passed and advanced to Trotaka. Right before she took his proffered hand, Rachel glanced at her own clothes. "Oh no. I have nothing on I was wearing that day." She tittered nervously.

Alexa did a quick estimate between her own frame and Rachel's. As she moved around behind a nearby crate she said, "My pants can fit you." She began to strip them off.

Donny looked back and forth between the two women, then at his own clothes. "My undershirt is from that day." He slipped his top shirt over his head.

While Donny was taking off his undershirt, however, the unmistakable noise of a motorized boat sounded from the river. Everyone in the building stopped moving for a split second, and then sprang into action.

Donny took two steps forward, handed his yellow smiley-face T-shirt to Rachel and whispered, "I love you."

As she accepted the shirt, she reached up and kissed him. "I love you," she responded.

A dog nearby barked furiously.

During this time Alexa called out, "Pearson," and tossed him her trousers. As Donny rushed at the door, Pearson turned toward Rachel, handed Alexa's trousers to her and also headed at the door.

Rachel gazed at Trotaka, holding cargo pants, T-shirt, and her ever-present white plastic bag clasped to her chest. He positioned her in front of him with her back to the door, then asked her to close her eyes.

"Crystal" popped into Alexa's head. She yelled, "Wait!" and reached into her shirt and then her bra, and brought out the crystal. "Pearson," she shouted. He took two long strides to her. As Alexa handed him the crystal she said, "Give it to Rachel."

Pearson received it and swung around to Rachel in one smooth swoop. After Rachel received the crystal, Trotaka repeated his request for her to close her eyes.

During that maneuver Donny began pushing on the door, trying his best to keep it closed. A man forced his head into the room and Donny landed two quick punches into his face. The man growled something, perhaps an oath in a local dialect. Before Pearson reached the door the man brought up a laser. There was no sound when a flash of light momentarily blinded Alexa. Donny may have seen the flash, but he could not have felt much pain, because he was dead before he hit the ground.

Pearson stopped. He glanced side-to-side, perhaps searching for some kind of weapon.

The door slammed open. The shooter stepped aside.

A woman stood there, wearing a heavily embroidered sari and four inches of gold bangles on her wrists. Trotaka's orange robesmust have caught her attention first. Without a pause she strode over Donny's body, directly at Rachel and Trotaka.

Pearson reached for the woman. The guy brought up his gun and Pearson fell to the floor, sparks flying from his face.

As the woman drew closer to Rachel, Alexa whispered "no," while scrambling onto the crate in front of her.

Then Trotaka and Rachel winked out. Gone, with no trace of sound, light or smell.

Time seemed to stop; the sight was so surprising. Alexa had a brief thought that there should have been sparkling magic pixy dust, or something like that, remaining there, lightly drifting to the ground.

Then the woman thundered, "No!" The sound, drawn out, beyond any human voice, reverberated through Alexa's chest. The woman slammed a fist onto the crate where Trotaka had sat.

Rachel got away! Relief shooting through her, Alexa grinned crazily.

Elation dissolved to horror, however, as the woman swiveled toward her and human features became feral. Alexa crouched on the crate, transfixed. The person stomping at her appeared female, but felt like Corcoran when he almost crushed her windpipe. Bishop's angry face also raced through her mind.

When the woman reached the crate, her hand shot out and grabbed Alexa's shirtfront. It was rough in its search of chest and torso. "Where is the crystal?"

Alexa's breath rasped. Riveted by the fury in front of her, she could scarcely shake her head no.

The woman spat and shook Alexa so hard her head whipped back and forth and her legs dropped and her feet couldn't touch the ground. Her legs scraped over and over across the wooden splinters. "You are nothing," the woman snarled. "The dog SivSatyananda may have won this one, but I *will* be victorious. I would break your neck this moment, as I could have countless times. Still, you are his pet and *you* will be my path to him. Keep in mind, I know everything about you, as I did on the cruiser."

Alexa's body and then head slammed against the wall. *Hurt.*

"I will be your constant companion."

Alexa slid to her knees.

"In manners you cannot even conceive." With that, the woman's features went blank.

One moment later, the woman blinked twice and took a deep breath. She slowly turned to view the room. At the sight of the fallen bodies of Donny and Pearson, she appeared shocked and whipped around to Alexa.

"It didn't go well, did it," the woman stated, clenching her hands. "And you are the reason." Her eyes narrowed. "This affects me personally. I will not forget it." When the woman jabbed a forefinger at Alexa, her bracelets jangled. "I know who you are. You will not get away with interfering with my life."

With that, Varshana Vagwhatar turned on her heel, stepped over the two bodies and departed the building. She aimed at the river. The gunman sprinted in the other direction. About half a minute later, the sound of a boat's motor began receding from the shore.

Chapter 42

As the motor sound faded, Alexa leaned her forehead against the crate, wondering whether she might join Pearson and Donny if she kept totally still and quiet. Tears welled, spilled from her eyes, and slid down her nose. *Abandoned, in the here and now.*

For a bit she watched her tears drop from the end of her nose, one at a time onto the dirt floor. A rustling noise made her wonder if mice were reclaiming the emptiness.

"Alexa," came a low, electronic sound in an android voice like from the movies in her own time; well, used to be her time. The sound increased in volume. "Alexa?" It sounded tinny and forced. "Are you there?"

Alexa raised her head and scanned the room. Pearson lay on his back with his knees up, whereas his body had been in a heap minutes ago. She hardly dared believe. "Pearson?"

"Yes," came the mechanical sound.

Alexa used her arms to pull her body up. Goosebumps covered her legs, alongside the bleeding scrapes. It might be India, but it was also February and her underwear didn't cover much. Didn't matter. She ran around the crate and slid to a stop beside Pearson.

He raised his hands to his face, but was unable to hide the fact his skin, almost gone, covered a metal understructure with muscles made of rubber-type fibers. The side where the weapon made a direct hit betrayed a tangle of wires. Alexa fell to her knees beside him, silent with her view of his physical reality.

"You should depart," he said. His words unexpectedly slipped into a more human sound, like a thirteen-year-old boy's voice going deep momentarily. "Take the plane. That monster may change its mind."

Alexa closed her eyes. "Can you walk?"

Pearson checked various systems. His right foot moved, then the left; the right knee, then left; the hips; his arms. He sat straight up in one fluid motion. When he became aware a wire dangled from the left side of his face, he tucked it in. "Yes," he said, in even another tone. "Vocal programming is not responding to my commands. I apologize."

"Not necessary," she said. "Let's go. I am not leaving without you."

At the plane, they maneuvered Pearson through the door and around into the co-pilot's seat. After he settled, Alexa closed the door.

Someone with a western stride was walking toward her. It turned out to be Zaire, who caught up with Alexa on her way to the shack. "You guys left me," he complained, falling into step beside her. "I was arguing with Varshana on the beach and that Pearson joker peeled out. I have to say, Varshana's tough normally. Tonight though, she went far beyond her prior limits. Eh, your skirt, is this some new fashion? I thought burlap was 'done' two years ago."

Alexa stopped at the door and waited for Zaire to notice Donny's body.

"Holy crap," he yelled and jumped. "Did Varshana do this?"

"No, a man with her."

The weapon must have seared almost all blood vessels as it pierced Donny's chest, because the dirt had absorbed everything. The hole in his chest was distinctly evident. The expression was blank. Alexa reached down and closed Donny's eyes.

"Where's Rachel?"

Alexa did not feel like explaining the impossible. "She's gone."

"Wow, and left this guy behind? I can't believe she would be that cold."

"She didn't see this happen." Alexa knelt beside Donny's head, reached under his shoulders and heaved up.

"You want to move him? Do you think that's a good idea?" When Alexa ignored his question and struggled with the dead man's weight, he said, "Here, let me help." Zaire edged in to take over the heavier part of the body and Alexa crawled down to the feet. He reached under the armpits and lifted while Alexa scrambled up holding Donny's legs. Zaire moved back, and Donny's rear end rose above the ground.

"Where to?"

"I am not leaving him here," declared Alexa. "Let's take him to the plane."

Zaire looked like he thought she was crazy. Twice they stopped to adjust. The first time Donny's head lolled back too far for Zaire to keep a good hold. The second time, Alexa's fingers slipped on the ankles. It took forever, but they arrived near the plane.

She could not allow Zaire a view of Pearson in his current condition. "Stand there." Alexa didn't wait for agreement because her energy for such niceties was all used up. She opened the plane's door a bit. "Pearson? Are you okay?"

"Yes," came the mechanical reply.

"We have Donny. The back seat is as far as we will be able to get him." Without comment, Pearson held his right hand up to shield against the view from outside. Alexa blessed the darkness that kept most everything hidden. Zaire, eyes wide, didn't ask stupid questions. She turned to Zaire. "Okay, I'll climb in, you heft him up to me and I'll pull." It turned out not so simple, but after much pulling and pushing, Donny lay across the backseat.

Standing on the beach, Zaire looked up at her in the plane. "Take me with you. I can help."

Alexa looked him in the eyes, and found them to be reasonably honest. "No. I'm sorry. This is as far as we can go together. Thank you for everything." He didn't try to argue. Few would, against the tone she'd used.

He wasn't completely done though. "Where is Rachel?"

"She's gone." Alexa reached out to grab the door handle.

This time, Zaire stood his ground. He wouldn't let go of the door. "Gone where? Is she all right?"

"I don't know. I honestly don't know." She cocked her head. "Maybe you will tell me someday."

Down the beach, three vehicles sped around a corner and headed toward them. Lights flashed on top, sirens warbled. Zaire saw them too, but stalled. "Come on, give me a hint."

Alexa relented. "Look for her—Rachel Mulligan—on the east coast of Florida."

"Florida!" Zaire's tone implied any person being in Florida had lost their sanity. "You mean in North America?"

"Yep." Alexa shooed him away from the plane. "Stay out of the way of the propeller." When Zaire did step back, she decided to give him one more tidbit. "You'll find her in the early twenty-first century." She didn't wait for Zaire to process the information and open his mouth to ask more questions. "G'bye," she said, and closed the door.

He yelled, "How will I locate you?"

She responded, "You did before. It wouldn't amaze me if you do again." As she stepped around and plopped into the pilot seat, Alexa realized she probably should have checked any number of things on the plane before taking off. She would have to trust how she left everything an hour—or a lifetime—ago.

In the air, having cleared first the vehicles and then the bridge, Alexa handed a headset to Pearson, clamped one on her own head and asked, "Where to? Which direction?"

"I believe we do not have enough fuel to return to the spaceport," said Pearson.

Alexa checked the gauge. "You're right, it's less than half full." At one point in her life she might have gone a little crazy over less.

Pearson drew a phone from his pocket and handed it to her. "Would you push the hash sign and the numeral five?" Alexa complied and handed it back.

A man answered. "Yes, sir, Captain Pearson?"

"We are in the air near Allahabad, with less than a half tank of fuel." Pearson spoke in a thin, mechanical voice.

"Are you hurt, sir?" asked the man, sounding concerned.

"I am in no imminent danger, Ensign. Thank you. We can reach the Lucknow airport. The city has a private hospital capable of assisting me. The Rama District hospital."

"We will contact them, sir."

"Obtain clearance for an ambulance for myself and one other, and arrange for it to meet us on the runway. And call us with the tower frequency for the Lucknow airport."

"Yes, sir."

"Tell the Lieutenant to meet us there. He is authorized to purchase any aircraft necessary to fly to Lucknow immediately, though one that could also transport this plane is best."

"Yes, sir. He's standing here and says he will see you in Lucknow."

As Pearson disconnected, Alexa turned around from looking at the tent city behind them. "We are heading north," she said. "Any idea where is Lucknow?"

"Head northeast, and look for the lights of a big city. The airport is on the southwest side."

Chapter 43

The pavement where Rachel stood scorched her bare feet, a fact that had registered as strange while she raced from the hangar toward the sound of Alexa's plane.

Dancing from foot to foot on the hot tarmac, she opted to drop the bag she held to the ground and step on. She felt totally abandoned by her friend. In fact she'd be kind of pissed off, except for the bizarre circumstances of her clothes. They were definitely not what she'd put on this morning.

And what to do with the impressions tugging at her mind? Were they memories, or dreams? She couldn't quite catch them. Before. They disappeared.

As gone as that plane.

The man who had sold her the newspaper under her feet arrived by her side; his old Jedi Master pullover almost made her remember—something. Morty said, "Rachel, what are you doing here? I thought you were flying with Alexa."

Thus, he verified that Alexa was supposed to wait for her to return from the hangar. *Okay, I'm not going crazy. Maybe.*

Rachel almost handed the newspaper over to Morty, but she noticed it had scribbles on it. The distinctive bold caps across the top stopped her.

ONLY FOR THE EYES OF MAC OR RACHEL
RACHEL, IMMEDIATELY CONTACT MAC

"Never mind," she whispered, clasping the message to her heart.

When Alexa awoke, a soft illumination seeped in through the room's one window. Treetops brushed against the building, perhaps moved by a gusty wind.

The inevitable was only postponed. The why of her location hit, and a band of some dense matter clamped down on her chest. All the hope that had buoyed her these past weeks vanished. As gone as Rachel, wherever she was; and as absent as Donny, who lay in the hospital morgue awaiting her decisions.

She remembered falling into this bed, in a hospital room next to Pearson's. It had been dawn, with rays of morning sun pouring in.

Alexa swallowed, working to keep the grief at bay. Flipping onto her back, *ow! bruises*, Alexa poked around reality inside her head to find some rightness. She couldn't be ecstatic about the result of last night. But it might help to perceive some order in the universe.

The door from Pearson's room opened and he walked through, looking much more orderly than when she last saw him. "Whoa," she said, propping herself on her elbow. "You clean up pretty good."

Pearson's eyes crinkled as he smiled. Alexa almost added, "and the programming is back, too." *Other than my father, wherever he is and if he is alive, Pearson is now the closest person to me. No snarky comments.* "Thank you," she said, "for all you did yesterday."

Pearson sighed heavily as he dropped onto the deeply cushioned love seat. Hospital it may be. Still, the furnishings were posh and Alexa got the impression confidentiality on all levels was a given.

"I failed you," he said.

Alexa shook her head. "It was my choice."

He seemed to find her actions unexplainable. "Why did you send Rachel?"

Alexa switched her gaze to out the window. She never told anyone. Now might be the time. "Because I am the reason Sammy doesn't have his father around." Alexa eyed Pearson, as she sat up and perched on the side of the bed. Since she couldn't give the truth to the parties involved, she'd tell him.

"When Rachel stole the man I loved." Alexa stopped. With a wry expression, she said, "We were eighteen years old and recently out of high school." Then she smiled wanly. It was so trivial, and so mean. "To get back at her, I told the guy that Rachel mocked his speech impediment, a slight stutter." She bit her lower lip, then admitted, "and that she did so in front of a group of people." After a couple of moments, she added, "and then, that Rachel laughed at her joke." Even years later, the guy's pain was clear in her mind. For years, she felt shame at her momentary triumph when he declared he would depart with his family the next day.

He did leave. And never returned.

"Less than a month later, Rachel realized she was pregnant." Alexa bowed her head. "She never knew why he refused to return her calls."

Chapter 44

Pearson didn't express shock at Alexa's lie. Instead, he gazed at the faux fireplace for a bit. "There is more to the story." He gestured to new clothes on the other side of her bed and a covered tray on the table. "I have another meeting with the specialist we brought in. It will take a couple of hours. Here is a snack. Can you wait for a proper meal until I return?"

The moment he mentioned a snack, Alexa knew food would be a really good idea. "Yes. I'll take a bite or two, then meditate until you return."

Within minutes, sitting up on the bed, she slipped into a stream of bliss and settled to the bottom of an ocean of light—the kind of place you would be happy to never leave.

By the time Pearson returned, the room was dark. When he opened the door, Alexa spoke from her spot on the bed. "I can be ready in ten minutes. Could you come back?"

"I will order soup and naan bread to be delivered in twenty minutes," he replied.

Twenty-five minutes later, she was finishing her first bowl of dahl and Pearson tucked a bite of bread and butter into his mouth. As she refilled her bowl, Alexa commented, "Your hair is short. The long hair was cool. This is handsome."

Pearson brushed his hand over the cropped locks. "This was easiest."

If they had not been eating, the next minutes might have been deemed awkward, though Alexa couldn't understand why. When she was full she put down her spoon, sat back, and folded her napkin. "You know, it occurred to me that we never fully explained to you what was at stake in our race to the Kumbh Mela." She raised her eyebrows. "You must certainly wonder about the drama in the garden shack."

Pearson laid down his knife and fork, folded his napkin, and looked at Alexa with intent. "I knew."

Alexa made a doubtful face. "How could you?"

"As I mentioned earlier this evening, there is more to the story." Pearson touched his chin. "You know my physical nature."

Alexa waved, "That does not matter."

He slightly inclined his head in appreciation. "I have contemplated many times about telling you. Innumerable times, in fact. And each of those scenarios bear no resemblance to this moment."

Alexa couldn't conceive where he was going with that announcement.

He spread both hands in front of him. "I never thought it would be this difficult." After a bit, he blurted, "I was *created* to help you, to help make sure you would return. To Mac."

Alexa felt her jaw drop, perhaps to the floor.

Pearson finished with, "Mac created me."

As she sat there, staring at him, it began to become clear. Moments passed, while the pieces fell together. "In his image," she ultimately stated. "He used himself as the pattern." Alexa brought her hand to her brow. "I wasn't blind, because I did see the similarity. But how could I have been so lacking in logic?" She gazed at Pearson in wonder.

"I failed," he stated flatly. "All the planning and preparations for every possible outcome were for naught." He sounded utterly depressed.

"What? How did you know?" She stopped. The ramifications of his declaration became clear. "Wait! Did Rachel arrive? Is that how you knew where and when to find us?"

Pearson nodded. "Yes, she arrived. And as long as everything happened the way Mac knew then, and I did not interfere and cause a problem, she is there now."

Alexa almost began crying with relief.

"What she wrote on her newspaper was confusing," said Pearson. "Over time, Mac began to believe you were not dead, and Rachel had somehow come back from the future. He decided that if she could return, perhaps he might arrange a manner for you also to return."

"Wrote on her newspaper? You mean the *Times*?" Alexa thought for a moment. "Yes, from what Trotaka said the newspaper might have made it back." She began to laugh. "And the pen! The silly pen!"

Alexa plopped her elbows on the table and her face into her hands. Mac aimed at the impossible to get her home. She chose to not go. And here she was without him, forever.

Her heart cracked.

Nausea hit first, then bile in her throat. Ultimately, tears would not be postponed. She rocked. She grabbed her hair, dragged it over her face, hoping to disappear. At some point, she was swooped up and held. Grief stormed, round and round.

Forever.

A thousand years later, quiet at last, Alexa sat on Pearson's lap, wrapped by his arms. At one point he'd handed her a handkerchief, which had become soaked. His shirtfront was also damp. She slid from his lap and gazed in front of her, out the window into the night.

Pearson shifted to be able to look at her. "There is something I can do," he whispered. "Mac thought of this possibility. He wanted to be able to respond. Therefore through the years, I worked to make it possible." Pearson stood up. "I will return."

Not too long later, he returned, took a stance behind Alexa and began massaging her shoulders, like Mac used to do. After a bit of time melting into the wonderful relaxing attention, Alexa glanced up and around.

Mac. It was Mac standing there.

She blinked twice and found him still there. He leaned his head to one side, like Mac would, to silently inquire if she was okay.

Alexa slowly stood and faced him.

She understood. She'd graphically seen how Pearson's facial

features were structured, and how logically they could be altered to present a different appearance. Still, in a way, this truly was Mac, getting himself to her in the only manner he could.

Alexa extended her hand. He took it and walked around to her. Perhaps violins soared in the background as she fell into his arms.

Chapter 45

Alexa and Pearson, and in private Pearson as Mac, remained at the hospital for a few days. This allowed Pearson to meet with additional technical experts and Alexa to sift through the pieces of her life to locate some forward impetus.

Once or twice a day if she was out and about, someone asked if she was the lady on the news that received the great prize. Alexa would respond yes, though no financial prize had manifested. Each person nodded sagely and let her be.

The second morning at the hospital, and after another truly profound meditation for Alexa, Pearson came to find her with a gentleman in tow, a Mr. M.K. Gupta, Esquire. "Very pleased to meet you, Madam," Mr. Gupta said. "If I may be of assistance at any time, please call upon me." Later Pearson explained he retained the man as his lawyer for certain matters and that Gupta had asked about the famous Alexa Jane Alden. They both enjoyed a chuckle.

The next day, Alexa decided to address the issue of Donny's death. The hospital had reported the body as an unknown person. She debated about that. But how could there be current family or connections, other than Rachel? The authorities didn't seem to have a problem.

She and Pearson took Donny's ashes to the city of Varanasi, to be spread onto the Ganges River.

For thousands of years the city had been important to several religions. For Hindus, a death ceremony on the steps to the river or remains deposited there into the river supposedly helped balance the deceased's karma. She didn't know the reality of this belief, but Donny certainly deserved her extra effort.

Upon return from Varanasi, Alexa had another tearful session of self-blame because she had flown to the Bahamas that day to sell the plane and fulfill her own desire for a silly cottage.

Afterwards, Pearson recounted the story of how Mac figured

out what happened while he was away on business.

"Rachel's notes were brief, perhaps because the pen ran out of ink," said Pearson. "What was there was fantastical. The number 2962 was supposed to be a year, and the name Adalans was supposed to be a planet, and someone named SivSatyananda was supposed to have retained a crystal."

To Mac's relief, when he was able to provide the information to Brahmaji, the crystal's fate did not seem to be a problem. "In fact, Brahmaji said that had been the intention. But declined to explain how and why," said Pearson.

It was almost two years before Mac realized the new investor who wanted to buy the plane had, in reality, been intent on luring Alexa to gain access to the crystal.

Alexa looked at Pearson in surprise. "Mr. Fahlsteder wanted the crystal? How did he know I had it? Was he the same person as John Lloyd?"

"Lloyd," repeated Pearson. A blank look appeared on his face. "Mac mentioned a John Lloyd once. He and another man visited Mac's office three days after you disappeared. There is no indication in my data that Lloyd and Fahlsteder were connected."

"Lloyd was at Brahmaji's school and figured out that I took the crystal away with me," said Alexa. *Do I implicate Donny, now it's all over? No.* "Iain Newcastle is related to Lloyd."

Pearson developed the blank look again.

"Iain knowingly accepted a decoy to give to his family."

Pearson nodded, and Alexa sensed she just saved Newcastle from a good deal of grief.

Pearson picked up on his story. "Brahmaji warned Mac that Sterling Fahlsteder was not to be trusted, indeed may have insinuated an informant at the school. But Mac could not resist, considering that Fahlsteder invested so freely. Ultimately, Fahlsteder copied or stole and almost captured via a ruinous lawsuit much of Mac's research on creating the prototype for… me."

Alexa put in, "Newcastle said his family wants the crystal because it's lucky. Did Mac's investor think that, too?"

"Probably not. Fahlsteder died of the same wasting disease as his family. Mac understood the man was convinced the disease was his own fault."

Alexa tried to connect the dots. "He thought the crystal would cure the disease?"

"Mac was unable to understand the man's reasoning. And Brahmaji ceased giving much information to Mac. Unfortunately, before the man died he produced a computer mimicking him, and me, which over the centuries developed into an artificial intelligence and went rogue in the worst manner."

"A rogue AI," Alexa repeated. Shaking her head a little, she wondered out loud, "Could it be that the AI is somehow the common link among Corky, Bishop and the Varshana woman?"

"Exactly. In the worst possible manner. The threats to you are not hollow."

Alexa sighed. "Heartening, isn't it." She studied the carpet.

"I will protect you."

She gazed at Pearson, in wonder. "And you. You have been around for all these centuries." She could hardly conceive of everything he'd seen and, yes, lived through. "One could think you would have become cynical, after all this time." Shrugging her amazement, she said, "Thank you."

Pearson gave a small wave of his hand in denial. "Mac designed the robot that would become me to work at improving my technology whenever possible. Nevertheless, there were a couple of instances when technology failed me so I shut down for a while. But search engines always trolled everywhere for any mention of the crystals, and you."

"I remember, now," she said, "that Brahmaji mentioned a 'link to a larger reality.' It's possible he was talking about the tall crystal."

The memory unfolded in her mind: Brahmaji propping his head with his left hand, while contemplating the tall crystal sitting to his right. Alexa noticed in her mind's eye that near the top of it was a much smaller crystal sticking straight up from off the side. Brahmaji said, "What to do?" The reason Alexa heard him was because she was unusually close by, collecting some papers she needed to collate.

Brahmaji began striking a yellow rose softly against the table in front of him, while looking the big crystal up and down. He switched his gaze off into the distance. He also continued to pound the poor bloom. Alexa remembered smiling to herself, recognizing the flower's plight. She and others knew how buds would inevitably blossom to their most magnificent state right at those moments.

Then Brahmaji murmured, "How far?"

That evening Alexa bore away the small package wrapped in gold cloth.

Whoa.

Perhaps, "far" *in time?*

Possibly, this was Brahmaji's intention?

As in, being hijacked to the future, wasn't *her fault?*

Alexa's breath stopped.

Huh.

Chapter 46

When Pearson acquired a couple of official passes, the two decided to revisit the Kumbh Mela during the day. The trick would be to navigate among millions of people, through avenues of flood-plain silt, and between tents set up for various saints and gurus and teachers. The goal was the sandbar built up over untold time at the meeting point of the three rivers. All attendees aimed to ritually dunk themselves at that place, to accomplish the most for the living before ending up in Varanasi as the dead.

Being an auspicious day when they arrived, immeasurable numbers of people pushed toward the Ganges. Pearson and Alexa clasped hands and managed to dunk three times without ending up separated amidst the crowds, nor drowned. Although right afterward Alexa felt a little chilled, soon enough the day's warmth dried her clothes.

Besides, what was more important than all the life going on around her?

Because attending the event was an important event in the life of any Hindu, mothers would discipline boisterous boys and family members would assist the elderly. Families traveled together and often walked arm-in-arm. With languages from all over the world being spoken, sometimes it was hard to focus. Strange men would stake their territory in the middle of a flow of people, to perform miracles, or magic, or feats of consciousness. Elephants bedecked with painted symbols ambled on the sides, when they weren't carrying people or images in a parade. Even the robots were decorated with what anywhere else would be Christmas ornaments.

On the stroll through the throngs Alexa and Pearson stopped at SivSat's tent, where more than a hundred pundits chanted in unison, slow and deliberate. The sound caught at anyone nearby and made you want to sit right down.

"It is the Rudra Abhishek," replied a gentleman. "Very favorable."

"That's the name I was trying to remember," said Alexa. "Do you happen to know what it means?"

"Rudra is the hunter and also is Shiva. The performance is meant to eradicate chaos, negativity."

They sat to hear the performance, and soon Alexa barely heard the pundits, instead drifting in the still, quiet places in her mind. She could practically track how the stress of the previous weeks seeped away. *The world needs more of this.*

Afterward, they decided to leave India for one of Pearson's several homes on Earth. Another night in the noisy Allahabad hotel, for which Pearson had forked over an outrageous sum, wouldn't be tolerable. Alexa was ready to leave.

Along the path the two stopped at a stall with beads and items dunked in the Ganges on other special days, and Alexa moved to the side as Pearson began to haggle. He seemed to enjoy that very human activity.

When a man approached her saying "Excuse me, Miss. Are you Alexa Jane Alden?" she turned, ready to again explain she had received no great fortune. Upon recognizing the saffron robes, she relaxed. "Yes."

"SivSat sent a message to you."

Alexa's heart leaped. "A message from SivSatyananda? Do you think he will come back soon? Should I wait for him?"

"He said he would not return for some time, Miss. But his message is," the monk paused, and then began reciting. "Ajay, job well done. You took exactly right action."

Tears welled up. She wondered about him using her initials. Family and friends might do that, but it sounded odd from this source. "Did you say A.J.?"

The monk nodded. "Yes, Ajay, as in A-J-A-Y. It means 'invincible' or 'unconquered.' SivSat must consider you as that."

With that, her definition of the events of the previous weeks shifted. Perhaps the situation that seemed as threatening as a snake might have been more like a string. "Thank you," she said.

Pearson strolled over and took his place beside her.

"SivSat also said, 'All efforts resulted in great accomplishment for trends of time.'" The man looked at her. "From SivSat, these words are not given lightly, Miss."

So, perhaps no mistake! Alexa clasped her hands. "Will I ever meet him, do you think?"

"SivSat always remembers those who assist him, as you did."

"I assisted him?"

"He was searching for an item that you delivered. From what I've seen in my years with SivSatyananda, it would not be surprising for him to appear, to find you, at any time."

At that instant a robot zipped by, emitting an unmistakable racket: Click-whiiiiiinnne–Click-whiiiiiinnne–Click-whiiiiiinnne.

Alexa recognized the orange cart-bot and shouted "Stop!" before it disappeared around a corner. Without hesitation, Pearson moved to chase it down.

She caught his arm.

After considering a moment, she whispered, "Whatever that monster wants—and you certainly pegged it correctly—I can't keep it from seeking." Gazing around at the joyous chaos tumbling by, Alexa said, "On the other hand, I refuse to spend the rest of my life in fear of what it can do. So let it be, and I'll just go find what is best for me."

About the Author:

Ms. Reminick loves reading and writing science fiction. The only science she officially studied, however, was while obtaining degrees in Finance and in International Business. One course was Chemistry for Business Majors (i.e. for Dummies); the others were Astronomy, including one as presented in science fiction novels.

Besides enjoying fifteen years as a New York City financial journalist and editor, she has worked as an amusement park ride operator, a stained glass artist, a pizza deliverer, draftsman and paste-up artist (BC, before computers), at a private post office, as an assistant at a Texas land-development company, a phone center caller, and teacher of most things she knows how to do.

Despite all those years of reporting just the facts, she now utterly enjoys making things up.

Her Brooklyn-bred husband and their canine princess Pomeranian—named Penelope—happily live on the prairie in Fairfield, Iowa.

She is also always on the lookout for real magic: knowing what's about to happen, changing a trend from inevitable to a choice, feeling bliss from nothing. Having been a teacher of Transcendental Meditation for a good long time, Laure has come to deeply appreciate the magic of silence—as well, those quirky thoughts that inevitably come up during meditation.

To return to her beloved son, Rachel left her friends behind. And by all reports, she showed up a thousand years previously.

How?

Knowing Rachel, it's not a simple story. Nor boring.

Copy this link into a browser to enjoy the tale.
http://bit.ly/RachelStory

Or hover your smart device over this QR code.
(You may need to download a QR code reader app)
Hope you enjoy!